# No Longer Oppressed

## Rai
## Lindsay-Wallace

First Blessed Press print edition published in 2017
Book cover designed by Same Rijn
Book Edited by M. Whitaker
Photo Credit: Kent Wallace
ISBN: 978-0-692-93827-0

Printed in the United States of America

# Dedication

*To my amazing hubby, Kent. We have journeyed this road twenty-six years...and I want to keep traveling with you, forever. You are the earthly love of my life! My heart still flutters, when you are near. You're the reason I smile...and keep on smiling!*

*To my church family – God's House of Healing...*
*Your support has been unfailing and unconditional. It's an honor and a privilege to be used by God to be your pastor. We are growing together and it feels so good! Thank you for allowing me to serve you. With all my heart, I love you.*

*To Molly Piner – an overcomer and true survivor of Lupus. Your faith inspires me. I've witnessed you endure days of pain, yet, you kept the faith. Quitting has never been an option for you. Love you!*

*Finally, in memory of Mary Scott Wallace. She lived life to the fullest. Mary loved everyone she met and laughed her way straight to heaven. Forever missing you. Until we meet again!*

# Contents

# Acknowledgements

Holy Spirit, thank You for leading and guiding me every day. Jesus Christ, thank You for saving my soul and interceding for me daily. Father God, thank You for being my Dad, and never giving up on me. It is because of You, that I live, I move and have my very being.

To my amazing, awesome family: Kent, Maurice, Karlton, Grace, Ashley, Kalya, Briana, Lauren, Mariah, Lamad, Alisa, Mary and Willie Watts, and Norris and Grace Wallace.

To my amazing mom, my #1 fan, there are not words to describe just how much you mean to me. All I can say is this: you are awesomely amazing! I love you!

To Marilyn, my new editor (lol)…thank you, thank you for coming through for me. I know you hate to hear this, but I'm old school for life…You're the bomb-dot-com!

To all my family, friends and fans, I dedicate this book to you. You have supported my dream of writing without fail. I appreciate you all and love you even more.

*"The Spirit of the LORD is upon Me,*
*Because He has anointed Me*
*To preach the gospel to the poor;*
*He has sent Me to heal the brokenhearted,[j]*
*To proclaim liberty to the captives*
*And recovery of sight to the blind,*
***To set at liberty those who are oppressed;***
*To proclaim the acceptable year of the LORD.*
*Luke 4:18-19*

*"Now I will break the yoke of bondage from your neck and*
*take off the chains of Assyrian oppression. Nahum 1:13*


*"For all have sinned and fall short of the glory of God."*
*Romans 3:23*

# Forward

Although this book is fictional, biblical principles still hold true. My beliefs in no way judge, condemn, nor censure anyone. We have all missed the mark...Lord knows I have. There is no big sin or little sin. Sin is sin, but the solution for all sin is the love of God. Because God so loved He gave us His Son, Jesus. Jesus loved us so much, He gave His life for the remission of our sins so that we could have everlasting life. Nothing can separate us from the love of God. Love covers a multitude of sin. Love is the key to healing, forgiveness, salvation, deliverance and seeing the good in everyone. So, let us not judge, but walk in love...and pray!

# CHAPTER 1

## Timothy's Secret

Sitting at the computer, Sherry Reed froze as she read her twenty-one year old son's email. Three, one syllable words stopped her heart from pumping normally. Seemingly, everything in her body shut down. Paralyzed, mentally and physically, Sherry couldn't think or move. She couldn't breathe. Excruciating pangs were squeezing her lungs, smashing her ribs, clogging her throat and somehow cutting off her blood supply. *Is this the end? Am I dying?*

Blinking repeatedly, Sherry stared at the screen, hoping that the message would disappear as if the words had never appeared in the first place.

**I am gay.**

She read the message again. *This is some kind of joke. Timothy likes to tease me. He is such a prankster. He's pulling my leg again.* Anxiously, Sherry waited for another email to pop up. Certainly, he would send a retraction, indicating that it was just a joke!

Timothy was the middle child of three sons. Tim's constant objective in life was making people laugh and making people happy. He kept Sherry laughing and on her toes all the time. She never knew from one minute to the next what kind of prank Tim would pull. Considering her health issues, which rendered her bouts of pain as well as times of pure melancholy, Timothy was both an antidote and distraction for her. On the other hand, her eldest child, Peter was an introvert, very reserved and a loner. After calling off his engagement with his childhood sweetheart Elaine, Peter became a totally different person. Now engaged to *wild-child* Imani, a woman who Sherry greatly disapproved of, Peter distanced himself more from the family. Daniel, the youngest son, was the more serious type. Now, a senior in high school, about to graduate as salutatorian, Daniel had a heart of pure gold. He had a deep-rooted, compassion for helping hurting people. Daniel never met a stranger he didn't make feel at home. He would give the coat off his back to anyone in need. Even though Daniel wore his feelings on his sleeve, often causing him heartache, Daniel was the epitome of love all wrapped up in the loving arms of God. He had a servant's heart.

All three children were born and raised by godly parents, having a solid foundation of not just going to church, but being *'the church'*. Peter, Timothy, and Daniel gave their lives to Jesus Christ in their pre-teens. They all were on the right path and it seemed as though they would stay on track. There was no indication that anything was amiss for any of them.

*And now this...*

Time was ticking by at a snail's pace. Seconds, minutes, twenty-three minutes to be exact, before Sherry's hope dwindled.

*It's not a joke!*

*Lord, how did I fail here? What did I do wrong? How do I cure him? How can I fix this?*

Another email.

*I knew Tim was teasing! That boy…* She winced as she read on.

Don't hate me. I cannot help it. I cannot help who I am. For the first time in my life, I feel free to be me. I was born this way. And, I think you knew it all along.

Sherry's heart plummeted lower than she deemed possible. "Born this way? What? All these years and now, he says he was born this way. The heck if I knew he was…" she couldn't even say it. "God...what happened to my child? Please tell me what to say. How do I respond?"

***In love...***

She opened her mouth to say something and then closed it tightly. Her bruised heart couldn't bear much more. The words of her pastor's last sermon came to mind. Apparently, God was preparing Sherry, and she didn't even have a clue.

***We have been given the task to Love our children TO Christ. While they are Christian and living right, we continue to love our children IN Christ. However, when they stray away from the Truth, we must Love them BACK to Christ. Through it all...our love remains. Love never fails!***

Sherry picked up the daily devotional next to her computer and reread her scripture reading for that morning. *No temptation has overtaken you except such as is common to man; but God is* faithful, who will not allow you to be tempted beyond what you are able, but with the temptation will also make the way of escape, that you may be able to bear *it. (I Corinthians 10:13)*

"Show me a way of escape from this nightmare." Sherry was still reeling from the shocking news. *Haven't I endured so much already? Isn't this battle with lupus enough? Isn't my illness enough?* She almost died twice because of complications due to Lupus, a dreadful autoimmune disease causing her to suffer kidney damage, heart failure, and many other troubling

3

side effects. *This disease is sapping my strength, confining me from things that I love. I am in pain all the time and yet, I endure. I grin and bear it.*

*Then there is the thing with my husband. You know what Frank did! He had an affair with Monique, my ex-friend— the same woman who ate at my table, for years. We went to the movies together. She was my shopping partner. We went on vacations with her and her husband Andrew, before they divorced. I told her my most intimate secrets. I trusted her. Then she sleeps with my husband!*

*I was such a fool! Frank made a complete fool out of me! I know I'm supposed to forgive him and I do...but I can't stand him! When he tries to touch me, my flesh crawls. All I feel is disgust for him. He makes me...* Sherry shook her head, trying to shake off the repulsion she felt for Frank. *Forgive him, yes, but forget—never!*

*And now my son...born this way? The devil is a liar! How can Tim be gay? How can he take this sinful route when he knows right from wrong? God, You made Adam and Eve, not Adam and Steve. How? It doesn't make any sense. He's had several pretty girlfriends. Nikita, Mallory, and LaShay. He likes girls! I just don't understand this.*

*Sure, Tim never liked sports. He was more of a bookworm. Instead of being outside with Frank, Tim liked being inside with me, reading a book or cooking. He's a great cook, now in his second year of college to become a Master Chef.*

This shocking news was taking a toll on her physical well-being and Sherry's peace of mind. Sherry was more than rattled. She was frazzled to pieces. She jumped when she heard the front door open and shut.

*Speak of the devil!*

"Frank!" she shouted.

She waited.

"Frank! Come here!"

He couldn't get to Sherry fast enough. "Can't you at least let me put my briefcase down before you start yelling?"

"I'm not yelling," Sherry said calmly. "I need you to look at this." She pointed to the computer, waiting on pins and needles for him to respond, as she clicked the first message and then the second.

His heart dropped to his feet, as Frank read those three words. He was too stunned to say anything at first. Never one to show emotions, Frank fought to contain what he was feeling. Words couldn't describe the struggle within.

"Say something! Didn't you read it?" Sherry shouted one thing after the other. "How can this be? He was raised by both parents. We took him to church, to Sunday school, Bible study! It's crazy! I never suspected that he..." she couldn't say it aloud, as her knees began to buckle. This was all too much for her physically to handle, as she became light on her feet.

Instinctively, catching her, Frank pulled Sherry into his arms and cradled her head at the tip of his shoulder. It had been a long time since he had held her close and it felt so good, so right. "It's just a phase or something. He'll grow out of it."

"He's twenty-one, Frank!" Her body tensed up in his arms. The barrier between the twosome had been there so long until Sherry was uncertain how to accept his comfort or if she even wanted to. Her heart was 99% guarded, leaving Frank with only 1% of wiggle room. However, deep down Sherry had to admit it felt good being held by Frank. It had been a long time since she felt supported and nurtured.

Sherry looked up at Frank, confused and sheepish, and then backed away as if she had just touched a hot stove. "This isn't some teenager thing, Frank. Tim is not just going to snap out of this! He's gay!" At last, she had said it, validating the fact that she could no longer deny.

"We'll get through this Sherry," he said softly. "It's bad, I know…but Tim knows right from wrong. He's a Christian."

"Apparently not! He's gay!" she said again. "What's Christian about that? There is nothing right about being gay, Frank. Nothing! You need to talk to him. Knock some sense into him, if you have to! Do whatever you have to. Make him see that he's wrong to be someone that God doesn't approve of."

"Let's just wait a few days and see what happens." Frank hoped that it would all just disappear and Tim would admit he was joking. He had done that many times.

"A few days! Are you crazy?"

"I can't deal with this now!" he stomped out of the room.

"Just like you, Frank! You're always running away! Why won't you just step up and be the man!"

"I don't have to!" he came back to the door. "You wear the pants in this family! Go ahead Sherry, figure this one out. Fix your son, like you try to fix everybody else…but yourself!"

She stood with her mouth wide opened, perplexed at how he was turning this on her.

"All that coddling you did with Tim is what made him soft!" Frank added fuel to the fire and left the room with the flames still scorching. Sherry felt its hotness and wanted nothing more than to turn the tables on him. *Let him feel the heat!*

"How dare you accuse me of making him soft! At least I was there for him! You were working all the time. At least that is what you told me and I believed you like a fool! I was so gullible back then but you do not fool me now, Frank! Once a snake always a snake!" She gave him a backlash, tongue-lashing piece of her mind, sounding like anything but a child of God. "You're weak, and that is exactly why Tim is weak!" She yelled so he could hear her.

This time Frank retreated not to the guestroom but trotted toward the front door.

"Yeah! Go, run away! Go back to your girlfriend!" She could not help it. No matter what the two argued about, it always ended with the girlfriend.

The front door slammed. A few moments later, the tires on Frank's car skidded out the driveway and into the street, full-speed.

"I've had it!" Frank hit the stern wheel. "I'm fed up with Sherry's shenanigans. One minute she forgives me, the next minute she is throwing Monique up in my face! Over two years ago! It happened two years ago and she won't let it go!" Frank rant and raved, driving nowhere in particular. "Lord, You forgave me, but why can't she? Now, this…Tim is gay. He's a sweetie-pie. He has sugar in his tank. Really, Lord? I can't take much more."

**I love Timothy…He's mine.**

*I love him, too!*

*My life is a mess! I'm married but living as a roommate with my wife, sleeping in separate rooms. She loathes me, and every time I touch her, it repulses her. Look at what happened today. I was just holding her to comfort her and she backed away as if I had contacted the Ebola virus. I'm lonely, Lord… really lonely. A man has needs. That's why I cheated. No excuse is good enough, but Sherry withheld her love from me.*

**Love your way back into Sherry's heart.**

Frank almost didn't hear the soft whisper during his on-going pity-party!

*I love her, Lord...with all my heart.*
**Show her.**
*How can I, when she argues all the time? She looks for ways to belittle me...to make me feel less than a man...to make me pay for my sins repeatedly. I am tired Lord, really tired. I just want to keep on driving and never go back.*
Silence.
*Is it worth it? Trying to save my marriage, when Sherry doesn't seem to care. Counseling was a waste of time. Sherry didn't participate the few times she did show up. We went through the motions, especially Sherry, masquerading the truth—that we are this perfect Christian couple. She wanted no one to know just how bad things had gotten. It was bad before the affair and now—well—I just don't know Lord. I messed up, but Sherry played a part in it as well. She may not have cheated, but she had left me a long time ago.*
**Love her back to you...back to Me.**
*Huh?*
Silence.
*Sherry is the most dedicated Christian woman I know. She plays the keyboards in the church. She oversees the children's choir and the Children Ministry. She is a vital part of the Help Ministry, always checking on the elderly, and making goodies for them. She prays all the time and fasts once or twice a week. Love Sherry back to You—that is crazy. Sherry never left You!*
**Martha's distraction.**
Frank remembered the familiar passage about Martha and Mary.
**Now it happened as they went that He entered a certain village; and a certain woman name Martha welcomed Him into her house. And she had a sister called Mary, who also sat**

*at Jesus' feet and heard His word. But Martha was distracted with much, serving, and she approached Him and said, 'Lord, do You not care that my sister has left me to serve alone? Therefore tell her to help me." And Jesus answered and said to her, "Martha, Martha, you are worried and troubled about many things. But one thing is needed, and Mary has chosen that good part, which will not be taken away from her."*

All the busywork in the church did not negate the truth. Sherry had left her first Love. She was simply busy being busy, so she wouldn't have to deal with the hurt, the illness, the betrayals, the disappointments, the shame, the church folks, the family issues, etc.

As the saying goes, 'you can run, but you cannot hide.' Everything was catching up to Sherry. She could not smile her way through it this time. She could not fake it until she could *make* it anymore. Now, Sherry was put in a situation where she would actually have to walk through it. The question that remained to be answered was—Would Sherry walk through it alone or would she allow Frank and God to walk with her?

# CHAPTER 2

## Enough is Enough

Making her way to the kitchen, Sherry peeped into the guestroom, where her husband typically slept. Exhausted from waiting on Frank to return the previous night, Sherry finally fell asleep after midnight.

To her disappointment, Frank's bed had not been slept in. Once again, it felt like a knife in the gut, being twisted and turned, puncturing her sensitive heart. Straightaway, her thoughts went to Monique Smith.

*He'd better not be with that hussy! How dare he not come home, and not even call me.* She rushed back to her bedroom to check her cellphone.

She had two text messages.

Mom,
I haven't heard from you. Please don't be mad at me. I'm still your son. Please don't turn your back on me. I need you...please! Tim

*Lord, I don't know how to respond. What do I say to him? He's my son and I love him dearly. That will never change. But I'm so hurt right now. So confused. So baffled by it all.*
**Love him.**
*I love Tim, Lord. I do!*

**Love him back to Me.**
*Help me, Lord.*

The second text message was from Frank.
Sherry,
Staying at Mom's. Will come by before work to change clothes.
*Such a Momma's boy! Always a Momma's boy! When will Frank step up to the plate and be a man? I'm sick and tired of dealing with all this stuff by myself! Sick and tired! And how do I know he's at his momma's? I'm sure not gonna call!*
**Forgive.**
*I have forgiven.*
**Forgive with your heart and not with your mouth. Confession is made with the mouth; but salvation is with the heart. It's not a confession issue. It's a heart issue.**
Sherry plopped on the bed, feeling as if she had been spanked…yet again. *Why am always feeling guilty, when I wasn't the one cheating? Frank hurt me. He let me down. I am still down because of it. How am I supposed to just bounce back from adultery? From betrayal? From lying? I don't trust Frank! Not one single bit!*
Moments later, feeling convicted, Sherry went to her laptop to respond to her son's text message.

Tim,
My love for you is unconditional. I will always love you, no matter what you do or say. However, my heart is in shock right now. I'm trying to process it all. You will always be my son and nothing will ever change that. But you know what the Bible says about homosexuality. It's an abomination to God. I cannot condone that lifestyle, but I will always love

you. I will always be there for you and support you, as long as it doesn't go against God's Word. Love always, Mom

Once again, the floodgates of tears opened up and flowed down her face. Staring at the blank screen, Sherry felt overwhelmed, forsaken, forgotten and downtrodden. All her emotions pooled together, Sherry was oppressed. Life was hard. How would she just move on from this, like she had done so many other times? No one even knew of the affair Frank had, excluding their spiritual counselor. She and Frank went to every Sunday service and every Bible study—not missing a beat of the various drums in their lives. It was as if nothing bad ever happened to them. Everyone thought them to be this happy couple. Frank was given kudos for enduring his wife's illness without ever complaining. Only Sherry knew the wall that stood between them. Even their children were spared much of their parents' unhappiness. Unfortunately, Daniel knew more than his siblings about their current sleeping arrangements. Albeit, Frank and Sherry explained that they slept in separate bedrooms because of Sherry's illness and Frank's snoring— Daniel knew everything wasn't kosher.

After wiping her eyes and taking her pain medication, Sherry put on a happy face and went to the kitchen to prepare breakfast. Daniel, bless his *good* heart, was already in the kitchen, flipping pancakes.

"Oh, I'm sorry I'm a little late. I was going to make the pancakes," Sherry stated to her son.

"You do everything Momma. I don't mind cooking breakfast. I burned the first batch."

"Give me that," Sherry playfully took the spatula. "Is this supposed to be bacon?" Sherry frowned, peering at the burnt black stuff on the plate.

"Well, I tried." Daniel threw up her hands. "Cooking just isn't my thing. I'll leave the cooking to you and Tim."

"But you're good at so many other things," Sherry smiled, always bringing out the positive in her children. "You're a great saxophonist; a leader in the church and outside the church. You're book smart and so very handsome."

"Like Dad!" Daniel tossed the bait, knowing something wasn't right with his parents. Wanting to surprise his mom, Daniel figured he would enlist his dad in on the surprise. Only, he was the one surprised when he went into the guestroom and found the bed hadn't been slept in. After observing his mom, it was obvious the two had another heated argument. Her puffy eyes affirmed it.

"Just like dad," Frank entered the kitchen.

Sherry rolled her eyes.

"Dad!" Daniel fist bumped him. Daniel thought the world of his dad. Frank could do no wrong in his eyes. What man would support and standby a wife, who was so ill all the time? Daniel watched his dad care for his mother and dote over her as if she was fine china. There was nothing Frank wouldn't do for his family and Daniel admired that. Frank was his hero. "I wanted to surprise momma by bringing her breakfast in bed.

Frank looked to his wife. Their eyes locked. The hollowness in her cheeks and bags beneath her eyes pierced him with deep guilt. He shouldn't have walked out. He should have stayed and taken it like a man. *Sherry just pushes my buttons. She strips me of my manhood. She tries to manipulate me into doing whatever she wants me to do. She never appreciates me—not anymore.*

Sherry broke eye contact.

"Thanks Daniel for the thoughtfulness," he patted Daniel

on the shoulder. "But I see Mom's cooking."

"I *kinda* burnt the bacon…"

"And the pancakes," Sherry added. "Sit down Danny and eat before you're late for school."

"Are ya'll coming to the game tonight?" Daniel was the drum major for the Western High School Marching Band.

"You know I wouldn't miss it," Frank replied.

"I'm sorry, Danny," Sherry began with her familiar excuse. "My joints are aching. It would be too painful to sit up in the stands."

Daniel nodded, trying desperately to refrain from saying how he really felt. "No problem! Least dad will be there." He swallowed the orange juice and fist bump his father again. "See you tonight after the game," Daniel said, and then turned to his mother. "Hope you have a good day."

"You too, Danny," Sherry felt sickened and somewhat miffed at Frank. He attended everything the kids did, but lupus held her back. At least that's what she told herself. Unquestionably, sometimes Lupus was controlling every part of her life. The pain was unbearable at times. There would be joint pain and stiffness, swelling in her legs and ankles, difficulty breathing, and more. In addition, the rashes etched on her face and hair loss, embarrassed Sherry. Her energy level was zilch…nada. Lupus also caused depression. During the rough times of the illness, Sherry resigned from the world and from her family. She hid behind the disease. She accepted its fate and refused to get back in the ring and fight for her life, for her family, and for her marriage.

The moment the front door closed, Sherry took her anger out on Frank. "You love doing that, don't you?"

"Doing what?"

"Don't play stupid! You love making me look like the uncaring parent, the unsupportive parent, while you get brownie points for attending the games."

"Sherry, don't start that again." Frank felt defeated already. "You can go to the game, just like me."

"How can I? I'm in pain."

"Are you in severe pain, or is it manageable where you can at least show your face for Daniel's sake?"

"How dare you call me a liar!"

"I'm not calling you…"

"Questioning my pain level! You wouldn't survive one day with Lupus! Not one day!"

"You're right, Sherry." Frank remained calmly, swiftly changing the subject. "Timothy called me. He will be in town today and plans on coming to the game tonight."

"Really! Why did he call you and not me?"

His shoulders dropped. There was no way he could have a decent conversation with Sherry. She was a rampant ball of fury and wouldn't stop until she had made Frank feel her wrath, totally and completely.

"He just wanted to make sure that he was welcomed."

"He's always welcomed. I told him that!" she snapped. "What did you say to him?"

"I told him the same thing," he paused. "He's bringing a friend with him."

Her eyes protruded wide. "Are you serious? Who? A boy… friend."

Frank nodded.

"He can't! That's embarrassing! We have friends and several of our church members attend the games! How dare he embarrassed us like that! That's so humiliating! I hope you

16

told him not to bring…that…that…person with him!"

"Sherry, be reasonable. The game is a public place. Timothy can bring *whoever* he wants. It's not the first time he brought a guy to the game."

She sighed loudly, thinking back at all the times he brought a male friend with him. Perhaps he was dating a guy even then. "Well, it's different now! I won't stand for it! I will not let him drag our name in the mud! We're an upstanding family and everyone knows we are Christians!"

"Sherry, this is not about us or what people think," Frank asserted. "It's about Timothy. We cannot drive him away… permanently. He needs us now more than ever."

"I will not condone his gay lifestyle, Frank! It's sinful! It's an abomination!"

"Timothy knows this. We've raised him right…"

"And look at what good that did! Our son is a…"

"He's confused, Sherry."

"Oh, so that's what they are calling homosexuality now. A confused behavior! Oh, please Frank! Stop trying to make it sound so…so less sinful! Sin is sin! You know all about that Frank, don't you? Sin…like sinning with Monique, my best friend. Is that where you were last night?"

And just like that, the conversation turned to Monique, as always.

"You know I was at Mom's. Monique doesn't even live here anymore."

"I don't know anything! Your word is *not worth a dime to me*!"

"I'm going to go get ready for work. I told Charles I'd be in by 10:00."

"Sure you did!"

Sherry was like a dripping faucet, nagging, aggravating, and never ending. Frank had nearly reached his limit with her. Enough was enough.

"How about I make this easier for you, Sherry. Since you seem incapable of forgiveness or trusting me again, how 'bout I look for my own place. This way, you won't have to worry about my whereabouts anymore. Isn't this what you want anyway? I know this roommate thing isn't working for ME anymore."

She was floored. Sherry never expected that Frank would leave. She had pushed him too far and instead of acknowledging that she was just stressed out and was wrong, Sherry blurted, "Leave then! That's what YOU want anyway…so you can go find another woman or go back to Monique! Don't let me hold you back!"

"I won't!" Frank marched off, refusing to let her have the last word this time. *Let her think what she wants. I'm tired of this crap! Every day she opens the wound and pours acid on it with her big mouth.* Slamming the door to the guestroom, Frank just couldn't take it anymore. He tried to work through their problems, earn her trust and forgiveness, but Sherry wasn't having it. She wanted him to pay for his indiscretions, forever. She didn't want to look at the role she played in any of it, not that she was at fault for the affair. However, a man has needs and Sherry refused to meet any of his. She refused to meet Frank halfway in anything.

Sherry literally dropped down in the kitchen chair, stunned by what had just happened. Her anger had gotten the best of her this time. She was losing everything that she loved. First, her eldest Peter was about to marry a woman Sherry inwardly detested. Imani had not only taken Peter from the family, she was changing him and Sherry didn't like the outcome. Her middle child, Tim, was a homosexual, living in another state. To add insult to injury, her baby boy was destined to leave for the army shortly after high school graduation.

*And now this...*

*Frank is moving out.*

Sherry's legs were aching terribly. She was hurting so badly, Sherry didn't think she could get up and walk to her bedroom. The stress of it all was taking a toll on her autoimmune system, causing another flare-up. Stubbornly, Sherry refused to call Frank to help her up.

Sherry sat, downtrodden and depleted of strength. When Frank's door finally opened, she pretended to be eating her pancakes, when truthfully, Sherry couldn't stomach the smell. Her appetite was gone.

Standing before her, Frank put down his suitcases. "Sherry, I apologize for the shouting match." Frank ran his hand through his thick salt and pepper hair, which made him look more distinguished and handsome in Sherry's eyesight. Although, she would never admit that to Frank. "But I do think it is best that we put some space between us. This just isn't working anymore. We argue all the time. *More you than me.* You don't trust me and I get that. Seems like the more I love you, the less you love me back. I'm tired of disappointing you and being a burden. Nothing I do or say makes you happy. Therefore, I'm going to give you your freedom. Sherry, I want you to get your joy back and if leaving you helps you have joy, then so be it. I don't know what else I can do to make you happy. Truthfully, we are both unhappy. Life is too short and...well, I'm tired of living like this."

"You should have thought about that when you cheated on

me," Sherry just couldn't help it. She had been living in the past for so long, Sherry just couldn't embrace her present life.

"Sherry, that happened over two years ago. When are you going to let it go? When?"

"Oh, I didn't know there was a limit on hurt," sarcasm oozed from her lips. "You hurt me Frank, really hurt me."

"Yes, I did Sherry and I've apologized a thousand times. I don't know what else I can do."

"Your apologies don't erase the hurt."

"No, it doesn't, but forgiveness helps. But, you refuse to forgive me."

"I have forgiven you."

"Come on Sherry," Frank scoffed. "You are holding onto un-forgiveness so tight it's like a noose around my neck and believe it or not…it's a noose around your neck…Daniel's… this entire family."

Sherry stared at Frank long and hard, unable to blackout her convicting conscious. Deep down, she knew Frank was right, but she was the victim and not Frank. Sherry feared if Frank left, he would never come back. Inwardly, that was the last thing she wanted.

"If you need anything just let me know. I will still pay the bills. For now, I'll be at mom's until I can find me a place." Frank paused, hoping and praying that she would say something—anything to stop him from leaving.

She blinked back the water gates of tears about to burst. Sherry's pride kept her from doing what her heart yearned to do. She refused to beg Frank for anything. All Sherry had to do was just ask him to stay and he would have—in a heartbeat.

"I will bring Daniel home after the game and maybe we can talk to him together and Timothy together. I'm not sure about Peter's plans."

Sherry remained silent and then finally nodded.

"Take care, Sherry," he leaned over and kissed her forehead. "I will always love you...always." His eyes misted as he picked up his suitcases and walked out the door and out of Sherry's life—hopefully not for good.

Placing her hand on her forehead, still feeling the warmth of Frank's touch, which she missed dearly, Sherry sucked in a shaky breath.

Edging slowly up from the chair, Sherry stumbled, the pain was sharp in her legs. Yet, the physical pain couldn't hold a candle to the pain of her heart. Oppression consumed her. Unquestionably, her life was one big fiasco and seemingly, Sherry felt there was nothing she could do about it—absolutely nothing!

*Oh, but she could...*

*Would she?*

# CHAPTER 3

## Peter's Secret

Frank was surrounded by his two boys at the high school football game, Peter was on one side and Timothy on the other with his friend Larry, who sat a little too cozily for Frank's liking. They were all here to support Daniel and the marching band. Though it was good to have all the kids in one place, Frank was in another world. His every thought was of his wife, Sherry. He felt like a coward for leaving her, especially since he knew she was trying to mask the physical pain she was feeling earlier. How could he leave Sherry when she was sick? How could he just walk away from 25 years of marriage? He vowed for better or worse, in sickness and in health, until death do them part.

*Here I am parting!*

"Dad, did you hear Peter?" Timothy nudged his father.

"Oh, I'm sorry," Frank mouthed. "My mind was elsewhere."

"Tell me about it!" Timothy joshed. "Your body has been here for thirty minutes, while your mind has skipped town."

"What were you saying, Peter?"

"I need to talk to you and mom tonight. You think it would be okay if I came over after the game and we have a quick family meeting?"

Frank scrutinized his son's expression, sensing that another bombshell was about to be dropped on his family. Terror hop-skipped on his back, refusing to budge. Knowing he was already planning to talk to them about moving out, Frank wondered if Sherry could take another blow right now. "Is it something serious, or can it wait?"

"It's serious to me," Peter eyeballed his father.

"Well, I guess its fine. I needed to talk to you all tonight anyway."

Moments later, Timothy's friend Larry was attempting to make conversation with Peter. Purposefully, Peter ignored him.

"Stop being so rude," Timothy barked at his brother. His bark surely worse than his bite.

"Why are you here?" Peter finally looked to Larry.

"Excuse me?" Larry replied.

"You heard me! This is family!" Peter pointed to his dad and Timothy. "You're not!"

"Timmy and I are a couple," proudly Larry said, sticking his chest out like a peacock with his bright pink shirt on. "I'm practically family."

Timothy braced himself for Peter's disapproval.

"Shut up you pink panther!" Peter verbalized his disgust. Then he addressed his brother. "A couple! So you're a fag now?"

"Now is not the time," Frank cautioned. "We're in a public place and we will not make a public spectacle of ourselves. Do I make myself clear?" Frank looked to both of his sons.

"If you ask me, Timothy has already done a good job of that. Look at him and that…that Pink Panther sitting all under him. Now everyone knows he's a fag!"

"Just like everyone knows you are a jerk!" Timothy

24

retaliated.

"So what does your Lord Jesus think about your son's homosexuality?" Cynically, Peter questioned his father.

*Your Lord Jesus.* "Enough Peter. We will talk about it later."

"Let's not!" Peter fumed. "I am disgusted and I do not want to talk about this evil crap another minute! If Timothy wants to live an evil, disgracing life then it is his choice! But I want nothing to do with it and I want nothing to do with him!"

"Peter!" Frank chided.

"You heard me, Dad. If you want to condone this lifestyle, then you go right ahead. But I don't want any part of it in my life and that includes Timothy if he chooses to be with that!" he pointed at Larry.

"So you're going to just drop me like that?" Timothy snapped his fingers, his heart breaking. He loved his brother and did not want to lose him or any of his family members.

"If you make this choice to be gay, then yeah!"

"Where is the love?" Timothy asked.

"Where is the love for doing the right thing?" Peter countered.

"Don't judge me!"

"I don't have to." Peter finished. "You know a tree by the fruit it bears. Your fruit is rotten, brother."

"Well, I just think it's a crying shame…" Larry interrupted.

"I don't give a darn what you think Sweetie Pie!" Peter crudely cut him off. "You disgust me! You've latched onto my brother, making him think he's something he's not! You're a blood-sucking leech and I despise your kind."

"Enough! That kind of hatred doesn't belong in our family, Peter." Firmly Frank stated. "We're here for Daniel tonight. Let's watch the game and his performance."

On that note, not another word was spoken, until Daniel came over in the third quarter after his superb performance during halftime. As drum major for the competition band, Daniel was a natural and he loved it.

"Great job, Brother!" Peter praised. "You really got some moves on the field with that cane."

"Thanks!" Daniel replied, sensing the tension in the air. *What in the world is going on now?*

"Daniel let me introduce you to Larry," Timothy made the introductions.

"Nice to meet you," Larry shook his hand.

"Larry is Timothy's boyfriend," Peter exposed.

"Huh?" Daniel frowned. "Like friends…two boys, who are friends?"

"No, like Adam and Steve, not Eve," Peter chuckled.

"You're such a jerk!" Timothy spouted.

"Rather be a jerk than a fag!"

"I don't have to take such abuse!" Larry stood up. "I'm leaving Timmy…"

"Timmy…" Peter mocked. "How sweet!"

"Peter, I've had enough of you tonight." Frank stood. "You are behaving like a child."

"Shouldn't you be chastising Timothy, oh I mean, Timmy. He is the one who is a sinner. He is the one who is messing up his life and bringing down the family's name. Do you know how many church people are here tonight? Everybody will know his secret now. I always knew there was something funny about him. He was too soft!"

"Shut up!" Timothy yelled, drawing undo attention to them.

"Hey, guys you're embarrassing me," Daniel calmly spoke,

looking around to see if all eyes were on his family.

"Sorry, Danniel," Peter stood. "You don't deserve this."

"Neither do I," Timothy stated.

Humph. Peter shrugged his shoulders.

"Are you coming with me or not Timmy?" Larry waited with his arms crossed.

"No. I'll catch a ride with Dad so I can be a part of the family meeting," he touched Larry's hand slightly, which Frank, Peter, and Daniel noticed. It sickened them all. "Besides, I want to know what goody-two-shoes," he looked to Peter, "has to tell us tonight."

"Not that I'm a fag!"

"Nope...just a number-one-jerk!" Timothy boldly reached for Larry's hand. "I will walk you to the car."

"Complete embarrassment!" Peter couldn't help himself.

"I can't believe it," Daniel sat down. "When did this happened?"

"Timothy sent your mother an email yesterday, confessing he was gay." Frank acknowledged.

"Just like him...a coward. He couldn't even face his momma." Peter was so disgusted by it all. "He's always been a momma's boy. Now we know why."

"Peter, for the sake of the family and for your mother's health, please keep your opinions to yourself tonight. I don't know what's got into you, but you are really getting on my nerves."

"Timothy is the messed up one, and you're mad at me. Go figure!"

"Your behavior is downright judgmental, mean-spirited and not Christ-like at all."

Peter bit his lips, pushing back the comeback itching to

come out. *Later! I will save it for later!*

"How is momma taking it?" Daniel always concerned about everyone else.

"Not good."

"Engaging in homosexuality is a sin. Timothy knows that. Why would he take this route? It's wrong and it's going to send him straight to hell." Daniel shook his head. "We have to talk to him, Dad. We have to make him see the truth again. Something has turned him in the wrong direction."

"Don't you mean someone?" Peter ridiculed. "Larry, the sweet cherry!"

"Dad is right," Daniel looked at his brother. "You are mean-spirited."

*He is also right about other things, too!*

Everyone was assembled at the family table in the dining area when Sherry entered, using her cane for support. It had been a long, trying, painful day, and she did her best to put on her happy face. Endeavoring to be strong and keep up the charade that she was hunky-dory, even though she was anything but all right. Sherry sat down at the opposite end of the table from Frank.

Looking around, Sherry was thankful to have all of her children together. It had been awhile. Unfortunately, after the news Frank was about to share, she wondered if they would ever be a family again, sitting and breaking bread together. It was highly unlikely. The thought caused her eyes to misty again.

28

"Mom, you alright?" Daniel was the first to ask what everyone else wondered.

"Just tired, Daniel. How was the game?"

"Of course Western won, 28-7. That's five in a row."

"That's good and what about the band?"

"We showed out, Mom. I wish you had been there. It was one of our best performances for the season." Daniel's eyes lit up. He was so passionate about everything he did.

"Of course!"

"Yeah, Daniel is a real professional," Peter chimed in. "He can really move on the field. He doesn't just direct the band, he uses that baton and makes it move to a beat of its on. *And* his cane is almost like yours. Maybe, we should decorate it, like his."

"Might be a good idea," Sherry looked to her eldest son. Something was different about him. She couldn't quite put her finger on it, but Peter was a changed man. *Hope that Imani has not warped him! I just do not have a good feeling about her.*

"So glad you could make it home. How long are you going to be here Timothy?" Sherry asked.

"I'm going back in the morning. *Gotta* work!"

"I hate that. Anyhow, I changed the sheets in your room. Everything is ready for you to stay tonight."

"I'm staying at the hotel tonight, Mom."

"Why would you do that? You will always have a room here. This will always be your home, Timothy."

"Thanks, Mom, but under the circumstances, I think it's best that…I stay at the hotel."

"He's not alone," Peter added the missing piece to the puzzle.

"Oh…I see," Sherry lowered her eyes, silently praying for

strength.

Clearing his throat, Frank took control of the awkward situation. "Your mother and I have something we want to discuss with you tonight. First, let me start out by saying that we will always be a family unit. We will always support you, love you, and be there for you. Nothing and no one will ever change that."

"We know that, Dad." Daniel smiled.

"But…I feel it is best that your mother and I take some time apart."

"Apart?" All three boys exclaimed in unison.

"Yes, your mother and I need time to figure out…what is best for us. Right now, we are uncertain about the future of our marriage."

"What!" Daniel shook his head. "I know you two haven't been sleeping together, but you said it was because of mom's lupus and your snoring."

"It was at first," his voice was raspy. Frank looked to Sherry, who was fighting hard not to cry. It seemed to be a losing battle. He ached for her and wished nothing more than to say this was all just a mistake, a simple misunderstanding. He and his wife weren't splitting up. Even though Sherry loathed him, Frank was very much in love with Sherry. He wanted to stay married to Sherry for the rest of his life. However, Frank couldn't go on another day living like roommates who didn't get along.

A cold shudder rushed through Sherry. Her heart was pounding like bongo drums. The intensity of her husband's stare greatly unnerved her. Unwillingly to admit to anybody, including herself, Frank still moved her.

"Mom, is this true?" Daniel was beside himself. He never imagined that his parents would separate.

She took a deep breath. "It is."

"Are you divorcing?" Timothy asked.

"No!" Frank shouted without thinking. "At least…that is not the intention right now."

"Nothing is solid anymore," Peter mumbled. "You've been married for almost 25 years. It's crazy to just give up on marriage."

"You don't understand," Frank tried to explain. "It's complicated."

"You're right. I don't understand." Peter uttered. "This is nonsense. Total nonsense. You just *gonna* separate the family like that. Already got Sweetie Pie over there, breaking up the family." Peter pointed to Timothy.

"Now is not the time." Frank cautioned.

"When will it be the right time, Dad? You'll be gone and nothing will ever be the same again. When are you leaving?" Peter asked.

"Tonight."

"Tonight!" Daniel and Timothy echoed their unbelief.

"Can't you guys work it out?" Daniel pleaded. "God hates divorce."

"He also hates homosexuality!" Peter threw in another jab, "but that doesn't seem to stop your brother from doing it!"

"I hate you!" Timothy banged the table hard.

Sherry screamed. "I can't take it! You hear me! I can't take all this!" She attempted to stand but fell back down.

Frank rushed to her side, trying to gather her in his arms.

"Don't touch me!" she squealed.

Frank backed off, and slowly went back to his chair. Silence engulfed the room. Several uncomfortable minutes went by before Peter broke the silence.

"Well, I might as well tell you my news," he looked around at his family, quickly looking over Timothy. "I resigned from all my Youth Leadership responsibilities at church."

"Why?" Frank asked first.

"Because I'm just not feeling it anymore," he paused. "Dad, Mom, you raised me in the church. You taught me about Your Jesus…

*Your Jesus*…both parents thought to themselves.

"You raised me the way you were raised," Peter continued. "But now I need to know the truth for myself. And the truth is…I'm not feeling this church thing anymore."

Sherry sighed so loudly, everyone felt her anguish. "What do you mean?" *It's that floozy, Imani? She's taking Peter away from his faith and us.*

"I don't know if I believe what you believe anymore. I'm not sure if your Jesus Christ is the only way to heaven or if there is a heaven or a hell."

"Who do you believe in?" Frank asked.

"I believe in God."

"Our God?" Frank continued.

"There is more than one God, Dad."

"Oh, my goodness!" Sherry's heart faltered. *How much more can I take?* "How can you deny Jesus?"

"Not saying that I'm fully denying him, but that maybe he was just a prophet," he shrugged. "Nevertheless, your Jesus has been denying me for a long time. I pray, He does not answer. I seek Him, I cannot find Him. I ask for help, He turns a deaf ear. Where is He? Look at the world! People, good Christian people, are suffering and He does nothing! Absolutely nothing! Why serve Your God, who does not seem to care about anything or anyone? Well, you can have it! Imani and I are on the path of finding our own peace. We do not believe in all that nonsense. It's brainwash."

"And you call me a sinner!" Timothy lashed out. "You're no better than me!"

"I'm way better! You are a punk, who pretends to be a Christian! Such a hypocrite!" Disdain dripped from his lips.

"You're going straight to hell, as you put it." Timothy threw his brother's words back at him.

"And you'll be right there with me!"

"Stop it!" Sherry shouted. "What is happening to my family? You have all gone crazy! You've all lost your minds!"

"Enough!" Frank shouted. "You're hurting your mother."

"I'm sorry if I'm hurting you, mother," Peter said calmly. "It's not my intent."

"You've broken my heart, Peter," Sherry cried. "How can one who knows the Truth, be so deceived? You let that Imani in your heart and she's taken you away from Jesus."

"I love Imani."

"You loved Elaine!" Sherry went on. "She was good for you and good to you. I never understood why you two broke up. You were so perfect together."

"Nothing is perfect, Mom. Definitely not Elaine."

"What do you mean?" her brows furrowed. "She's the preacher's daughter and she's a good girl."

"I don't want to talk about Elaine." he blurted. "I'm with Imani now."

"I'm going to pray for you, Peter. You are in such a sad state now. You don't have Jesus' covering anymore."

"If you ask me, I never did." Peter grabbed his jacket.

"Son," Frank stood up, resting his hand on his shoulder. "We have trained you in the way you should go. Taught you through the Word of God. Introduced you to Jesus. I don't know how long it is going to take…or how you will return to the Lord…but I know…one day, somehow, you will look to Jesus and with open arms, He will accept you back into the family."

"That will never happen, Dad."

"Oh, yes it will, Peter. Satan desires to sift you as wheat. But, I have prayed for you, that your faith should not fail. And when you have returned to Me, that you may strengthen your brethren." Frank quoted the Scripture in Luke, chapter 22.

"Let's agree to disagree," Peter embraced his father. Walking to his mother, he hugged her as if it were his last time. "I love you, Mom. I'm sorry to hurt you, but I must do what I believe is right," he whispered in her ear.

"You need Jesus," she whispered.

"Bye Daniel," Peter waved, ignoring Timothy and then he walked out of the front door.

Stunned, no one said anything for a while.

"Well, I guess I better be going," Frank slid his chair back. "Timothy are you ready?"

"I would just like to say something," Timothy stood. "Although I am with Larry, I still love the Lord with all my heart. And I'm not denouncing that I am a Christian."

Sherry shook her head. *How in the world was everything so screwed up?* "Sin separates us from Jesus. You cannot live a sinful life and think that it's alright with God. You have to choose either Jesus or Satan. There is no in between, Timothy. And you know this."

"I'm not sure being gay is a sin."

"The Bible doesn't lie," Frank replied. "It's an abomination to the Lord. He destroyed Sodom and Gomorrah because of it.

The Bible also says neither fornicators, idolaters, adulterers," he paused looking at his wife, swallowed and went on, "nor homosexuals, nor thieves…and the list goes on, shall inherit the Kingdom of God. Homosexuality is not God's plan; it is the devil plan. Do you want me to get the Bible and read to you what it says?"

"No, Dad, but instead of judging me…maybe you and mom should read it as well." Timothy hung his head, momentarily. "I love you both, all of you," he looked to Daniel, who sat in a dazed, confused and bewildered by everything. "But, I cannot help the way I was born."

"The devil is a liar!" Sherry exclaimed. "God didn't create you that way. We were all born in sin, shaped in iniquity, but because of Jesus, we can live a righteous life! It is a choice, Timothy. Just like it's a choice to commit adultery…"

Frank felt the jab right to his gut.

"…murder, lying, fornication…it's all sin. God doesn't look at any of it any differently. Right now, you are choosing sin. You are choosing satan's way over Christ Jesus' way. And that breaks my heart."

"I'm sorry, Mom," his eyes watered. "I'm sorry to disappoint you."

Sherry wept.

"Can we go now?" Timothy turned to Frank.

"When I call to remembrance the genuine faith that is in you, which dwell dwelt first in your grandmother…and mother… and I am persuaded is in you also. Therefore, I remind you to stir up the gift of God, which is in you through the laying on of hands. For God has not given you a spirit of fear, but of power and of love and of a sound mind." Frank quoted a passage of Scripture found in II Timothy 1:5-7, making it personal for

Timothy. "You were anointed as a child to do great exploits for the kingdom. No demon in hell is going to stop that."

Frank looked over to his wife, who gazed up at him, tears freely falling. He knew she approved of the Scriptures he had quoted to both his sons. One thing for sure, Frank was always well-versed in Scripture. No one could deny that fact. Not even Sherry.

There was nothing else to be said. Frank motioned for his hurting son. He walked out of the door and walked out on his marriage. Though hopefully temporarily, it didn't erase the stigma of separation.

# CHAPTER 4

## Absence makes the heart grow fonder

For two days, Sherry stayed in bed, bedridden and grief-stricken. Miserable and oppressed, there was no reason for her to get out of bed. With Frank gone, Sherry felt utterly alone. She didn't have the will to fight. There was nothing worth living for anymore. Her children, excluding Daniel, had thwarted her dreams for them. She expected them to be upstanding, productive Christians, influencing the world in such a positive way, that Jesus Himself would be pleased and smile upon them. They were so displeasing in her eyes right now. Certainly, God felt the same.

Life had flattened Sherry, flatter than a pancake, leaving bitterness instead of sweetness. The embarrassment she felt was overpowering. Receiving several voicemail messages from church folks, who attended the football game Friday night, each mentioning Timothy holding hands with some good-looking guy left Sherry feeling humiliated. How would she ever show her face in church again? Especially now that Frank had moved out.

Sherry had never felt so alone and inadequate, like damaged

goods. Useful for nothing and *nobody*.

*I wonder how many people know about our separation. Bad news travels fast. Surely, Ms. Nosey Peabody has already told everybody about Timothy.* Ms. Peabody was the head usher and the head of the Blabbermouth Gossip Squad. Hers was the first voicemail message! *I am mortified!*

Oppression was slithering its creepy poisonous way back into the crevices of Sherry's broken heart—subtly, but strongly. Its poison was worse than lupus. Whereas lupus affected her organs and autoimmune system, oppression infested her soul… slowly killing her.

Frequently, Daniel checked in on his mother, worried that she would slip back into the lifeless state she had been in before when Lupus had been at its worse. Sherry didn't want to live. God had other plans. With their home being so topsy-turvy now, Daniel didn't know if his mother would survive this time. She appeared defeated.

"Mom," Daniel entered the room, carrying a tray. "I have some delicious chicken noodle soup and your medications."

"I'm not hungry," Sherry said. "And I don't want the pills."

"You need the pills, Mom."

"Danny, please…"

"Mom, I know you're hurting right now, but no matter what is going on with dad, Peter, or Timothy, I still need you," he put the tray down and sat on the corner of her bed. "I will always need you."

Sherry believed that Daniel would do anything for her. He would give his life for hers, but she also recognized that life could be so cruel. Though Daniel had good intentions of always being there, he could not control his fate. He had no more control over it than she did.

"Thank you, Danny," she reached for the tray. "I'll try and eat a little."

"Good," he stayed, making sure she did just that.

After swallowing almost half of the soup, Sherry motioned for Daniel to the take the tray. "You heated up the can of chicken soup, just right," she grinned.

"Didn't I?" Daniel's eyes twinkled. "Umm, dad called several times. He was checking on you and wanted to know if he could come by and get a few things that he left, like his brown shoes?"

"Can you take them to him, Danny? I'm not ready to see Frank just yet."

"Mom, don't give up on our family. God put us together as a family and He knows how to piece us all back together, one piece at a time," Daniel spoke with wisdom.

"I'm not so sure this time, Danny," Sherry's faith wavered. "Some things just cannot be fixed."

"All things are possible to him who believes," Daniel quoted. "Isn't that what you always say?"

"Not sure…what I believe anymore."

"You can't lose your faith, Mom. You just can't!"

"I'm trying," fresh tears spilled over, blurring her vision. Tightness squeezed her throat making it impossible to speak any further.

Swiftly, Daniel wrapped his arms around his mother, feeling her pain. He, too, was hurting. His mother was the backbone of their family, holding them all together with her prayers, support, and strength. Now, she needed someone to uphold her. Witnessing her in such a fragile state was nearly Daniel's undoing. *God, we need You now, more than ever!*

"It's going to be all right, Mom. I know God will not fail us."

Suddenly, Frank appeared at Sherry's bedroom door. "Is everything all right?"

"What are you doing here?" Sherry wiped at her eyes.

"I needed to get some things."

"You don't live here anymore! You cannot just come by when you want! This is my home now!" Sherry reiterated. "You can just leave your key with me now!"

"Need I remind you that my name is on the mortgage? I am paying the bills. This still is my home." Frank didn't bat an eye.

"You left your home. You left your family."

"Sherry, stop being so unreasonable."

"Unreasonable! You're the unreasonable one. You want to have your cake and your ice ice-cream, *ain't* that right Frank?"

"Please folks, don't argue!" Daniel was mentally tired of it all. "Mom isn't feeling well, Dad."

"I'm sorry," Frank mumbled. "But I do need to get some items I left behind."

"Get them and go!" Sherry closed her eyes, trying to shut him out. If only it were that simple.

"Daniel, please leave your mother and me alone for a moment."

"No Danny!" Sherry sat up.

"Daniel, please," Frank asserted. "Now."

Reluctantly, Daniel left the room, praying that neither of them would hurt the other...not necessarily physically, but emotionally.

"Listen, Sherry, we don't have to be enemies," his voice was soothing. "We still have Daniel to raise together."

"Kind of hard to do that when we are not together."

"I left because I thought you wanted it," Frank hoped she

would deny it. He waited, but Sherry said not a word as she reclined back on the bed with eyelids closed. "Anyhow, I thought we needed the space. I am confused, Sherry. On one hand, I love you so much I do not want to leave or lose you. On the other hand, I love you enough to let you go…to be free from me…so maybe you can be happy again."

His confession confused her and comforted her at the same time. Pride kept her silent. Bitterness kept her hardhearted. Harboring offense kept her oppressed.

"I know you hated going to counseling, but perhaps, we can try it again. You can choose the counselor. We owe it to ourselves and to our sons…to at least try it one more time. If it does not work, then…we can end this marriage."

Sherry's eyes popped opened as she looked to him. Intermittently, her lungs collapsed and her heart spasms out of control. Frank was thinking of going all the way with this separation—possibly divorcing. No matter how much she denied it to herself, Frank still mattered to her. She wanted to hate him forever for what he had done to her. How he betrayed her with Monique. However, hidden and stifled where no one could see but God, was a heart that still cared for Frank, very much so. He was her first and only love, which made the betrayal that much demoralizing and deplorable.

"Will you at least think about it?" His eyes pierced hers, speaking more than audible words.

For the first time, Sherry saw what she saw every day when she looked in the mirror—hurt. *Frank's hurting, too!* The realization of that shook her like an earthquake. Though Frank kept his emotions at bay, somehow his eyes always revealed the truth. Sherry could read his eyes like an open book. "I'll think about it."

"Pray about it?" He pushed the envelope a little further.

She nodded.

"That's all I ask," Frank smiled. "Now, as for the body, how are you feeling? Is there anything I can do?"

She shook her head.

"When is your next doctor's appointment?"

"Friday."

"Can I take you?"

"Frank, everything has changed. You can't go around acting like it hasn't."

"I'm still your husband, Sherry. I want to take care of you just as I have in the past."

She closed her eyes, thinking it through. Daniel could not take her because he was in school. Timothy lived a two hours away. Well, Peter, who knows where he was? Sherry hadn't heard from him since Friday night, four days ago. She could not drive herself unless the pain eased and the inflammation decreased. That left only Frank. Sherry felt weak and helpless. Guarded feelings, she purposely wanted to stay in a prison of isolation. She didn't want to need anybody, especially not Frank.

"Okay," grudgingly she gave in to the only option she had left.

"Nine o'clock as always."

She nodded.

"Can I pray with you, Sherry?" Frank felt the need.

Surprised, Sherry nodded. It had been a long time since the two had prayed together.

"Dear Father God, we come to You thanking You for touching Sherry right now, from the crown of her head to the soles of her feet. Remove every pain, every ache, deflate any inflammation, and cure the Lupus and all side effects. Restore her health. Give Sherry peace of mind and joy in her heart. Moreover, Lord, bless our sons, Peter and Timothy. Father, they are lost sheep, in need of the Good Shepherd to lead them back into the fold. Cover and protect them from harm's way. Have mercy on them and on us. Bless Daniel. I know he is trying to brave this out, but he is hurting, too. And, Lord, if possible, mend our hearts…Sherry and mine, back together again. We thank You for hearing and answering our prayer in Jesus' name, amen."

"Amen."

"Well, I'll get my things. See you Friday."

She nodded.

With shoulders sagging, Frank exited the room.

"Everything okay," Daniel met him outside the door. "You were in there a long time."

"Not long enough," Frank grinned. "Mom is in pain. She has a doctor appointment Friday, but if you notice something out of the ordinary between now and Friday, please call me and I'll take her straight to the hospital."

"Mom hates the hospital."

"Rightly so, but it's for her good."

"I talked to Timothy a few minutes ago," Daniel stated. "He and Larry live together."

"I didn't know that."

"They go to some church, where the pastor supports gay marriages," Daniel frowned. "The world is becoming worse than Sodom and Gomorrah, Dad. Surely, Jesus is coming back again soon."

"He has to be," Frank put his hand on Daniel's shoulders, as he often did when he was saying something important.

"We must remember, God loves Timothy. He hates sin but loves the sinner. Also, we must be mindful that we don't treat Timothy like he has leprosy. He's God's child. The woman who committed adultery…what did Jesus say to her accusers?"

"He without sin cast the first stone," Daniel replied.

"None were sinless…and neither are we, Daniel. We strive not to sin. However, our righteousness is as filthy rags. It's only the blood of Jesus that cleanses us. With that being said, we have to continue to love Timothy and Peter, in spite of the paths that they have chosen to chart now. We may not condone their lifestyles, but we still must love them and pray for them."

"Peter is crazy. I called him and he was talking nonsense. He was saying all this anti-Jesus stuff. He's not sure about there being one God. Jesus Christ isn't the only way to heaven. He doesn't eat this or he doesn't do that. He said he wasn't coming over for Thanksgiving or Christmas…pagan celebrations. He doesn't celebrate man-made holidays. He seemed really out there. What happened, Dad? How could he stray so far from the Truth?"

"It's true that Christmas has become so very commercialized. Even Christians have forgotten why we celebrate our Savior's birth. It's not about the day, because no man knows Jesus' exact birthday. It's about the purpose. The Savior of the world was born… as the Greatest Gift ever given to mankind. Anyhow, Daniel, we just need to keep praying for him."

"What about you and mom?" Daniel hesitated. "Should I keep praying that you two will get back together?"

"Most definitely!"

"What are you going to do to make that happen, Dad? Mom seems depressed about it. It is oppression all over again. Like she's giving up. I don't want her to go back…"

Frank knew his fears because he had the same ones. "Sherry won't. I'm going to do everything in my power to keep that from happening."

"How, Dad?"

"I'm going to win her back."

"But you moved out," Daniel was confused.

"So your mother could miss me," Frank admitted. "Absent makes the heart grow fonder. Staying here was not working. So, I figured by leaving your mother would miss me and somehow…want me back. I know one thing, it has only been four days, but it seems like forever. I miss Sherry more than I thought possible."

"I pray your plan works and not backfire."

"When did you become a pessimist?"

"Friday, when my family fell apart."

"Have faith, son, God will put us back together again.

Sitting on the couch, watching the news, Frank wanted to be any place but at his childhood home. His mother was driving him crazy. His life was in a shambles, his entire family in disarray, and Frank felt worthless. However, being away from Sherry, gave him time to re-evaluate his life. To really take the time and glimpse how far he had fallen from grace. Although he was endeavoring to live a life pleasing to God now, the consequences of his wrongful actions weren't going away. He had to accept that his family's problems were greatly his responsibility.

Why had he drifted away from his marriage, seeking

comfort from another? Seeking attention from a woman, who was his wife dearest friend. Yes, Monique stroked his ego, making him feel wanted, desirable, important and needed. Truth be told, Monique was the pursuer. Because Frank was lonely, he easily became vulnerable to satan's plan and buckled under pressure. Afterwards, Sherry made Frank feel small as if he was nothing but a provider for the family. It seemed, she tolerated him but didn't respect him—anymore.

And their love life? What love life? He hadn't slept in the same room with his wife since the affair. However, before the affair, Sherry used her health issues as an excuse, wanting no intimacy with Frank. They were just two roommates living in the same home but living separate lives. Their hearts weren't connected anymore. Sadly, their only connection was the children.

How did he let this happen? Why didn't he fight for his marriage before the affair and even after the affair? Like a coward, Frank just gave up. He let everybody think that he and his wife were happy and they had this happy family. Now, the joke was on him. Soon, everybody would know that his family was a mess. For the first time, Frank didn't care. All he wanted now was for his family to be restored. The oppression that had settled over his family, Frank wanted it to be lifted for good.

*God, I need You. I release it all to You. Show me how to get my family back. And...give me patience with my mother.* For Frank feared he would snap if his mother didn't hush up. Her constant negativity, regarding his family, was wearing Frank down.

"I think Sherry is faking her pain!" Martha continued with her derogatory remarks about Frank's wife. "She looks fine to me. I mean, one minute she is prancing around, playing the keyboards in church, then the next she cannot get out of bed. She just wants the attention, if you ask me."

"Mom, I'm not asking you," his sentiment just slipped out before Frank could retract it.

"What?"

"Mom, Sherry is still my wife."

"Yeah, but she's not a good wife. She treats you like dirt. She barks orders at you and you jump like a trained dog. She has never treated you right. Never!"

"Sherry is a good wife and a good mother. And yes, she plays the keyboards at church, but most of the time she is in pain even in doing that. She tries not to let the disease get to her. The only time she stays in bed is if she cannot help it," Frank defended his wife's honor. "I'm blessed to have Sherry and I don't want to lose her."

"She's blessed to have you…if you ask me!"

*I did not ask you!*

"Perhaps you would be better off without her," Martha pushed further. "There are a lot of good women out there who know how to appreciate a good man."

"Mom, I haven't always been good. You know what I put Sherry through with Monique."

"Well, she pushed you into her arms."

"You can't blame Sherry for my indiscretions. I made the choice to be unfaithful to my wife. It was all my fault and not hers."

"Well, how long is she going to make you pay for messing up…like she's some kind of saint!" Martha huffed. "She *ain't* no saint. People talk you know."

"Enough!" Frank had had it. "This conversation is over. If you can't say anything good about Sherry, then don't say anything at all, Mother."

Martha's eyes stretched in disbelief. Frank had never talked to her in such a crude tone before. "Your family is a mess, Frank," she couldn't help herself. "Now Timothy is a *homo.* That's because Sherry babied him. Peter is an atheist. That's because Sherry let him do whatever he wanted to do. I *sho* pray that Daniel turns out right."

"Sherry is not to blame for the Peter or Timothy's choices. If anyone is to blame it's me," Frank acknowledged. "Working all those late hours and never being at home. It is only recently that I start going to Daniel's activities. Sherry used to attend every game when the disease was in remission."

"That was a long time ago." Martha refused to give Sherry credit for anything. Frank was her only child and no woman would ever be good enough for him.

"Mother," Frank eased up from the chair and looked his mother straight in the eyes and said, "let's get this straight. I am here for only a short while. I intend on winning my wife back. I intend on wooing her all over again and making her fall in love with me. I intend on being the best husband, the best father, the best man of God, I could ever be. I love you and respect you, but I will not allow you to say another negative thing about my Sherry. If you do, I am checking into a hotel, immediately. Do I make myself clear, Mother?"

Dumbfounded, she replied, "Perfectly." A widow of eleven years, Martha didn't want to lose her only child. For that reason alone, she would bite her tongue to keep the peace between them, while secretly hoping he would leave Sherry for good. In her eyes, Sherry didn't deserve him. *Frank done grew a backbone!*

# CHAPTER 5

## The Reed Sons

"Your mother never liked me," Imani contended while folding the clothes. Peter had moved in with Imani a few days ago. Imani was glad Peter was living with her, an hour away from his hometown. Away from his family. Away from his religion. Away from everything and everyone that could separate Imani from the man she loved. "She always gave me the evil-eye when I came over."

"Mom just never got the chance to really know you," Peter safeguarded his mother's honor. No matter how distanced they might be he loved his mother and would let no one put her down. Peter loved his family, including Timothy, whom he just didn't respect right now. "You've only been around her a few times."

"Enough to know she hates me. She thinks she's better than me. Acting all high and mighty, snubbing her nose at me, like I'm filth!" Imani true feelings surfaced. "She hates me and I don't care!"

"My mother doesn't have a hateful bone in her body."

"That's what all those Christian people say. A bunch of hypocrites. My mother used to be the same way, praying to a God that she believed would help her. But he didn't. He sure didn't keep her from getting beat upside her head by my drunken dad, or punched or shoved or kicked!" she laughed wickedly. "Night after night, she prayed and nothing. God... what a joke! There's no God. No higher being."

*A fool has said in his heart, there is no God!* The familiar scripture echoed in Peter's heart.

"Oh, I grew up with that foolishness! Pray—believe— receive! Your faith can move mountains. Really, the mountains were moving us, while crushing us to the poor house. Where was God when my dad hit my mother one too many times? He was nowhere to be found. Instead, my mom ended up dying, while my no-good father shot himself in the head. Where was God when I ended up in a shelter, then a terrible a foster home that I ran away from at age of sixteen? Been on my own ever since! Please..." she sneered. "Spare me that kind of God." Anger and bitterness ejected from her mouth, like venom.

*In the beginning was the Word, and the Word was with God, and the Word was God. He was in the beginning with God...*

Again, a familiar scripture his father quoted Friday night whispered in Peter's heart, stirring his heart with uneasiness. *Satan has asked for you, that he may sift you like wheat, but I have prayed for you, that your faith should not fail; and when you have returned to Me, strengthen your brothers.*

Imani continued. "If your people want to continue to believe that foolish stuff, then go ahead...but I want us to be free from it, Peter. We don't need it. And really we don't need them."

"I think we better change the subject," Peter cautioned.

"I'm just saying!" Imani pouted. "I just want us to be happy. With your family acting so crazy...thinking we are devil worshippers or such evil people, I just don't think we need to be around any of them."

"No one said that we were those things," Peter defended.

"Timothy said a few choice words. At least that's what you told me."

"Timothy was mad. It was my fault. I pushed him and said some awful things myself."

"You were just calling a spade a spade. He's a queer—gay. I mean, what does he expect you to say…that it's okay to be gay?" she scoffed. "Gays are taking over the world. They all need to be brought together and poisoned like Hitler did the Jews."

"Hold up!" Peter shouted. "That's my brother you're talking about. I mean…hey, I can talk about him, but you are not going to just go on dogging him, wishing he would be killed or something! That's evil! Timothy is my brother," he repeated firmly, "and I don't care who he is or what he does, I will always love him. We're blood…*and you're not!*"

Imani knew she had crossed the line. "I'm sorry, Babe," she went to him, wrapping her arms around his fit waistline. "It's just that I don't want your family to come between us. I love you, so much. And yesterday, after talking to Daniel, you were upset. He was trying to convert you back to that crazy religion of theirs. He thinks you're gullible enough to go back to being brainwash," she pecked his lips. "I don't want anyone to hurt you, Babe. They don't understand you like I do. What we have is special and I fear they will try to tear us a part."

Slowly, but surely, Peter calmed down, taking in several deep breaths before speaking. "I'm my own man and you know that."

"I know," she toyed with his hair, "but I don't think they

know. Let's just keep a distance from them for now... that's all I'm asking. Like you said, you need space to figure out who you are and what you believe."

"I will always love my family, Imani. Nothing will ever change that—not even you."

"I don't want to change that," she lied. "I just want to be the most important person in your life. I don't want to be second to anyone, not even your family. When a man marries, the wife becomes first."

"We are not married, yet." Peter reminded, suddenly feeling like things were going way too fast. He had known Imani only six months and she was practically rushing him down to the altar to be married. It was one thing to go against his beliefs of shacking up, but to marry someone who despised his family, was another. "And until we do, I think its best that we do not talk about my family."

"I think you are right," Imani felt defeated—for the moment. However, deep down, Imani believed that eventually, Peter would be eating out of her hands, especially since she had taken him away from his *holy-roly* family.

Meanwhile, Timothy and Larry were sharing dinner in their new place. He, too, had stepped out of the bounds of their moral upbringing not to shack up or fornicate. As usual, Larry was chatting away, talking about his customers at the salon, while Timothy just listened. He didn't feel like talking. His mind was elsewhere. Still shocked by his parents' separation, Timothy's heart was troubled. He hadn't talked to his mother in four days, which may not seem like a long time for most people. Typically, Timothy talked his mother every day, whether through email, texting or talking on the phone. She was more than just a mother and a friend. She had been his spiritual advisor. This silence between them was shattering his world, leaving him oppressed. He missed his family immensely.

"Are you even listening to me?" Larry screeched in his high tone, which secretly grated Timothy's last nerve.

"Yeah, you were talking about Tressia…your manager at work," he answered.

"Twenty minutes ago! What's with you? This melancholy mood is putting a damper on our evening. Not to mention the oppressing vibes it's putting in this apartment." Larry was always the dramatic one.

"Listen, this is new to me," Timothy voiced his feelings. "I'm close to my family. We love one another and always stick close to each other. But now…well, things are different. My mother has lupus and I don't even know if she is well or not."

"You don't seem that close to me. Your family is a mess! Your mother and father aren't even together. Daniel is a little-goody-two-shoes, but too good to be true. If you ask me, he's hiding something. Look at Peter! He hates you!" Larry jigged the nail into Timothy's bruised heart. "And now he doesn't know if there is a God or not? Please! You're better off without that nutty family."

"My family is not nutty!" Timothy firmly contested. "My parents are just going through a bad patch right now. Peter doesn't hate me. He's just mad right now. Daniel is a good person…always has been. There is nothing sinister or hiding in his closet."

"Don't be so sure," Larry continued. "Everyone has some

skeletons in their closets…even Daniel."

"I'm not arguing with you about Daniel or any of my family members."

"We're not arguing, just having a discussion," Larry amended. "I just think your family hides behind religion. People on the outside see something different from what is really going on behind closed doors. Your family is judgmental. Though your father didn't say anything, I could tell he didn't like me being at the game. It was as if I was some diseased being. As for Peter, after only meeting me once, he accused me, tried me, judged me, found me guilty and sentenced me to life without parole!"

"Stop being so dramatic, Larry. We were raised differently. My family believes homosexuality is a sin and wrong."

"That's because they are judgmental. People cannot help if they are born this way. It's still no excuse for the way Peter behaved. He hates me and he's a mean bully."

Timothy didn't deny that. "He'll come around."

"I think you better get used to being ostracized from the family functions," Larry continued. "Not only does Peter hate me, he hates you, as well."

"Peter doesn't hate me. We're blood," Timothy refused to accept such presumptions. "And I will never believe otherwise. The Reed family sticks together. We have each others' back. My family is and will always be very important to me."

"Timmy, the family unit you once knew is no more. Your parents are divorcing," Larry repeated, "and Peter is now an atheist."

"My parents are not divorcing. They are on a hiatus for right now. They will find their way back to each other and so will Peter. He is lost, that's all. He'll find his way back."

"And you..." Larry fretted, knowing that Timothy was fighting tooth and nail to live right, not really on solid ground with their relationship yet. "Are you going to find your way back, too?"

Timothy didn't answer. "I'm confused, Larry. I believe the Bible. I believe that God's Word is true. But I cannot deny that these feelings are real. What I feel for you is real." Timothy found himself between a rock and a hard place. He loved God and his family, but he had strong feelings for Larry, as well.

Larry reached for his hand. "Just as what I feel for you is real. I love you, Timmy. You're special to me. I believe wholeheartedly you're my soul-mate. I've been waiting for you for twenty-six years. Now that you're here, I don't want to lose you. Don't allow your family to come between us. And don't let religion tear us a part. Pastor Dave says God accepts us as we are." He was an active homosexual, married to his partner for three years now.

"God loves us just as we are...but I'm not so sure, He accepts our sins. In the Bible, He doesn't condone murdering, just as He doesn't condone adulterers...or homosexuals."

"Timmy!" Larry snatched his hand away. "You're not changing your mind, are you? I cannot go through these roller-coaster emotions of yours. One minute, you're sure it's okay and then the next you're running like a scared chicken! My heart is at stake. You need to make up your mind once and for all because I refuse to be looked at as if I'm wrong for loving you and being with you."

"I know," Timothy felt his lover's pain. "I don't want to hurt you."

"Then don't! Let go of the past and let's move forward—together."

"I'm trying, Larry. Just give me time."

"I will, but for right now, until you're stronger, I think it's best that you stay away from your family and their antiquated views. It's only confusing you more. Talk to Pastor Dave again. He'll help you see the truth."

"Maybe I will."

Meanwhile, Daniel was out on a date with his girlfriend, Molly. The twosome had been officially dating for a year but had been best friends since elementary. Molly was a member of their church, working in the children's ministry, alongside Daniel and his mother. She was like family.

Both were still pure before God, wanting to save that special oneness for marriage. Daniel believed fully that he would marry Molly someday. He loved her wholeheartedly. It didn't matter to Daniel that Molly was paralyzed from the waist down, due to a car accident when she was just twelve years old. Molly insists that she has some feelings in her legs at times. However, according to the doctors she will never walk again. Still, her free-spirit and determination to overcome many obstacles moved Daniel with deep admiration. Molly would let nothing get her down. Daniel and Molly were both optimists, seeing the glass half full instead of half empty.

"You're quiet tonight," she said at the restaurant. "What's wrong? You didn't like the movie, did you?"

"I hate horror," Daniel frowned. "But I'll do anything for you."

"I appreciate that. You have to admit, it wasn't that scary."

"No, it was more stupid than scary," Daniel chuckled.

"Watch it!"

"Next time, I get to pick the movie."

"As long as it's not a science fiction."

"You know I hate science fiction."

"I guess, action it is," Molly smiled.

"Yep!"

"Seriously, Daniel, what's wrong?" Molly reached for his hand, caressing it gently.

"What's not wrong? My dad is living with his mother. Peter doesn't believe in Jesus Christ anymore and he's moved to another city to live with a lady who appears heartless and cold. Timothy has come out of the closet, living with Larry. And Mom, she's giving up on life!" He tossed up his hands. "And here I am trying to stay strong in my faith. Well, Molly, my faith is shaken a bit. I'm praying, but I just don't know if God is hearing me anymore."

"He hears you, Daniel. God knows the hurt you're feeling right now and in time, He's going to work it all out. You just have to keep praying and holding on, even if it's only by a thread. All He needs is mustard seed faith—something to work with."

"That's good because that's about all I have right now."

"I remember when I first had my accident and the doctors told my parents I would never walk again. I was so mad at them for believing the doctors and not God's Word! I wouldn't talk to them for days. I kept saying to God, prove them all wrong. You can do it, God. Prove them all wrong and make me walk again," she paused. "A year went by and I still couldn't walk. I kept praying and believing, until one day I just gave up."

"You did?" Daniel's forehead crinkled with confusion. "To

this day, you still confess that one day you'll walk again."

"I will, Daniel. Maybe on earth or maybe in heaven. I still believe, but I'm not God. I believe He can heal me and will manifest His healing, but I choose to leave…when, how, and where up to Him. When my faith was at the lowest, I met this old man in a wheelchair during a doctor's visit and he said to me, *God don't make no mistakes. If you're in this wheelchair, He's going to use it for His glory. So you need to get to rolling and do whatever He wants you to do.* That's when I start volunteering with the special needs foundation, working with other kids, encouraging them to take the limits of others' expectations off them. I have made a difference, Daniel, just as you are making a difference with your family. You're the bridge that will bring them all back together."

"You really believe that Molly?"

"I really do. Just keep praying Daniel and hold onto God. When you cannot hold onto Him, He will hold you in the very palms of His hands."

"See, that's why I love you so much," Daniel leaned over and kissed her cheek. "You always know what to say to make me feel better."

"And don't you forget that when you're in boot-camp. I don't know how I am going to make it without you for twelve weeks. We've never been separated, Daniel."

"I know," he understood. "I was thinking, Molly…I was thinking why wait another year to marry? Why don't we get married before boot-camp?"

"Are you serious, Daniel?"

"Very! I don't want to wait. I love you so much and knowing that after twelve longs weeks, I would be returning to my wife, would make boot-camp that much easier. Plus, when

I get my assignment you can travel with me. And you can get the surgery you need."

"Oh Daniel!" she leaned over for a hug. "I think it's a great idea!"

"Hallelujah!" He shouted and then his lips claimed hers more passionately than they ever had before—Saving such passion for marriage. The twosome were so much in sync, their love radiated and consumed the atmosphere.

"Wait!" Molly pulled away. "It's not official until you give me a ring."

"Got it!" Daniel dug into his pocket and retrieved the little black box he had been carrying for months. Dropping to his knees, he officially proposed. "With all my heart, I love you, Molly Myers. You complete me. You make me laugh. You make me stronger. You make me so very happy. I want nothing more than to spend the rest of my life with you. Will you marry me?"

"Most definitely!"

Daniel put the ring on her finger and kissed her again, sealing their engagement.

"I have a lot of planning to do since you're going to join the army a month after graduation.

"With all the drama in my family, let's go to the courthouse."

"Daniel Reed, I will not go to the courthouse," with her hands on her hip, Molly's tone didn't waver. "I want to get married in the church we both grew up in. I don't care if it is just the preacher and our immediate family, but I will not go to the courthouse."

"Okay," he cajoled. "We can do whatever you want. But can we make it for immediate family only…your parents and my crazy family."

"That's fine with me."

"So, let's say the week after graduation, we make it official. That's gives us three weeks of being on our honeymoon," he winked.

Her cheeks colored crimsoned. "Sounds good to me."

"What do you think our parents will say since we both are just eighteen?"

"It's not about age, Molly. I know God created you for me and me for you. That's all that matters. My parents want me… and you to be happy. Besides, my parents already consider you as part of the family. I believe everyone will be excited."

"I hope so."

"I know so."

# CHAPTER 6

# Lupus Relapse

Today wasn't a good day, health wise for Sherry. Besides her joints aching and hip feeling like it would pop out of the socket, Sherry's stomach was in constant pain. She felt like someone was grabbing her stomach pouch and squeezing it. Thus, Sherry stayed in bed, because the pain meds made her sleep through most of the day. When she wasn't sleeping, she was crying.

For nearly a week, day and night, Sherry's eyes overflowed with continuous tears. She couldn't stop weeping for her sons and even for her marriage. Despite all the dirt, Frank had swept into their marriage, it never crossed Sherry's mind that Frank would leave her. Never! When she gave her wedding vows before God, Sherry meant them and assumed Frank did, also. Now, everyone she once believed in had let her down.

She had endeavored to keep the faith. Tried to hold her family together. Tried to be strong. It all had been a facade. She was weak, weary and plain old, worn out. Life just didn't seem to be worth living anymore.

A steady flow of tears streamed down her hollow cheeks. Sherry was carrying a burden much too heavy for her to carry. She found herself too distressed to even pray. She wished for the good old days when children were seen and not heard. When her boys were riding their bikes or playing street basketball. The boys would sometimes have minor injuries, but she'd bandage them up and they'd go right back outside and play as if nothing ever happened. If only a bandage could cover the wounds of her heart now or mend their detached family. Oh, how she longed for them to gather around the piano, while she played and the family harmonized familiar tunes. Those were the days when much laughter and joy filled their home.

*So long ago!*

Things change. Her sons had changed. Her husband had changed. Admittedly, she had changed, too.

Sherry was in mourning for her two sons. Her joy had been snuffed out. Her eldest had walked away from God, denouncing Jesus Christ. Timothy had chosen to fulfill the lust of the flesh and to willfully accepted homosexuality instead of resisting and running away from it. Both were spiritually in trouble. Seemingly, there was nothing she could say or do to shake them to their senses.

*Lord, I'm lonely and hurting. My troubles have increased. I don't know what to do anymore. My life is out of control and I can't stand it.*

Heart writhed in pain, Sherry did not want to see anybody, let alone Dr. Hills for her nine o'clock appointment. She would have to see Frank, who was driving her to the appointment. This caused more dread than pleasure.

Looking at herself in the mirror, Sherry grimaced. Her eyes were swollen and bloodshot. Her cheeks were gaunt, skin color pale and her once glorious hair was thinning as she pulled it back in a ponytail. Sherry wanted to look her best for Frank today, reminding him of what he had left behind.

However, undeniably, she was a sight for sore-eyes and Frank would notice it the moment he saw her. There was absolutely nothing pretty about the face staring back at her in the mirror. With disgust, Sherry put on lip-gloss and hurried away from the mirror.

Slipping on a pair of stretch jeans and light blue sweater, which Timothy had given her last Christmas, almost brought fresh tears. *I wonder if Timothy will spend Christmas with us this year...if any of the children will be here for Christmas dinner. Daniel had mentioned going to the mountains with Molly and another couple.*

Sherry sighed loudly, finding it suddenly difficult to catch her breath. Is it my imagination or am I really having a hard time breathing? *Lord, do not let it be my heart again. Not now. Don't let my heart pulse rate drop low again. I cannot deal with another hurdle right now.*

Not to mention how badly her legs were aching and sore. Sherry was having yet another flare up. They were happening more frequently now and lasting longer, too. Sherry would have to mention this to her doctor. Perhaps her medication needed to be changed—yet again.

Just before heading downstairs to wait for Frank, her phone chimed.

*Ms. Nosey Peabody! Now what?*

"Hello," Sherry faked her cheeriness.

"Hi Sister Sherry," Ms. Peabody greeted. "How are you feeling?"

"I'm fine," Sherry rolled her eyes, "I'm in a hurry though. I have a doctor's appointment."

"Oh, I was just wondering about Timothy. My daughter Sarah saw him at the game last Friday."

Here it goes. *Sarah is just like her mother! Nosey! Gossiper!* "Yes, he was in town…"

"And she said he was with this nice looking guy and they were holding hands. The world is warping the minds of our young people. They are living gay lifestyles and..."

"Ms. Nos…Peabody," Sherry caught herself. "I really must be going, but for the record, Timothy is not gay!"

"But Sarah said…"

"I don't care what Sarah said!" Sherry lashed out. Taking a deep breath, Sherry composed herself as best she could. "Sorry to shout, Ms. Nos…Peabody, but I really have a lot going on right now and I'm going to be late to my doctor's appointment if I don't get off this phone."

"I'm praying for your family. I know it is hard watching your children living in sin. It's a shame when we raise them the right way, then they turnout…"

"Timothy is fine! My family is fine!" Sherry contested.

"And your heart must be broken over Peter leaving the church," she ranted more. "He shouldn't have *broken* up with Elaine. Pastor Law has raised her well. Now, I hear Peter is with this tattooed girl, tattoos all over her body," she hissed. "Such a shame!"

"Ms. Peabody, I really must go," she said frustratingly.

"Sister Lykes says Franks' car has been parked at his mom's house for several nights…" she paused. "Is everything all right on the home front? "

"We're all fine. I must go, Sister Peabody! Have a good day!" Sherry practically slammed the phone done. "How dare she gossip about my family with her nosey self! She ticks me off!" she fumed. "The nerve! Now everyone will know about Timothy and that Frank has moved out! What's next?" *When it rains, it pours!*

Sherry was still fuming by the time Frank arrived. She was so worked up, she was about to explode.

"You're late!" Sherry was waiting at the door when Frank entered.

Looking at his watch, he frowned. "It's only 8:30."

"I asked you to be here at 8:20, so we can beat the traffic."

"There is hardly any traffic."

"And if you would have gotten here on time, I wouldn't have had to talk to Ms. Peabody, with her nosey self. Everybody knows about Timothy being at the game with that…" she refused to say it. "I told you to tell him not to bring him to the game."

"And I told you, Timothy has the right to bring whoever he wants. It is a free country, Sherry. He's old enough to make his own decisions, even if we don't approve."

"God doesn't approve!"

He took a long breath before speaking again. He knew that it was impossible to reason with Sherry when she was in one of her fighting modes. "We should go."

"Then she talked about Peter not being in church anymore and Ms. Lykes already told her about your car being parked at your mom's at night. Therefore, they know we are not together. It is just so humiliating! Can't you just park in the back or something? Do you have to make it so obvious for everyone?"

"Really? You're blaming me because of nosey people. I can't win for losing with you, Sherry. When will you stop making me the scapegoat for everything that has gone wrong? When?" His tone remained calm as his heart cried out for understanding.

His words cut off her rage. Sherry witnessed the hurt

displayed in his eyes. His countenance was sad. Instead of apologizing, she said, "Let's go. I'm going to be late."

He opened the door and then rushed outside to the passenger's side, so he could open her door for her. *Lord, please give me the strength.*

An awkward hush infiltrated the thirty-minute ride to the doctor's office. Disappointment engulfed Frank. He was so looking forward to seeing Sherry. Even though he was just taking her to the doctor's office, the thought of being near his wife pleased Frank greatly. A week apart was too long. Despite their problems, his love for Sherry remained solid. True, she grated his last nerve. Case-in-point, soon as he walked in the door Sherry attacked him, like a hammer, smashing the desires to be with her to smithereens. Frank loved his wife, till death do they part—despite their relationship appearing so dead at present.

Meanwhile, Sherry felt remorseful. The hurt in Frank's eyes cut her to the core. She caused it. Why couldn't she just let go of all the animosity she felt toward him? Why couldn't she just forgive him and move on? The anger and resentment that she held towards him were destroying their marriage. Yet, it was easier to blame Frank than to deal with the truth—her life was a sham—a façade!

Parking his car and turning off the ignition, Frank turned to his wife and placed his hand gently over hers. "I'm sorry Sister Peabody upset you this morning with mean-spirited gossip. You don't deserve any of that Sherry. Right now, I just want you to clear your head, mind, and heart so that you can have a good doctor's visit and a good rest of the day," he paused eying her intently. "Things are going to work out for us, Sherry. I'm not giving up," his voice faded.

That was just like Frank to apologize for something he had no control over in order to smooth things out. His words melted her icy heart. Sherry stared at Frank long and hard before she finally opened her mouth. "I appreciate that, Frank, but it's not your fault. Sister Peabody accomplished what she set out to do and that was to upset me. I gave her the power to do so. So, I guess it's my fault."

"I miss you, Sherry," Frank confessed, still focused totally on her.

Sherry was flustered being in close proximity of Frank. There was no denying, he still had a way of making her heart beat faster. Guarded feelings kept Sherry's heart imprisoned and oppressed. She loved the man, who could smile and warm her heart all at once. Frank still meant the world to her and yet, she couldn't tell him. To be vulnerable to such betrayal all over again, kept the wall around Sherry's heart. "We better get inside."

"Sure thing," Frank squeezed Sherry's hand and hurried outside the car to open her door.

Once inside the waiting area, Sherry looked to her husband and whispered, "I miss you, too, Frank."

His eyes sparkled as his smile widen. For the first time in a long time, Frank felt hopeful. At least Sherry hadn't slammed the door in his face again. Instead, she cracked it slightly open, with the possibility that one day Frank could enter in again.

Hope was a beautiful thing!

"Mrs. Reed, you're right the SLE (Systemic Lupus Erythesmatosus) has flared up. That is why you are experiencing severe joint stiffness. I know you hate it, but you need to use the walking cane again." Dr. Hills reviewed Sherry's chart again. "I am going to give you a steroid shot before you leave today."

"The steroids always make my blood pressure elevate." Sherry went on to explain that she had been feeling dizziness, shortness of breath and being tired more than usual.

Dr. Hills closed her file and looked at her with much concern. "The tests also indicate that your heart pulse rate is 30bpm and we're striving to maintain at least 40 to 60 bpm. The medication doesn't seem to be working. Perhaps, we will try another medication in low dosage since the effects can make you tired."

"So am I in danger of heart failure again?" Sherry worried. She barely survived the last time. *Not another setback!*

Frank fretted, his heart rate kicking up several notches. He reached for Sherry's hand. Surprisingly, she placed it gently in his care, looking at him with fear presenting itself. Squeezing her hand, Frank whispered in her ear, "We'll get through it… together."

Her lips quivered. Her shoulders sagged, as she shifted anxiously in her chair. *This was not good…not good at all.*

"I'm going to send you to Dr. Lloyd, the cardiologist you had before," he closed the file. "I don't want you to worry, Sherry. It is obvious to me that you are under a lot of pressure right now and stress is the last thing you need. Let me speak frankly," Dr. Hills, turned to Frank. "Your wife cannot deal with any stress right now. Her lupus is aggravated, which means her autoimmune system is not functioning properly. She needs rest and peace. And she needs to stay on all medications." He eyed Sherry, assuming that she wasn't taking her medications as prescribed, "and she needs to eat healthier and to stop skipping meals."

"I understand, Dr. Hills," Frank asserted. "I will make sure Sherry is following your orders," he winked at Sherry. Something he had not done in a long time.

The simple gesture thrilled Sherry to no end. Despite the bad news, Sherry was glad she would not have to battle this alone. For the first time, in a long time, she appreciated Frank. He was the one solid thing in her life that remained. No, he wasn't perfect and had hurt her deeply, but he was trying to make things right. For a long time, Frank endured Sherry's bitter treatment, her nagging, her outlandish wishes, knowing that no matter what he did, it was not good enough.

After administering the steroid shot, Dr. Hills handed Sherry her prescription. "I'll have the nurse give you some samples. Again, if you feeling any unusual pains in your chest or having difficulty breathing, you call my cell phone immediately, and go to the hospital."

Sherry was alarmed, reading between the lines, she knew her health was not good. "I will."

After checking out and scheduling with the Cardiologist, Dr. Lloyd, Sherry accepted Frank's invitation for brunch to her favorite café *Jacksons*. It was a homey eatery with the best soul food in town.

"Let's bless the food," Frank extended his hands to Sherry; she complied. Her hormones were all over the place. The simple touch of his hands sent her insides quavering. The touch was electric, which unnerved Sherry greatly. *My hormones are all over the place. It must be with the uncertainty of my health that has me acting like a lovesick puppy.*

As always, the food was superb, Frank enjoyed a hefty plate of mash potatoes with homemade gravy, two pork chops, collards, candied yams and a large slice of pound cake. *So much for a light brunch.* Frank was eating lunch and dinner all at once. "Sherry, you have to eat." Frank encouraged as he watched Sherry moving the fork around her plate of squash casserole, candied yams, baked chicken, and cabbage.

"I'm really not hungry."

"You heard Dr. Hills. You have to eat, Sherry."

Fighting to hold back the tears, Sherry avoided looking at Frank. "It's too much," her voice cracked.

"I know," he put down his fork. "But we'll get through this together, Sherry. I moving back home today and…"

"What?" Her head shot up, and her eyes popped wide opened.

"I'm not going to let you go through this alone, Sherry. I was hasty in moving out," he admitted. "With the test results today, there is no way I can stay away. I know we are not in a good place, but…I want to be there for you, Sherry. Please let me."

One fat teardrop escaped her eyelid, sliding down Sherry's cheek. Impulsively, Frank was on it. Scooting his chair next to his wife, Frank gently wiped her tears, which were coming slowly, but steadily. Letting her guard down briefly, Sherry rested her head on his shoulder. "I'm afraid, Frank."

"I know, Honey, but we have to counter fear with faith," he replied. "I know it's not easy, but we have to."

She nodded, unable to speak.

"You are going to have to release Timothy and Peter to the Lord and stop stressing over them," he paused. "And you are going to have to give Him your fears about me, as well." Frank noticed how immediately Sherry's body stiffened. "I know I have hurt you, badly, but I love you, Sherry…always have and always will. Please say it is okay for me to come back home and be there for you," he pleaded. "I will still sleep in the guestroom, as usual. I just want to be near you, Sherry. I want to come home."

"I don't want your pity, Frank," she looked at him.

"It's not pity, Sherry," his eyes locked on hers. "It's love." A teasing smile played on his lips, echoing in his eyes his unconcealed feelings.

Sherry sat up, endeavoring to gather her composure, while color singed her hollow cheeks. Shamed, she looked around feeling certain that everyone was looking at them.

Frank stood up to scoot his chair back over, but before he did, Frank bent over and kissed her forehead.

Again, her cheeks colored. Sherry suddenly felt dehydrated. Her throat was dryer than the desert.

"After I take you home, is it okay if I go get my things from mom's and come home today?"

Within, a war was raging. Partly, Sherry did not want to need Frank for anything. He had left her. He moved out. Yet, she could not deny the fact her lupus was out of remission, flaring up again, for who knows how long. Sherry needed help. She could barely walk even now.

To the point, Sherry needed Frank. Point—blank—period!

"I'll stay in the guestroom like before," Frank repeated.

"You can come home…"

"Great!" his smile was wide.

"You can move back in our bedroom," her lips quivered. Sherry not only needed Frank, she wanted Frank. She wanted her marriage to work. Being separated for just a week had given her a glimpse into the future. A life without Frank was bleak, colorless, lonely, miserable, and just not acceptable.

Surely, he did not hear right. Frank was speechless. His wife was actually inviting him back in the bedroom. "Are you sure?"

She nodded.

"Oh, Sherry…"

She held her hand up. "Frank, we will take this slow and see how it goes."

"That's all I ask," he could not help it, as he leaned over and planted a soft, gentle kiss on her lips.

It was over before it even started, but at any rate, Sherry did not pull away.

*Absence does make the heart grow fonder.*

# CHAPTER 7

## Daniel's Big News

"Dad," Daniel met his dad coming out of his parents' bedroom. Dressed in his boxers and t-shirt, Frank stood before his son.

"Good morning, Daniel," he greeted. "Slept well?"

"Uh huh. And you?"

"The best sleep I've had in a long time."

"You moved back in with mom?" Daniel held his breath.

"Yes."

"Really?" Daniel waited for his father to say more, but he didn't.

"What do you want for breakfast?" Frank walked away.

"Doesn't matter," Daniel followed. "Why are you cooking?"

"Mom is still sleeping. She needs her rest." Looking through the pantry, Frank took out a box of Pancake mix. "Blueberry pancakes, it is!"

"Dad, what's going on?" Daniel was perplexed. "You're cooking? You're back home. Does this mean what I think it means?"

"Your mother and I are going to try to work things out. We cannot do that living apart. We're taking baby steps."

"Wow!" Daniel finally sat down.

"Aren't you happy?"

"Of course, just surprised," Daniel ran his fingers through his thick hair, like his father. "Just things are so confusing around here. Things change from one minute to the next. I'm happy, but cautiously happily, if that makes sense."

"It does, Son," Frank eyed his son. Daniel was carrying the weight of the world on his shoulders. Sensitive to the craziness of his entire family, no doubt Daniel had been taking everything to heart. He was hurting, confused and skeptical whether or not anything would ever be the same again. "Listen, Daniel," Frank put his hand on his shoulder, "we're going to be all right. All of us. It will all work out for our good. It may not seem that way, but it will. Keep the faith. However, I don't want you to worry about any of us. I just want you to be happy. Enjoy life. Enjoy your senior year of high school. Enjoy Molly."

That brought a smile to Daniel's lips. "About Molly…"

"Yes…" Frank waited. "What about Molly?"

"We're getting married."

"Tell me something I don't already know," Frank ruffled Daniel's hair. "You need a haircut."

"Think I'll just wait a little longer to cut it," Daniel replied, "But seriously, Dad…Molly and I are getting married."

Frank turned to his son, giving him his undivided attention.

"Soon, like right after graduation. Before I enlist. We're getting married sooner than planned."

"Sooner?"

"The Saturday after graduation."

"Daniel, that doesn't make sense. I thought you told us that you would wait until after boot-camp…after you're stationed somewhere."

"I don't want to wait, Dad. Seeing how life is, how things

happen so fast, I don't want to wait. I love Molly and she loves me."

"Marriage cannot be entered into lightly. You both need counseling." Frank began. "Marriage is hard work and with you being away from each other at the beginning of your marriage, I'm not sure if that's a good thing, Daniel. I just want you to be sure."

"I am sure, Dad. Respectfully, there is nothing you can say to change my mind."

Frank gazed at his son, seeing such determination in him. Before his eyes, Daniel had become a man overnight. A good Christian man, who held strong to his beliefs, not wavering because of peer pressure. Daniel had always made him proud. Frank couldn't deny his son, the one thing he knew Daniel wanted the most—his approval.

"I support your decision, Daniel."

"Thanks, Dad!" Immediately, Daniel embraced his dad.

"What's going on in here?" Sherry entered the kitchen.

"Just congratulating our son, Sherry. Daniel asked Molly to marry him, the Saturday after graduation.

"What?!" she frowned, fearfully that she was now losing her son. "That's too soon, Danny!"

"Daniel!" he disliked the boyish nickname.

"You will always be Danny to me," Sherry kissed his cheeks.

"Danny is a boy's name. I am a man, Mom," Daniel amended.

"Well, Daniel, it's too soon for you to marry," Sherry began, trying to control yet another thing in her life. "I love Molly and you know that. But marriage isn't for the fainthearted and well, Molly still needs to grow up a little. She thinks everything is all fairytales and magical. She needs to be more grounded and down to earth."

"Yes, Molly is free-spirited," Daniel acknowledged. "That's what I love about her. She doesn't take everything so seriously. Considering all that she's been through, that's a good thing, Mom"

"Her health is an issue, as well."

"Her health is fine. She's paralyzed, but that changes nothing. I love her more the way she is now than before the accident."

"But Daniel…"

"Sherry, Daniel knows what he wants," Frank interrupted. "We have to let him make his own decision."

Sherry wanted to knock the smile right off Frank's face. Why was he so easily letting her son go? He of all people knew that marriage was hard. She just wanted Daniel to wait. Couldn't Frank back her up on that? Once again, she and Frank didn't see eye to eye. Once again, they were on opposite sides of the fences, regarding their children.

"Excuse us, Daniel," Frank sensed that Sherry was taking a step back in their fragile relationship. Frank escorted her to their bedroom.

Closing the door, Frank spoke calmly, "Sherry, take a deep breath. I'm going to talk, and I want you to listen before you say anything. Please, Sherry," he felt her resisting. "Please." She nodded. "Sherry, we cannot control Daniel. We have to let him grow up. He will be leaving for boot camp shortly after graduation. Let's enjoy every moment of his stay with us and not be at odds with him. Sherry, 1 feel certain that if we reject his wishes to marry Molly sooner than later, we stand a chance of damaging our relationship with him. Do we want to spend those precious weeks with him that way? Daniel is a prayer-warrior. He never jumps into anything without seeking God's counsel or approval. We have raised him to seek God's will for his life. We must trust that he has done exactly that."

Though Sherry had entered the bedroom ready to fight for her son, she listened to Frank, really listened to him. Her heart dropped. Her shoulders sagged. Her eyes glistened. "I don't want to lose Danny, too!"

"Shh," he hugged her to his chest, "we'll never lose Daniel. He will always be our son. We must let him go, Sherry. Just as God had to let Jesus go because others needed Him. Others need Daniel. He has such a big heart. And well, Molly, she's wonderful. She loves our son. That's all we really want is for all of our sons…to each have someone to love them."

"You're right," Sherry looked up at him. "It's just hard."

"It is. I'm going to miss him, too," Frank's eyes glistened, as well. "But I am so proud of the man he is becoming."

"Me too," Sherry sniffed.

Looking at his wife with such longing, Frank was more attracted to Sherry now than when they first married. Maturity had taught him a valuable lesson. True love wasn't based on feelings but on the heart—good or bad. True love saw beyond the physical, connecting on a deeper, soulish level. Indeed, Frank was in love with Sherry—far beyond words.

Sherry couldn't remember the last time Frank had looked at her like that. Or maybe he had, but she was too busy being mad at him to notice. Her heart rate soared at the thought that Frank was going to kiss her and she didn't think she had the willpower to deny him this time. Better yet, Sherry didn't want to.

Bending his head, Frank gave into his desire. He wanted

nothing more than to endow his wife with a passionate kiss. As their lips almost touched...*Dang it!*

"Can I come in?' Daniel cracked the door.

"Of course, son," Frank replied, releasing his wife.

"Ah, you guys stop all the crying," breaking the *sacred* moment. "No matter where I go, what I do, or who I'm with, you will always be the greatest parents and nothing can separate us." Daniel hugged them both. "I love you, both and I love Molly. She is the special one that God has created just for me. I know this one hundred percent."

"We are proud of you, Dann...Daniel," Sherry smiled. "Very proud of you."

"You can call me Danny, Mom. I will always be your Danny."

"Yes, but you're right...it's boyish. Daniel suits you better now."

"I love you, Mom!" Daniel hugged her.

"I love you even more."

"Now let's eat breakfast!" Daniel chimed. "I'm starving!"

At the breakfast table, Frank cautiously approached his wife's health. "Daniel, your mother's visit with Dr. Hills wasn't what we expected.

Daniel stopped eating, heart pounding, fearing the worst. "What is it?"

"Your mother seems to be out of remission and at risk of having heart failure."

"Don't worry, Dann...iel," Sherry chimed, beholding her son's demeanor change. Always the nurturer. "I'm going to be fine."

"She sure is," Frank added. "But, we have to keep her stress level down, especially in this home."

"Does Peter and Timothy know?" Daniel asked.

"No, not now," Frank replied. "I think for right now, we're going to keep this news between us. I don't think it's good for Peter and Timothy to be here. With Timothy and Peter at odds with each other, your mother doesn't need the stress."

"Frank, my children are always welcome here. This will always be their home," Sherry chided. "I want them here. Thanksgiving is around the corner and then Christmas. We have to be together. Family means everything to me."

"Peter told me he won't be here for Thanksgiving or Christmas," Daniel revealed. "He doesn't celebrate those days anymore."

"What?" Sherry gasped.

"Now, now," Frank touched her hand. "See, you're getting all worked up. It's not good for you."

"Frank, I'm not a baby. I am not going to just have a heart attack because I am upset that my boys aren't going to be home for Thanksgiving or Christmas. I'm a mother. I am disappointed and rightly so."

"Please, Sherry, trust me on this," Frank said gently. "Until our boys find themselves, family gatherings won't be as peaceful and joyous as they once were. We are just going to keep praying for them and let God work a work in their lives and changed their hearts. We can't change them, Sherry, only God can."

Hesitantly, Sherry agreed and so did Daniel. After finishing breakfast, Sherry went back to her room to rest. Later that afternoon, Daniel and Frank enjoyed watching a football game. Molly parents dropped her over, during halftime. Molly loved football, actually any sport, just as much as the Reed men. Definitely, she was already a part of the family.

"Hey, I'm going to go check on Sherry," Frank stood. "I'll be back before the third quarter. Oh, by the way, Molly, congratulations! Welcome to the family!"

"Thanks, Mr. Reed!"

"You can start calling me dad," Frank winked.

"How about I call you, Papa. Thanks, Papa!" Molly beamed.

Quietly entering the room, Frank gazed down at his sleeping wife. Sherry still took his breath away. At forty-five, she was still beautiful beyond words. He was glad she was napping. Sherry endured much pain during the night. She barely slept. Although they shared the bed together last night, Sherry wanted no part of intimacy. She stayed on her side of the bed and he stayed on his. Giving thanks, just to be home and sharing the bedroom, Frank inwardly prayed that in time the wall that separated them, keeping them from being intimate, would be torn down completely. He desired his wife. He wanted to touch her and to be united in oneness again. He ached to love his wife fully. He would have to take things slow. Physically, Sherry was in a lot of pain, but emotionally she was delicate like porcelain. Frank had to handle her with extreme care.

"What time is it?" Sherry's eyes opened.

"It's four."

"I slept that long?"

"Yes, and that's good," Frank sat on the bed. "You needed it." He gently moved her hair out of her face.

"I know I look a mess." Sherry was cognizant of how she must have looked.

"You never looked more beautiful, Sherry."

Her cheeks shaded pink at his compliment. Despite her resentment toward Frank, which she was working on changing, Sherry still loved him. She couldn't turn her love on and off life a faucet, even though at times she wanted nothing more.

"Molly is downstairs, watching the game with us. It's half-time, I wanted to see if you needed anything."

*I need you!* Instead, she said aloud, "I'm good, Frank. I think I'll just freshen up and join you all. I could bake some honey mustard wings…"

"My favorite," he smiled.

"Yes, I know and seasoned French-fried-potatoes for Danny and Molly."

"Their favorite," Frank chuckled. As Sherry attempted to get up, Frank held her hand and fastened his eyes on her, and said, "My darling Sherry, we're going to be alright. I just know it. Because I am totally and completely head-over-heels in love with you."

Her eyes glistened. "In spite of everything Frank, not once did I ever stop loving you."

"Thanks for saying that Sherry. It means more to me than you will ever know."

# CHAPTER 8

## *Let God Fix it*

Opening the passenger's door for his wife, Frank assisted Sherry out, keeping her hand in his as he escorted Sherry up the church steps. Holding hands is what they used to do all the time, and then things changed. The little things didn't seem to take precedent anymore. As the children needed more and more of Sherry's attention, Frank drifted in the background, taking care of the bills, making sure the family was safe and secure. Frank needed to be the provider since Sherry's health was so debilitative, and she was unable to work anymore. Therefore, in order for the family to be well fed, clothed, and sheltered, Frank worked long hours. He had been promoted three major times, now a partner at a reputable accounting firm. Yet, along the way, Frank had lost his way. Work became his primacy. For Sherry, the focus was on the children. Neither Frank nor Sherry made their marriage a priority.

Their eyes met and locked. Frank felt privileged to be holding his wife's hand again. If only he could glimpse the sparkle in her eyes again. Frank had deep regrets. If only, he could go back in time, he would do things differently. For sure, he would steer far away from Monique as possible. The month fling had nearly caused him to lose his family, his wife—all that mattered to him. It took almost losing everything to realize that Frank had had everything he needed and ever wanted already. *You don't miss your well until the water runs dry.*

"Are you okay?" Sherry finally asked.

"Sherry," he swallowed, trying to find the right words, "I know I've said it thousands of times before, but I am truly sorry for hurting you...for bringing sin into our family and into our lives. For being so stupid not to see I had the best wife and the best life. God gave me His best twice – Jesus, His Son and you," he choked. "I was a fool to forget that and to allow my flesh to become so weak."

"Frank, let's not go there," Sherry wasn't ready, "not here. Let's just enjoy the church service."

"You're right," Frank wiped his eyes and then seized her hand again. Taking a few steps, he halted and said, "You look lovely today. I love the teal dress. Is it new?"

"It is," Sherry blushed.

"Your hair looks great down," he touched her long locks. "With age, you have become even more beautiful. I am so blessed to have you in my life." Frank was laying it on thick, but he meant every word.

"Thank you, Frank," Sherry enjoyed the attention. It brought back the memories of the old days, when Frank would lavish her with compliments, making her feel like she was the queen of the ball—even if they were only at the grocery store, or in their humbled home. He noticed her and had no problems of letting her know it.

"You look quite handsome yourself," Sherry complimented, something she hadn't done in a long time. "Your brown suit is my favorite on you."

"Thank you, Darling," he said and kissed his wife on the cheek. "Let God use you today as you play for Him."

"I will."

Entering the church, immediately the devil showed up. None other than Monique stood in their path. She practically crashed into them, heading for the restroom.

"Oh, excuse me," she spoke first.

Sherry rolled her eyes, still unable to let go of the resentment she felt toward her former friend. Instead of letting go of Frank's hand, she held it tighter, nearly crushing it.

"It's good to see you, Sherry. I saw your name on the prayer list. I didn't think you would be here."

*Bet that would have made you happy. I'm so sorry!* "I'm fine."

"I'm glad," Monique continued. "It's good to be back in town and at the church, I grew up in. No one can play the keyboards like you, Sherry."

Sherry remained quiet, not believing a word that came out of Monique's mouth. "We really must go."

"Good to see you too, Frank," Monique added as the couple walked away.

Frank thought it best not to respond.

"That little tramp has the nerve to speak to me...to us!" Sherry said between tight lips. "Why is she back at OUR church? She left and now she's back! She just won't leave us alone!"

"Sherry, please don't let her steal your joy," Frank whispered.

"Too late for that! She did that two years ago!" Sherry marched ahead, carrying anger, bitterness, and un-forgiveness with her.

Sighing Frank sat down next to Molly and Daniel. "Are you both not singing today?"

"No. The youth choir is singing," Daniel replied. "Are you okay, Dad? You look peaked."

"Everything is fine son," Frank forced a smile. "Everything is fine." *Lord, maybe we should change churches. We married in this church. Sherry grew up in this church, but since Monique is apparently back, being in her presence isn't healthy for our family. Maybe, I'm wrong. Please forgive me, Lord, if I am—but it's almost as if Monique is taunting Sherry. She deliberately pushes Sherry's buttons. Why can't she just stay clear of her, of us? Just the other day, she called me. I didn't answer, but why is she calling me again? The fling was over two years ago. Why now?*

"Dad," Daniel called again, "we're standing for prayer."

"Oh," Frank stood. "I guess I was elsewhere."

"For sure. Are you sure, you're all right, Dad? You don't look like it," Daniel mumbled. "And mom looks like she's about to bust a gasket. Instead of playing the keyboards, she's banging on them."

Frank gazed at his wife. Sherry appeared madder than a bear, trying to protect her cubs from an intruder. That's exactly what Monique was now—an intruder coming between their family. Frank winked at her, but Sherry only turned away.

*Lord, every time we take two steps forward we end up ten steps backward. I don't know what to do.*

**Trust Me!**

Despite Sherry's attitude, the worship service was beautiful. God's presence saturated the sanctuary, making it possible for Frank to forget about everything and everyone for a while.

Pastor Law's sermon had pricked the Reed's family, in different ways. Even Daniel received a confirming message, comprehending that only God could change their family. He didn't need to carry the load.

"We have a problem with letting go," the pastor said. "We say we want God to handle things. Yet, we are constantly putting our two-cents in. Constantly, trying to fix things and fix people. However, it's not our job to fix it…its God's job! He said for us to cast our cares on Him. Why? Because He knew the load was way too heavy for us to carry. He said for us to come to Him, all who are weary and heaven laden. Why? Because He knew it was too much for us to bear alone.

"Stop trying to change people, because you cannot. We expect people to live up to our expectations, to do what we want them to do, to be who we want them to be…but just like no one could change you, you cannot change others. That's God's job. Get out of the way and let God handle it.

"We all come to Jesus Christ our own way. Look at Paul. He tortured the believers. Doing everything possible to make their lives a living *hell*. It wasn't man, who changed Paul. No, Paul's encounter with Jesus Christ changed him. See, people will mess up. People will disappoint us. People will hurt us. People will let us down. That's a fact. You only have to look in the mirror, and realize that you, too, have done those same things. You aren't perfect. So why do you expect others to be perfect? You're trying to change everything and everybody when you should ask yourself, what do I need to change about myself?" Pastor Law paused, giving the church family time ponder the question.

"Many of us are hiding behind smiles, while inwardly we're messed up. We're depressed, oppressed by the enemy. He's literally zapping our joy and stealing our strength. He's taking things from us that on the outside, looking in, people cannot see. However, we cannot fool God. He knows the real truth. He knows what goes on behind closed doors. And He knows, sitting here today, are people who are oppressed by the devil."

Sitting at the piano, Sherry wanted to run and hide. She wanted to be anywhere but in the church. Sherry, felt like all eyes were on her. She felt exposed and naked. The spotlight was shining upon her soul for all to see—to see the real Sherry. She was a fake. A phony. A fraud. Unhappy, miserable Sherry. They could see that her marriage was not so perfect. Sons were living messed up lives. They had failed because somehow she had failed. Ms. Goody-Two-Shoes couldn't keep her family together. Sure, Frank was back, sleeping in the same bed with her, but she kept him at bay. She kept the wall between them. They weren't the happy couple everyone thought they were. Their happily-ever-after marriage was bogus!

True, she expected Frank to be perfect, to walk the straight and narrow path, every day and in every way. She expected her sons, Peter, Timothy and Daniel, to live their lives in perfection. When things weren't perfect, Sherry wanted to change them. She wanted to change her loved ones, to see it her way. She wanted to control them…

"You cannot control people." The pastor invaded her thoughts, reiterating the truth. "You cannot control people," he repeated. "God is in control, not you. That's the problem, today. We want to control everything, not realizing we are only making a mess of everything. It is the Lord, Jesus Christ, who is the Author and Finisher of our Faith…not man. Not you. Not me. There was only One Perfect Man that walked the earth and they killed him. Who are you killing today with your high-and-mighty attitude? Who are you killing today with your judgmental behavior? Who are you killing today with your unforgiving heart?

"Turn it all over to God. Let Him work it out. You pray about it and let God do what He does best and that is to handle it. To fix it. To change it. He's God. He knows what to do, how to do it, when to do it and who to do it to. There is absolutely nothing too hard for God. But God can't do His job, if you're constantly trying to do it for Him," Pastor Law spoke in love.

"God knows your hurts. He knows your pain. He knows your discomfort. He sees your oppression. It's not that He has forgotten about you. No. It's the other way around. You have forgotten Who He is and what He can do for you. You are in the way. Move out of the driver's seat and let God do the driving. Let Him drive you where you need to go. Let Jesus take the wheel. Let Him direct your steps. Let Him heal your heart.

"The Word says in Psalms 72, verses 12 and 14, 'For He will deliver the needy when he cries, the poor also, and him who has no helper…He will redeem their life from oppression and violence.' He will do it, not you or I. Let God fix your problems, fix your careers, fix your children, fix your marriages, fix your health and fix your life. He can and He will…but you must let Him," Pastor Law concluded. "Cast your burden on the Lord and He will sustain you."

Convicted, Frank bowed his head, right where he sat and released it all to God.

*I cannot do it, Lord, but You can. I let go of my children, Sherry, our marriage…I give them all to You. Whatever you want me to do…or not to do I will obey. They belong to You, not me. I surrender. Your will, not my will."*

**Forgive Yourself.**

The words startled him. *But, I'm unworthy.*

***I have forgiven you. You are worthy. I have removed your***

*transgression from you as far as the east is from the west, and I remember your sins no more. Forgive yourself.*

*I forgive myself,* Frank's heart silently cried.

*Now you are free my son. No longer oppressed by un- forgiveness.*

Thank You, Lord. Now may Sherry forgive me, truly forgive me.

*Just as you forgave, she too must forgive.*

Equally, Daniel released the reigns of control over to his Heavenly Father. His family was God's family. Indeed, God knew how to fix it.

Likewise, as Sherry was softly playing, while the pastor was at the altar praying for the congregation, Sherry's spirit was convicted. It was hard for her to release control in her life. All her life, she had to be strong, to fight to live, to keep the family together, especially growing up with her neglectful mother. After her father died, her mother lost her will to live, so Sherry had to do everything. Take care of her younger siblings, make sure they were fed and clothed, while her mother drank. She drank herself to death, unable to live without her husband. Never realizing how much her children needed her. How much Sherry needed her. She had practically lost both parents; thus, losing her childhood years.

*Lord, I don't know how to let go. I don't know how to be free of carrying the burdens of my family. But, I'm tired. Tired of feeling so…depressed…so oppressed. I want things to change…but…*

*You cannot change them. You can only change you.*

*I'm not the one who messed up. Timothy is messed up. Peter is messed up. In addition, well, Frank messed up and he expects me just to move on as if nothing ever happened.*

*Monique betrayed me.*

**You can only see the speck in their eyes, but not the bolt in your own.**

Trying to push back the truth, Sherry played louder, wanting to drown out the truth…but couldn't.

*Forgive.*

*I have.*

*Forgive.*

*I have.*

*Forgive.*

Silence. She hadn't forgiven, not really. She was mad at all of them. They had all let her down. Her mother. Peter. Timothy. Monique and Frank.

***Forgive if you want to be free!***

Adding salt to an open wound, leaving the church with Frank, Sister Peabody stalked the couple just before they got outside the church doors.

"Well, well, isn't it good to see you two together," she began. "My sister said your car wasn't parked at your mother's for a few days. Does that mean that you two are back together?"

"We have always been together," possessively, Frank pulled his wife close to him, wrapping his arm securely around Sherry's waistline.

"But you stayed with your mother. That's strange, don't you think?" Sister Peabody chuckled.

"What I think is strange is that two Christian ladies have the time to gossip about their sisters/brothers when they should be praying," Frank asserted. "Sister Peabody, if you don't know the whole story, you shouldn't be spreading any story. Good day."

"Well you don't have to be so rude!" she hated being dismissed like that.

"Look up the word, Sister Peabody," Frank turned to her, keeping his wife from saying anything. Someone had to stand up to the woman and put her in her place in a nice-nasty way. Frank wanted to do the honors. "See if the shoe fits?"

"Well, I never!" she screeched. "You are in God's house and being so unkind. All I was doing was showing concern for your family."

"Then pray for us," Frank said lastly. "As we will for you." On that note, Frank escorted his wife out the church, noticing the stiffness of his wife in his arms.

As they drove away, Sherry finally spoke. "Thank you, Frank. I had nothing in me to deal with that nosey woman. She grates my last nerve."

"She's just a lonely woman, that's all."

"I don't know about that. She has Sarah."

"Yeah, but Sarah is married and unhappy, as well. They both need our prayers."

"It's hard to pray for the enemy."

"But I say to you, love your enemies, bless those who curse you, do good to those who hate you, and pray for those who spitefully use you and persecute you." Frank quoted the words from the lips of Jesus Christ. "We have to, Sherry. God expects us to."

"I know," she concurred. "Today has truly been a trying Sunday. First Monique, then Pastor Law's tough message, followed by Sister Peabody. Not to mention, I'm aching all over."

"Sorry Sherry," he touched her hand with one hand and drove with the other. "For everything, especially Monique."

"She still has feelings for you, Frank," Sherry stated, which hurt deeply. "I hope you can see that and stay far away from her as possible."

"I cannot control her, but I can promise you that she is no longer a problem for me. The truth is, I have no real feelings for Monique and never did. Maybe we can finally talk about this, Sherry. Deal with what happened, so we can move forward."

"Not now, Frank!" she pulled her hand away. "I just want to go home and go to bed." She turned to look out the window, letting Frank know the conversation was over.

*Lord, did the sermon convict her as it did me? I release it all to You and I'm not taking any of it back. It's all in Your hands.*

# CHAPTER 9

# Thanksgiving Part I

Things were shaky in the Reed's family home. Sherry was battling her own demons, spiritually, physically and emotionally. The sermon had perforated her heart, leaving a hole that only God could fill and heal if she would just allow Him. It had been almost a week and still, she hadn't heard from Peter or Timothy. Her heart ached, nearly breaking. She did her best to put on a happy face for Daniel, but she knew he saw right through her.

As for Frank, he did his best to keep the mood light in the home. Frank catered to Sherry's every need, making sure she ate, took her medicine on time and routinely, he massaged her legs. Yet, Frank was greatly concerned about Sherry's tiredness. He feared her heart pulse rate was still too low. Sherry needed a miracle. Faithfully, Frank prayed for God to grant it. In spite all his efforts to make Sherry comfortable, sometimes, he felt it was for naught. Sherry didn't seem to appreciate anything. She nagged and complained. The food wasn't hot enough. Bath water too cold. His massages were too rough. He was too slow in answering her beck and call. Nothing was good enough. Oftentimes Frank was at his wit's end, his hair turning grayer by the minute.

However, there were those precious moments when Sherry seemed to soften. Times when she relaxed and allow Frank to be the husband she needed him to be. More than just a provider, but her companion and friend. Maybe not lovers yet, but Frank believed that would happen with time.

"Thanksgiving is two days away," Sherry began. "But I don't think I can prepare a big meal, Frank. I'm just too weak and too tired. Besides, we still haven't heard from Peter or Timothy."

"I wanted to talk to you about that. How about we have Thanksgiving with my mom…at her place?" Frank prepared himself for a quick lashing, as always, for spending time with his mother. Martha could be a *pill* at times, so he understood Sherry's reluctance to spending Thanksgiving or any other time with his mother. As his mother aged, she became more ornery, especially toward Sherry.

Resolving to stay calm, Sherry eyed her husband, accepting that he was the peacemaker in the family. Mostly, she appreciated the solid faith in him. Against her better judgment, Sherry did the unthinkable. "Okay."

Stunned, Frank held his breath, waiting to see if she would take it back. This was a huge step for his wife, and Frank didn't take it lightly. "Really?'

"Really," she nodded, half smiling.

Frank's eyes zeroed in on his wife's full lips. His desire to kiss her heighten as Sherry's cheeks flushed, making her even more beautiful than ever.

Sherry had never felt this nervous before being this close to her husband. Her heart was pounding in her chest so fast. A teasing smile formed on her lips, anticipating the kiss as Frank leaned forward.

Her cell phone chimed a familiar gospel tune.

Frank sighed, too loudly.

"Hello!" Sherry didn't know if she was glad for the distraction or not. Her feelings were all jumbled inside, like a jigsaw puzzle, pieces everywhere.

"Hi Mom!" It was Timothy. "Just calling to check in on you. How are you doing?"

"I'm feeling better now that you called." Sherry eased away from Frank, which disappointed him.

"I can't talk long. I'm on my break at work. Just wanted to say hello."

"Are you okay, Timothy? You sound a little down."

"I'm fine, Mom. Everything is fine," his mouth uttered, though his mother wasn't convinced.

"Well before you go, what about Thanksgiving?"

"I won't be home," he replied. "I'm spending Thanksgiving with Larry and his family."

"Oh, I see,"

"Sorry Mom, but I have to go. Tell Dad and Daniel I said hello. Talk to you soon. Love you!"

"Love you," she replied, not sure if Timothy even heard it because the phone clicked off.

Sherry fell into Frank's waiting arms. "I know we have to trust God with our sons, but it's hard, Frank. Timothy is spending Thanksgiving with Larry and his family."

"It's going to be alright, Sherry," he caressed her back smoothly. "Remember the sermon...we cannot change them. We have to trust God to change them."

A steady flow of tears streamed down her hollow cheeks. Sherry felt helpless.

"Try not to let it get to you." Frank rubbed her tears away.

"Timothy will come around."

"I pray that we will have the family around the table for Christmas," she still held a hint of hope. "I miss my boys."

"Me too," Frank agreed.

Thanksgiving Day.

Sitting around his mother's table with his wife, Molly, and Daniel, Frank prayed that this Thanksgiving Dinner would be peaceful and that his mother would just enjoy being with her family. Martha had no filter on her mouth. No telling what would come out today. She was on her own turf, with no need to please anybody.

Frank never understood what his mother had against Sherry. To Martha, no woman would ever be good enough for her only son, especially not sickly Sherry. In his mother's eyes, Sherry took far more than she ever gave. Despite Frank's rebuttal over the years about his wife being selfish, with Martha, it went in one ear and out the other.

Frank stole quick glances Sherry's way. He couldn't help himself. She was stunning. Wearing his favorite color, the baby blue peplum sweater he purchased for her recently. Also, Sherry wore the silver earrings he gave her for their tenth anniversary. With her hair pulled up, she appeared younger and fresher. The fact that she took the time and put on a little make up, with a soft peachy lipstick impressed Frank. It was evident that Sherry wanted to please him and she succeeded.

"This ham is superb, Martha," Sherry complimented. "It's perfect. I wish I could get my ham to be this moist."

"It's all in the way you cook it. You must let it marinate, cook slow," Martha advised. "You can't be in such a rush like always. Good things take time to develop."

"Okay," Sherry read between the lines. Nothing she would say would mean a hill of beans to Frank's mother. Martha hated her without cause. She even blamed their failing marriage on Sherry, knowing full well that it was Frank who cheated on her, not the other way around like she initially thought.

"I hear Timothy is having Thanksgiving dinner with his gay lover." Mother took another jab at Sherry.

*Here it goes!*

"I told you, Frank, that Sherry was smothering that boy. She didn't allow him to be tough, like Peter. When Timothy fell, you coddled him too much. You should have just let him cry and just get back up. He was always hiding behind some book. Now, look at him. He's as sweet as my sweet potato pie."

No one responded. Sherry was fuming inside. She wanted to just knock the smug chip off her mother-in-law's shoulder. Mostly, she wanted to grab her purse and leave.

Martha continued to jab at her with insults. "And where is Peter? He and that gal of his don't even think there is a reason to be thankful anymore."

"Mom," Frank cautioned. "Let's enjoy our family time together."

"Grandma, did dad tell you that Molly and I are marrying on June 10, the Saturday after I graduate," Daniel intervened, trying to bring some joy in the atmosphere. Molly squeezed his hand, slightly uncomfortable with Martha's judgmental attitude.

"That's just ridiculous!" she barked. "You're too young for that Daniel. No disrespect, Molly, but you two have dated no one else. How do you really know if you are made for each other when you have nothing to compare the relationship to?"

"Because God brought us together," Daniel answered before Molly could respond. "Just like He brought mom and dad together."

"My point exactly," Martha smirked. "I've never been convinced that God played a part in this unhappy marriage."

"Mother!" Frank's tone was stern. "I'm warning you. One more negative comment and we're leaving."

"I didn't mean any harm, Frankie," she said, smooth like butter. "I'm just saying Daniel is too young to marry."

"Grandma, you were sixteen when you married grandpa."

"That's because back in those days, we had no choice. Besides, who will take care of Molly when you're going to fight in the war?"

"Who says I'm going to fight in the war?" Daniel replied.

"I don't need anyone to take care of me, Ms. Martha," Molly intervened. "I may be in a wheelchair, but I am fully capable of taking care of myself."

"Marriage is hard work, Daniel," Martha went another route. "And even with hard work it still might not turn out like you want it to. Look at your parents. They go to church, pray, know what the Good Book says, and yet, they are unhappy people!"

"We're not unhappy!" both Sherry and Frank rejected.

Looking at each other, Frank felt pleased that Sherry wasn't unhappy and defended their relationship against his mother.

"You don't even sleep in the same room," Martha added.

"That was because of Sherry's illness," Frank replied, not revealing that they were sharing the same room together, again. It was none of his mother's business.

"Never stopped you before," Martha continued. "All I am saying is that Daniel, you should go to boot camp like you have planned. Get a feel for the military life, and then say in a year or so, if you still feel God wants you to marry Molly, do so."

Gazing at Molly, her eyes threatening to spill, Daniel did his best to temper his words. "Grandma, I respect you, but I love Molly with all my heart. I know without a shadow of a doubt that God brought her into my life, so she could be my wife. I am not so naive to think that we won't have problems, every couple does...including my parents. However, with us being connected to God, like a threefold cord, we will not be easily broken. We will be together forever, just like my parents," Daniel looked to his parents. "My mother and father love each other. They just needed to remember how much they love each other and that God put them together. For who God puts together, no man *or woman*," Daniel eyed his grandmother, "can put asunder."

"Well, I'll just mind my own business!" Martha was miffed.

"That's a good idea, mother," Frank replied.

"This is my home, Frank and I will say whatever I please!" She put her foot and her fork down at the same time.

"You're right, mother," Frank slid his chair back, "but we don't have to listen to it. Sherry, Daniel, and Molly let's go!"

"Frank," Sherry stayed seated. "We're okay. Let's finish this wonderful meal. Martha went to so much trouble to make this dinner great," Sherry said soothingly. "Sit, Honey, please."

Frank remained standing, torn on what to do. He didn't want his family to endure another brutal word from his mother. Yet, his wife pleading made his heart tender to comply. *She called me Honey.*

"Yeah Dad, let's finish."

"We're good, Papa," Molly admonished. "Ms. Martha means no harm."

"I can speak for myself," Martha blurted. "Frank knows I love you all."

*This kind of love makes you crazy!* Sherry thought.

"We love you, too, Mother…but not one more negative word!" his eyebrows raised.

Martha kept eating, not agreeing to anything. Truthfully, she was happy that Frank and his family came for dinner. Otherwise, she would have been home alone, refusing once again to share dinner at Frank's home. She had cleaned the house thoroughly, and prepped for two days for the lavished thanksgiving dinner, wanting everything to be perfect. If her late husband Dwayne were still alive, he would be upset by her rude behavior to Frank and his family. When had she become so mean-spirited?

*When Dwayne went home to be with the Lord, leaving me all alone.*

Meanwhile, Timothy was feeling homesick. Thanksgiving with Larry's family was weird, to say the least. Larry's parents were extremely different from his parents. His parents were more conservative, old-school type. Whereas, Larry's parents were radically adventurist, the fly-by-the-seat-of-your-pants type. They accepted Larry for who he was and saw nothing wrong with their relationship. You could say, anything goes in their family as long as it wasn't illegal—and even that was up for discussion.

Dinner was a store-bought turkey, boxed mash potatoes with gravy, canned string beans, canned cranberry sauce and a store-bought cake. Nothing was homemade like his mother cooking. Then to top it off, they drank beers and vodka at the table.

Nothing felt right for Timothy. He missed everyone, gathering around the table and individually giving thanks before eating. His father, cutting the turkey, while his mother gave a prayer of thanks, followed by the blessing of the food from his father. Timothy missed *cutting up* with his siblings, including Peter. The strange atmosphere made him cringe with heaviness resting on his chest. Further, Timothy wondered about his mother's health. The last time he saw her, she wasn't doing well.

"You look like you just sucked on a lemon," Larry leaned over. "I know we're not like the traditional family for Thanksgiving, but we enjoy each other and accept each other without condemnation. Stop looking so sour!"

Timothy forced a smile, while his heart ached for his family.

"You're putting a damper on today, Timmy. You have been doing that a lot lately and I'm getting tired of it. Stop acting like a spoiled brat and grow up."

"You're a jerk!" Timothy lashed back and stood. "Excuse me, Mr. and Mrs. Landers. I'm not feeling well, so I'm going to leave. Thanks for the dinner."

"I'm not ready to go." Larry blurted, not moving.

"I drove, remember?" Timothy stated. "You can stay as long as you like."

"Fine!" Larry shouted. "Go home to your parents."
"Jerk!"

Meanwhile, Peter was overwhelmed with the news Imani had just shared with him.

"I'm pregnant," she repeated.

The words settled in his heart like a ton of bricks. "But how? I thought you were on the pill."

"Pill or no pill, aren't' you happy?"

"Imani, I told you I wasn't ready for children. Did you do this on purpose? Did you stop taking the pills?"

"No!"

"Then how?" Peter was flabbergasted.

"The pill isn't a hundred percent, Peter!"

"We cannot afford this right now, Imani!" Peter ran his hands roughly through his single braided hair.

"Peter!" she yelled. "I'm pregnant and you're making me feel bad about it. Be grateful. I'm carrying your seed, your son or daughter. A part of you is in me."

"Imani, things aren't *good* between us and a baby sure won't help that," Peter reasoned. "Adding a baby to our already strained relationship is like lightening a match to kerosene. It's arsenic."

"You're too serious, Peter. Lighten up a little. A baby shows the love between two people. A baby will enhance our relationship."

Peter remained silent and calm, while inwardly he was in

turbulent waters. A flash from the past, gripped him, literally sucking the life out of him. His complexion became ashen and dull.

"Are you alright?" Imani worried. "You look sick."

"I'm upset!" he shouted. He and Imani would not see eye-to-eye on the matter right now. A baby was the last thing he wanted to share with Imani. The last thing!

To add to his misery about the child, Peter was feeling homesick for his parents. Though he was still miffed by his father's moving out in the first place, he wanted to spend Thanksgiving with them. This was the first Thanksgiving he hadn't spent with his family and he missed them terribly... even Timothy. Though he had declared Thanksgiving was a celebration of the genocide against the Indians and that there should be no celebrating, just mourning. Still, was it wrong spending time with family, feasting and fellowshipping? Was it wrong to take the time to give thanks on this day? Isn't it about having a heart of gratefulness and thankfulness...not about the day?

Imani had enough of Peter sulking around the house. Acting as if he had lost his best friend. Wasn't she supposed to be his best friend now? His first love? She knew that faraway look. She had seen it too often. Peter's mind had traveled back in time to his family...and perhaps to his former girlfriend. No matter how hard she tried, Imani felt outranked to the people in Peter's past. Fed up with Peter's selfish behavior, Imani threw a plastic bowl at him. Anything to get his attention.

"What the heck!"

"Why can't you just forget your family?"

"I'll never forget my family, Imani! Never! No matter what happens in life, my family will always be of utmost important to me. We may not agree on things, but one thing that is forever sure—that our love for one another is forever...no matter what!"

"I'm your family now! Me and our baby."

"You're not hearing me!" Peter yelled. "I don't want this baby! I'm not ready for this...and neither are you!" he reached for his jacket. "I'm going out for a few."

"What about dinner?"

"I'll be back. I need space."

"I can't believe you're going to just walk away. I just told you I was carrying your baby and you aren't happy," she pouted.

"No, Imani, I'm not happy. Something isn't right...not just between us. But I feel lost. I don't know anything anymore. My life was *pretty* steady before I met you. Now, I don't know who I am, what the heck I'm doing and where I'm going?"

"You're Peter, the man I fell in love with."

"You feel in love with Peter, a Believer, that's who I was then. Now...I don't know who I am anymore," he threw up his hands. "Who am I?"

"Yes, you used to believe in all that nonsense. You were brainwashed to believe all that spiritual garbage. But deep down, I don't think you ever bought into it or you wouldn't have so easily walked away from it all."

"Nothing has been easy, Imani," he said remorsefully. "I walked away from my faith, my church, all the teens who depended on me, and my family...*Elaine*," he paused. "There's nothing easy about any of that, Imani."

"Was I not worth it?" she held her breath for the answer, fearing it wouldn't be what she wanted to hear.

He gazed at her. Definitely, Imani was a beautiful, chocolate queen. Standing nearly six feet, an inch shorter than he, she was stunning. Standing there with tight jeans and a tank top, even though it was cold outside. There wasn't an ounce of fat on Imani. In her line of work, modeling, there wasn't any room for a pudgy midriff. Especially since Imani mostly model lingerie and bikinis. Yes, he cared for her. But, was it love? Or lust? Secretly Peter knew that what they had couldn't compare to the solid affection his parents shared growing up. Was his parents' marriage all a sham with the recent acknowledgement of them separating? Didn't anything last anymore? Was anything sacred anymore? Were there any genuine, honest people left. People who didn't keep life-changing secrets?

"Well…" Imani impatiently patted her foot.

"I'm not sure," he spoke the truth.

"Are you serious?" she blew up. "Are you saying that I'm not worth it Peter?!"

"I'm confused."

"Confused. Confused about what? The baby? Us? What Peter?"

"I need time alone before we both say things we cannot take back later." Peter went to her and kissed her on the cheek. "I'll be back in about an hour."

Imani fretted that she was losing Peter. She would do anything to keep that from happening. Putting on a happy face, she conjured up a smile and replied, "Dinner will be ready by then."

"Okay," he left. *Dinner! All can food—no turkey, no ham, no dressing, no homemade sweet potato pie! Some Thanksgiving! Oh yeah, we don't celebrate Thanksgiving!*

Peter walked through the neighborhood to blow off some steam. When had things gotten so bad for him? When had he lost his joy? His way? His faith? Always one to make his own decisions, even if he had to learn the hard way, no one could force Peter to do something he didn't want to do. Therefore, he couldn't blame Imani for anything. He walked away from his old life and all that went with it.

He just didn't bank on it being so hard and so confusing. Why wasn't he happy? Why couldn't he find peace? Why was life throwing him yet another curb ball? He was going to be a father. How in the world was he going to train a child the right way, when right now he had no clue what the right way was or was not?

How could he even thinking about raising one child when another child…

***Therefore, to him who knows to do good and does not do it, to him it is sin.***

The familiar scripture came to mind. Lately, scripture after scripture had been invading Peter's thought, day and night. The more he tried to stifle the Word, the more it took up residence in his mind and his heart. Peter couldn't shake it off. He couldn't run from it or hide from it. For it had been imbedded in the depths of his very being as a young child. The Word was still living and powerful in him, no matter how hard he tried to suppress it.

Looking up in the sky, as always Peter was amazed at God's beauty. How could he not believe in God—the Creator of the Universe? The Author and Finisher of everything? Only God could create such a beautiful sky. With darkness in the horizon, the stars were glowing. How often, he and his father had sat on the porch gazing up at the stars. His father would point out the Big Dipper and the Little Dipper and planet Jupiter, right next to the moon. Countless times, he had made wishes on the stars. During those times, Frank would share spiritual wisdom with his son, and practical ways to live and see things. Those precious moments with father and son were priceless. Now, everything had changed.

"Where were You when I really needed you?" Peter looked up into the big sky, seeking answers. Seeking solace. Seeking closure. "I lost my baby and didn't even know about it. Elaine killed our baby and there was nothing I could do about it. I wanted our baby. I don't even know if it was a boy or a girl. I'll never know.

"I despise Elaine for not giving me a say-so about the abortion. She was embarrassed, ashamed at what her father would think, what the church folks would say…everybody but me! She didn't even care what I would think!" Peter crumpled to the ground. "Where were You then God, when I needed You? You said you would not have me ignorant of the devices of the enemy. Sure, I messed up. We shouldn't have had sex outside of marriage, but to take my baby…my innocent baby and I not know it. Elaine was a believer. She knew it was wrong to abort and she did it anyway. You turned a blind eye, never making me aware of what was going on. You could have stopped her, Lord. You could have stopped her from aborting my baby. How can I live, when my baby didn't have the same right?" He wiped his eyes, refusing to shed another tear. If only Peter could erase the pain like he erased the tears.

Peter's walking away from God started the day Elaine confided in him. At first, Peter was depressed and oppressed about it. He couldn't eat or sleep. He distanced himself from everybody and everything. Mostly, he distanced himself from God. Then bitterness stepped in, with anger on its footsteps. Peter was a mess. Elaine wasn't any better. She also didn't eat or sleep. She felt guilty for secretly going to an abortion clinic. She called herself a murderer, and Peter let her. Deep down, he wanted to sympathize with her, to comfort her, but he was too angry with her. She didn't trust him enough to be honest and up front. Elaine knew Peter would object to her having the abortion. How could she have felt it was the right thing to do? It all came down to her disappointing her father or disappointing him. Elaine couldn't stand disappointing her father. *But what about me, Lord? She disappointed me even more. She let me down and for some reason, I cannot get back up.*

A part of Peter died with his unborn child. Abruptly, Peter called off the engagement with Elaine, unable to forgive her. It broke her heart. She begged Peter to forgive her and to love her in spite of what she did. But he refused. He couldn't, with all the hatred he had built up inside. Peter slowly withdrew from all that was familiar with his relationship with Elaine. Now, she was dating someone else in the church, which affected Peter more than he would ever admit. Since he and Elaine partnered in working with the teens in church, he resigned. They were both active in the singles ministry, so he resigned from that too. Both worked in an accountant firm, so he went to another firm. And they both loved the Lord God with all they hearts and were raised in God-fearing families, with a strong faith in obeying the voice of God, so he rebelled and walked away from God.

At his lowest and most vulnerable state, Peter met Imani, who heightened his feelings of doubt against God. She subtly persuaded him to think outside of the religious box he had been raised in. To see that there were many gods. To open up his narrow point of view, observing the world in a different way. People had to take care of themselves, like she did, working her way from the bottom to become a well sought after model.

She convinced him to attend her meetings with a group of radicals who believed in fighting for the rights of black people. They didn't call themselves atheist because they believed in a High Power—*just not his God.*

Peter felt trapped, like a bird in a cage with a broken wing, unable to fly out of the open cage. Desiring freedom and yet, what was freedom? Oppressed, Peter felt as if his life was over.

"I can't have a child now. I don't deserve it. My firstborn never made it into this world. I don't deserve a second chance. I don't want this baby, Lord. Not now. Not ever." Peter couldn't stop blaming himself.

"God, if You're out there…really out there, show yourself! Give me a reason to believe again." Unknown to Peter at that exact moment, his parents were on bended knees praying for their sons. Praying for God to bring them home again. Not just their home, but to the Lord Jesus.

Peter waited, not sure on what. Surely, he didn't expect the sky to open up and God Himself to come down and see about him. Peter just needed a sign.

"Just what I thought!" Peter got up, ready to head back home.

All of a sudden, from out of nowhere, the sky opened up, like a faucet from heaven had been turned on full force. The rain came down rapidly. It hadn't rain in weeks. There was a drought in the area and there was no expected rain in the foresight.

*It's not supposed to rain!* Peter sprinted home, becoming drenched.

*Well, Lord…*

While Peter was away, Imani was busy preparing dinner. Suddenly, she felt ill. Something wasn't right. She rushed to the bathroom, feeling even more certain that she was pregnant. She had taken two pregnancy test but neither positively confirmed her suspicion. She wanted to be pregnant so badly, she told Peter before she had concrete evidence. Since she was a week late on her period, which was unusual, Imani believed wholeheartedly that she was carrying Peter's child. Her monthly was like clockwork. This pregnancy meant everything to Imani. Certainly, this would keep Peter from leaving her and returning home. She loved him and would do anything to keep him.

"Oh no," Imani gasped, shaken that her monthly visit had finally arrived. What was she going to do? She already told Peter she was pregnant. "I'm not taking the pill anymore. Surely, I'll ovulate this month and get pregnant. It's only a matter of time. Simple as that and Peter will stay and do the right thing." Imani planned her next move —to trap Peter.

***They dig a pit to trap others and then fall into it themselves. The trouble they make backfires on them. The violence they plan falls on their own heads.***

*Lord, have mercy!*

# CHAPTER 10

# Thanksgiving Part II

Later, while Daniel shared the rest of Thanksgiving Day with Molly's parents, Frank and Sherry changed into something more comfortable with the intentions of watching a Hallmark Christmas movie —Sherry's choice of course.

"Frank," Sherry entered the bedroom, "I have this bad feeling, this urgency to pray for our sons. Something is not right and I can feel it.

"Okay," without hesitation, Frank reached for her hands. The two dropped to their knees in the middle of the bedroom and prayed in the spirit for some time until they both felt a peace come about.

"Father God, shield and protect all of our sons. Have angels encamped all about them. Draw our sons back to You by Your Spirit. Show yourself mightily in their lives. Give them a sure sign of Your Presence and Your Power. Remind them that You are the reason for their existence. Remove the scales from their eyes so that they can once again see You. Cover them with Your divine protection, keeping the enemy far from them, where he cannot harm them in any way. And Lord, have mercy on Imani. Somehow bring her to You," he squeezed Sherry's hand, sensing her struggle. "And Lord, Larry needs to know You as well, so we pray for his salvation. Lord, bless Daniel and Molly as they plan to marry. Let Your will be done in their lives. May their marriage be happy, healthy and blessed. We believe that You have heard and answered our prayer, in Jesus' name, amen."

"Amen." Sherry opened her watery eyes and gazed at her husband. She never really gave him credit for leading their family, spiritually. However, Frank was a spiritual leader. He loved the Lord. She didn't realize just how one-sided her vision had been of him. Frank was a good man. His good definitely outweighed his bad. Not only was her husband flawed, but she was also flawed.

"Thank you, Frank," she began. "For being the man of this household. I appreciate you for that."

Her words touched him deeply. It had been nearly a decade since Sherry spoke such kind sentiments. To hear words of adoration was good for his soul. "Thank you for saying that Sherry. Truly thank, you," he stood up assisting his wife gently up.

"Ouch!" Sherry expressed her pain. "I don't know why I thought I could get on the floor like that."

"Sit for a moment," Frank helped her to the edge of the bed. "Do you need anything? Pain pills? Water?"

"No. I'll be fine. Just give me a minute."

"Are you sure?"

She nodded. "You can go pop the popcorn and get everything ready for the movie. I'll be there in a few."

"Okay," Frank boldly pecked his wife on the lips. "See you in a bit." He winked and departed, leaving Sherry wanting more —more of her husband."

♥♥♥

"Tell me you're not crying," Frank asked, as the love story ended.

"It was so touching," Sherry wiped her eyes. "I'm a sucker for a good love story. Too bad it's not real life."

"I don't know about that Sherry," he eyed her. "I mean even in the love story the couple had problems. Everything wasn't all roses. They almost didn't make it. Their faith was tried by fire. Life almost pulled them away from each other. Somehow, they found their way back...just like us."

"You think so," Sherry wasn't convinced. Her heart was still bruised and tender. Unquestionably, she loved her husband. She still didn't trust him.

"I have to believe that Sherry. All things are going to work out for our good...no matter how bad it looks. I have faith in God. I have faith in us."

"Real life is nothing life Hallmark, Frank. You cannot just do wrong and pretend everything is okay. You cannot just kiss and make up. Life is not like that."

"I think a sweet kiss doesn't hurt. As a matter of fact, Sherry, I'm going to kiss you right now." Frank didn't wait for her to reject. With a longing he could no longer stifle, Frank's lips claimed her mouth. All of his passion came to the forefront of the kiss. He was hungry for the taste of his wife, thirsty for her love to fulfill him. Slipping her arms around his neck, Sherry kissed him back, giving into the desires of her heart. Forgetting her trust issues. Forgetting her children issues. Even forgetting her health issues. That single moment in time was all that mattered. She was all wrapped up and tied up in the embrace of her husband, emotionally and physically —and it felt good—really good.

Coming up for air, Frank gazed into her eyes, relishing the sparkle in her eyes again. Sherry hadn't looked at him like that in a long time. It quickened his heart rate, stirring feelings within Frank. At that precise moment, his love for his wife amplified. Frank felt as if his heart would explode.

Straightway, panic encompassed Sherry's being. For a moment, her guard had been let down and regret took possession. "Ah…I…I'm not feeling well," Sherry pushed herself off the couch. She was all tied up in knots with conflicting feelings of romantic notions and fearful desires. Frank was making her feel things she hadn't felt in a long time. He was getting under her skin, making Sherry uncomfortable. "I think I'm going to turn in."

"Sherry, please don't go. Let's talk. Let's watch another movie," Frank pleaded. "Anything, I just want to be with you."

She stood still, desiring to give into his request, but fear got the best of her. Nippily, her thoughts went to Monique. Every time, she felt vulnerable to Frank, wanting to toss caution in the wind, and become intimate with her husband, she used Monique as her defense mechanism. Sherry never wanted to experience such betrayal and hurt ever again. To surrender her heart fully to Frank would lead to other things. After two years, Sherry still wasn't ready.

*I don't know if I'll ever be ready.*

"I'm tired, Frank," she finally said. "It's been a long day. I think its practical tonight that you sleep in the guestroom. I'll be tossing and turning all night, with the way I'm feeling."

His heart dropped. They were right back where they started. One-step forward, two steps backwards. "I don't mind, Sherry. I prefer sleeping with you."

"Not tonight, Frank." Sherry didn't trust herself. She was lonely and that kiss ignited a fire in her that she wanted to quench. Sleeping near the man she loved tonight would make it almost impossible to keep herself from giving into her secret longings.

"Sherry," Frank went to her, "don't do this. I'm sorry if kissing you repulsed you, so much that you don't want me in our bed again. However, I'm not apologizing for wanting to kiss my wife. I love you." His gazed locked with hers as he put his hand to her cheek. "Please don't pull away from me again. I need you."

Sherry's eyes glistened hearing Frank's heartfelt plea. Oh, how she wanted to just fall into his arms and to just be held by the man who held her heart in his hands and he didn't even know it.

"Goodnight Frank," she pecked his cheek. "I'm sorry."

Defeated, Frank watched his wife slowly walk away, until she vanished from his sight. It felt as if his chest was being squeezed in a constricted bottle, with a lid tightly in place so there was no room for his heart to beat. The ship of saving his marriage was sinking and sinking fast.

*Lord, I don't know what to do anymore. Sherry will not let me into her closed heart. She cracks the doors and then shuts it right in my face.*

**Love her through it.**

Sitting on the couch, Frank stared at the television, not hearing or seeing what was going on. His heart ached. His spirit cried. He felt numb. He wanted to fix their marital problems. Yet, nothing was working. How would he ever earn Sherry's trust again? How could he make her fall in love with him all over again, as he was falling for her?

Interrupting his thoughts, his phone vibrated. Looking at his watch, Frank figured it was Daniel calling saying he was running late since it was almost midnight. No other person would call him at this late hour.

*Boy*, was he wrong. The enemy of temptation is relentless, always roaming seeking whom he could devour.

"Hello," Frank answered.

"Happy Thanksgiving!"

"What are you doing calling me at this hour?" Immediately, Frank recognized Monique's voice. Paranoid, he looked behind him, fearing his wife was near.

"Frank, I need to talk to you," Monique began. "It's very important."

"We have nothing to talk about," he mumbled, rather annoyed at her gumption. "Are you crazy? Don't ever call me again!"

"I must talk to you!"

"There is nothing that we have to talk about. Stay away from me!" he hung up. Frazzled, Frank paced the living room. Why on earth was Monique calling him now? What was she up to?

*She has some nerve calling me! I don't need this confusion now, Lord!*

His phone vibrated again. And again. And again.

"Stop calling me!" he nearly yelled.

"I will keep calling until you agree to meet with me."

"Never! You're loco."

"You may choose to forget that we had something special, but I cannot," Monique shouted, persisted in her pursuit. "I need to tell you something, in person. It's in your best interest that you see me or else you will definitely regret it."

Breathing hard, unable to control his anger, Frank wanted to go through the phone and smack Monique. Not a violent person by nature, every part of his being wanted to harm

Monique, just as she was trying to harm him now. If he stood any chance with his wife, he had to stay clear of Monique. Now, she shows up. Why?

"Are you threatening me?"

"It's not a threat, Frank."

"I can't," Frank affirmed. "I love my wife and I'm not going to do anything else to jeopardize my future with her."

"I'm not trying to break you two up," she said, "not that you two were really happy, remember? You came to me."

"No, you hunted me down like a dog in heat," Frank rebutted. "You chased me."

"Maybe, but it didn't take much chasing," Monique added. "You were lonely and I fulfilled your needs."

"Enough of this, Monique…"

Unbeknown to Frank, Sherry had had a change of heart. She was coming to tell Frank that he could sleep in their bedroom when she stopped dead in her tracks upon hearing Frank say Monique's name.

Sherry's breath caught in her throat, as her heart dropped to the floor, frozen in anguish. Writhe in pain like a woman in labor, Sherry felt sick! Her heart was bashing against her ribcage.

*Once again, he has betrayed me. How dare he speak to that woman in my house! How dare he bring his sin back into this house! Oh, he had me fooled. Fool me once, shame on you! Fool me twice, shame on me!*

*Well Frank, never again! Never!* Like a flood, the currents of the little trust she had left, had been swept away. She was crushed in her spirit. More determined than ever, Sherry vowed to keep her heart closed to Frank Reed. Sherry tiptoed away, her heart torn to pieces, anger riding her coat trail.

"There is nothing you and I have to say to each other! My marriage was almost destroyed because of a month of sleeping around. I never loved you. Like you said, I was lonely and stupid. Nevertheless, I love my family. I love my wife. God has forgiven me and Sherry is working hard on doing that. Now, with all that being said…leave me alone! I don't know why you ever came back in the first place. And to come back to our church…that was just cruel," he rambled. "Move! Go to another church! Do whatever, but stay away from me and my family!"

"I have a right to go wherever I want to and to do whatever I please," Monique defended, riding high on her high horse. "Sherry is not my concern."

"Why do you hate her, Monique? She was your best friend."

"I don't hate her," she paused. "It's just that Sherry has everything and she doesn't appreciate it. As her friend, I listened to her whine all the time. About her family. Her children. Her marriage. Her health. She never appreciated you, Frank," her tone softened. "She had everything and I had nothing."

"You had a career," Frank said. "And you had Sherry. Your parents are still alive and well, Sherry had a rough childhood. Anyhow, none of that matters. All that matters now is that we both have learned from our mistakes and moved on, both endeavoring to be better Christian people."

"Frank, I have to see you. Just once. After you see me, I promise I won't bother you ever again," Monique pleaded. "Just one time. Frank, I have to see you."

"Monday, I have to meet a client in Dales Village. Meet me at the coffee shop there at two o'clock," he gritted his teeth. "And this will be a very brief meeting, you understand?"

"Thanks, Frank," Monique triumphed. "I can't…"

Frank hung up.

*Lord, what is Monique up to? She just shows up now of all times and wants to see me. Lord, I know I opened the door of discord in my family, but You know I shut the door completely, two years ago.*

**I open doors that no man can shut; and I close doors that no man can ever open again.**

*Is this your doing Lord? Or is it the enemy?*

# CHAPTER 11

# What's done in the dark, will come to the light.

"What is going on between you and mom?" Daniel asked at Monday morning at the breakfast table. Once again, it was just he and his father sharing a meal together. It had been that way since Thanksgiving. Sherry didn't join them for breakfast or dinner, feigning illness.

"I'm not sure, Daniel," Frank ran his fingers through his hair. Perplexed, he was at a breaking point in trying to reach Sherry. She had withdrawn so far back in her shell, she wouldn't even look at him. Something was troubling her and it was more than him kissing her. "She won't talk to me."

"Now you're sleeping in the guestroom again. This sucks, Dad! I hate seeing my parents on the verge of a divorce... again."

"We're not getting a divorce, Daniel!" he raised his voice. "I will do anything in my power to keep that from happening, but your mom is going to have to give a little."

"Two years ago, did you cheat on mom?" Daniel finally asked, afraid to hear the answer. Rumors were that he had cheated and got caught. Repeatedly, Daniel defended his dad, refusing to believe that his father wasn't flawless.

Frank choked on his orange juice. He had to get through the coughing spell before he could answer. "How did you know?"

"So it's true?"

"Sadly, so."

"How could you?" Daniel slid his chair back angrily. "Mom is the best! And she's sick! How could you do that to her?"

The look in Daniel's eyes stabbed Frank's heart to pieces. He never wanted to see that look. A look of disappointment. A look of loathing. A look of letting everyone down. A dismal look of shame. "I was stupid. Really stupid. I didn't mean to hurt your mother…"

"But that's exactly what you did!" he lashed out. "And me! And our entire family. So, mom stayed with you even though you were a jerk!"

"Watch it, Son," Frank cautioned. "I'm still your dad."

"Well excuse me Dad, but you were a jerk to do that to our family! What about God? Didn't you fear Him?"

"Of course, I did."

"Humph! Must not have feared him too much to do such a thing."

"Daniel, that was over two years ago and I paid for it dearly, trust me," Frank drew near. "I was dead wrong, no doubt about it. I messed up. No doubt about it. I missed the mark and fell short of God's glory, but in His mercy He forgave me."

"But mom hasn't?" Daniel assumed.

"Sometimes, I think she does and then sometimes, I don't know if she ever can or will," he sighed deeply. "I'm trying to win her back. I am fighting for our marriage with everything that is in me. You have to believe that."

"I do, Dad," Daniel's eyes watered. "But right now, I'm

hurt. You were my hero. I looked up to you. I wanted to be a good husband and father like you."

Frank was crushed. He'd lost his son's respect. "I will never do that again, Daniel. I will never hurt your mother or our family like that again. Please believe me. Please forgive me."

"I forgive you, Dad," Daniel sniffed. "I just don't understand. I'm confused. I'm hurt."

"I'm so sorry," Frank embraced him. "I love you, Daniel, and I don't ever want to lose your respect."

"I love you, Dad," Daniel pulled away. "God forgives and forgets. Therefore, I purpose to do likewise. I just need some time to process this. Just, don't give up on mom. Win her back, please! I want my family to stay together."

"Me too," Frank wanted nothing more.

"I better go, or I'll be late for school," Daniel reached for his book bag. "Mom wants me to take her to the store later."

"Good. Least she is getting out of the house."

"Baby steps," Daniel smiled. "Love you, Dad."

"Love you too, Son."

Frank couldn't concentrate at work. His mind was occupied with two women. His wife and Monique Smith. Dominating his thoughts was his wife, who had seemed more distant that ever, not looking him in the eye, avoiding any contact with him and she didn't even go to church yesterday. Knowing Sherry well, Frank perceived that she was withholding something from him. But what? Then there was the thorn in his flesh,

Monique. He felt guilty about seeing her behind Sherry's back. But what choice did he have? Monique's hint of regretting not meeting with him somehow worried him. Something wasn't right and he needed to find out what, hoping to prevent another train wreck in his marriage.

Later, arriving at the restaurant, Frank felt sick to his stomach. How had his life turned out like this? Meeting the woman he had an affair with, behind his wife's back. This was so wrong in every way, and Frank knew it.

Looking around, Frank immediately spotted Monique, sitting near the back, waiving her hand for him to come over. Each step he took toward her Frank thought he would regurgitate his breakfast. He felt like evil was all around him and he was walking straight into the enemy's camp. *Lord, help me.*

"Oh Frank, it is so good to see you," happily Monique greeted, touching his hand as he sat down.

Immediately, Frank pulled back. "It's not like that," a strong reprimand was in his tone.

"Frank, we were once friends," she demurely spoke, "all of us."

"Yeah, well what we did ruined that friendship. Why am I here?" Frank wanted to cut to the chase. "What is so urgent that I had to see you?"

"I'm leaving for Germany in January."

"So!" he shrugged, his usually calm temper was rising. "Good! Go!" he scooted out of his chair. "This is ridiculous! I need to have my head examined for agreeing to meet with you in the first place. I shouldn't be here. You interrupted my life to tell me you're going to Germany. I'm sorry, but I can't do this!" Frank was ready to bolt.

"Frank!" she shouted to stop him. "You better hear me out!"

"Better!" he turned, his eyes blazing. "Get a life! And leave me the heck alone!"

"Frank!"

He stumped away.

"Frank, you have a daughter!" she blurted. Thankfully, there weren't many people in the restaurant to witness their public dispute.

Frank slowly turned around, gazing at Monique as if she had something on her face. "Say what?"

"Come sit down, Frank. We don't want to cause a scene."

"Too late for that," the frown on his brow deepened, as he undesirably sat across from the woman he wanted to make disappear forever. Clearing his throat, Frank finally spoke through the constricting clog and said, "I don't believe you."

"It's true, Frank," she spoke softly.

"You said you and Troy couldn't have kids," he ran his fingers through his hair nervously.

"We couldn't," she replied.

"Then, if you couldn't..."

"I never said I couldn't," she interjected. "Troy had a vasectomy before we were married. Neither of us wanted kids. Troy divorced me when he found out that I was pregnant... with your child."

Shaking his head in disbelief, Frank couldn't absorb the colossal chaos his world was spiraling into. This was way too much! He expected nothing like this. "You should have told me this...that...you could get pregnant. We are adults. We could have prevented this. Shoot, it should never have happened in the first place. One month of sin has caused a lifetime of anguish!"

"What's done is done, Frank. We cannot go back and change things. Her name is Farah if you're interested."

*Farah! My twin sister's name who died at birth.* Frank clench his fist, anger consuming him. Of all the horrible things he had done to his wife, by having a short affair with her friend, he never expected to hurt her even the more. Surely, this would push Sherry over the edge. She would leave him for sure now. He had fallen into the pit of despair and feared he would never rise again. Frank was jarred with guilt and condemnation. His marriage was over! His life was over!

"Why didn't you tell me this before?" he finally asked.

"Because everything was a mess. I didn't want children, still don't want children, and you were trying to work things out with Sherry. I didn't want to…breakup your marriage. I never wanted to hurt Sherry," she swallowed, still feeling guilty for betraying her once closest friend. "I always had a crush on you, Frank. We were both unhappy and well, I acted on my feelings for you. I regret hurting Sherry, but I don't regret the month we shared together. It was the best month of my life."

"Shut up!" Frank lashed out. "How can you say that? You lost your husband and friend. My wife cannot trust me and probably never will! It was sinful and stupid! I wish I could go back and turn the clock. I'd run away from you as fast as I could! No, but you kept calling, kept making passes, kept showing up. I was at my weakest and you knew it."

"Oh, no you don't!" Monique objected. "You won't blame me for all of it. I didn't force you into bed with me."

"No, but you did everything in your power to seduce me," Frank mumbled. "So why now? Why are you telling me about Farah now?"

"All this time, Farah has been living with my parents," Monique revealed why she was really here. "I would have put her up for adoption, but my mother wouldn't have it. She begged me to let her raise her, hoping that I would change my mind. Well, I didn't and I never will. Kids are not what I see in my future. Anyhow, my mother has dementia and it's getting worse. My father's health never was good and he cannot raise Farah. So, before I leave, I will put Farah in a children's home not far from where my parents are until she is adopted…unless you want to raise her."

Frank's mouth dropped wide opened, staring at Monique as if she had turned into The Joker. Yet the joke was on him, and it wasn't funny. He sank further into his chair, in utter confusion. He closed his eyes, wishing he could close off everything. To face reality was too painful at the moment.

"You've got to be kidding me?" he finally spoke.

"I'm not kidding Frank," she stated. "I didn't want to tell you, but I promised my mother I would give you the option. Now, I have given you the option. You can walk away as if I never told you about her. On the other hand, you can raise her and she won't have to be adopted. But the choice is yours."

"Some choice!" he croaked, blinking back the tears. "It would have been best that I never knew." Frank was calm on the outside, but inside he was a ball of fury. Mad at the woman sitting across from him, talking as if her words weren't affecting anybody but herself. Mostly, Frank was mad at himself, for putting his family in such a terrible predicament. *Well, you reap what you sow.* He sowed his lonely oats and now got a heap of coal smearing his name, his honor, and his family. *What else could go wrong?*

She shrugged. "You say that now, but you may change your mind." Looking up, Monique saw a familiar face, and for some cruel reason, she reached over and put her hand over Frank's hand. "Farah is a beautiful child…"

Meanwhile, Daniel had driven his mother around to do a few errands and was parking the car, while Sherry went inside the restaurant. She wasn't hungry, but Daniel insisted that they have a late lunch together. As she waited to be seated, Sherry looked around the place. She had never been here before since it was rather far from her home. As her eyes darted to the back, she gasped, putting her hand over her mouth to stifle the sound.

*Monique…and Frank!* She clutched both hands over her mouth, to stifle the scream oozing to come forth. Sherry's heart hammered, thumping erratically. Were they having another affair? Her heart was paralyzed in anguish, barely beating. The stressing scene made Sherry feel like she was on the verge of having a heart attack. Bitter anguish infiltrated her being. Her heart melted under the pressure of it all. Seeing her husband with that woman, Sherry's knees buckled. She fought to stay upright and to keep calm. Every inch of her wanted to go over to them and let them both have it. She wanted to shout 'AHA! What is done in the dark, will be brought to light.'

As she turned to just face them —to confront her husband and his mistress—her heart spasm and the lights dimmed, as she fell.

"Mom!" Daniel entered just in time.

Recognizing his son's voice, Frank turned, "Sherry!" he jumped up. *Oh my God! What have I done now!*

# CHAPTER 12

## Finding hope in despair

"How could you?" Daniel cried while sitting in the waiting area of the emergency room.

"It's not what you think?" again, Frank ran his shaking fingers through his thick hair. Today topped the list of being one of the worst days of his life. How would Frank ever dig himself out of the hole that he helped dig? Was there a limit on reaping the negative he had sown in the past? Would he forever pay the piper for his past discretions? Would he ever be respected and cherished by his wife and his sons, again? Was his marriage over for good? Frank mind reeled with questions, of which, he had no answers to at the moment.

"You were at a restaurant on the outskirts of the city, with the woman you had an affair with," Daniel's heart ached even saying the words. His hero had once again fallen from his pedestal. "What should I think? What do you think mom was thinking before she had a heart attack?"

"We don't know that it was a heart attack," Frank was clearly upset, knowing he was responsible for causing his wife more pain.

"I heard the EMT whispering that it was a heart attack," Daniel mumbled. "And it's all your fault! Just when mom was trying to really work things out with you, you go and meet up with Ms. Smith, of all people!"

The accusing words nearly did Frank in. He didn't need Daniel to blame him. He was doing a *pretty* good job of it all by himself. His wife was fighting for her life, when it should have been him having a heart attack, and not Sherry. There was no end to the misery he felt. He deserved it. He deserved to be the one suffering, not Sherry. "I know," he cringed in terror, fearing the worse. He could lose his wife, without even making it up to her, without even getting the chance to say he loved her—to say he was sorry.

Daniel felt his dad's pain, but he was just too mad at him to offer any comfort. "Why Dad? Why were you with her?"

"I can't talk about that right now," Frank looked at his son, hating the look of disdain in Daniel's eyes. "Right now, we just need to keep praying for Sherry."

"If mom doesn't..." Daniel couldn't hold back the his fears through his tears.

"Shhh," Frank embraced his son, not wanting to go there with his thoughts. Sherry had to make it. Sherry had to pull through. She was his world and if he lost her now, they might as well bury him right next to her.

His phone vibrated.

Glancing, Frank read the text.

I'm so sorry.

"Is that her?" Daniel pulled away.

Frank showed him the text.

"That she is...real sorry! The nerve of her texting you now. What's wrong with her?"

Before Frank could think of an answer, the emergency room doctor came out, informing them that Sherry was undergoing emergency surgery for her heart and that her kidneys were failing…again."

What Frank feared, had come to past. His wife's life was hanging in the balance, by a small thread. Guilt and shame consumed him—*Rightfully so*.

"Oh my God!" Daniel screeched. "Help my mom," he sobbed. "Please don't let her die!"

"She won't, son," Frank spoke, not convincingly. With all that she was enduring, he wondered if Sherry had any fight left in her to want to live, to survive it all.

After the doctor left, both Peter and Timothy arrived a few minutes a part, thankfully without their significant others. The waiting room was already filled with tension and worry— didn't need to add more stress to it. Frank wanted his family back together, but not this way.

"How is mom?" Timothy was the first to ask.

"She's in surgery," Frank answered, Daniel too distraught to repeat the words of the doctor. "She had a heart attack and her kidneys could be failing."

"What? How did that happen?" Peter asked. "I knew she wasn't doing good, but what triggered it?" Like his father, guilt pierced his conscious. Purposefully, he had been avoiding his mother's calls. Not wanting to talk to her or listen to her trying to convert him all over again. Right now, Peter would do anything to hear her voice—anything!

Frank sighed, feeling the weight of his transgressions upon his shoulders. If he could just snap his fingers and make everything like it used to be…before he became a statistic of infidelity.

"Dad?" Timothy called. "What happened?"

"We were about to have lunch and she collapsed?" Daniel answered, eying his father.

"Were you there?" Peter asked his dad, sensing there was a lot more to the story. "Were you at the restaurant?"

Frank nodded.

"With mom?" Peter continued.

He shook his head.

"Huh?" Timothy was confused. "What? You were there, but not with her?"

"It doesn't matter," Daniel interjected, once again coming to his father's rescue. "All that matters now is mom getting better. Our focus should be on her."

"Were you there with Ms. Smith?" Peter's tone changed. He wasn't a kid anymore. The rumors he had heard before about his dad and Monique Smith, his mother's friend, always stayed in the back of his mind. Never spoken, but never forgotten.

"What?" Frank was caught off guard. "Why would you say that?"

"Were you?"

Frank didn't respond.

"Dad, were you with Ms. Monique, mom's friend?" Timothy asked, also having heard rumors before, but taking it with a grain of salt. He refused to believe that his father would do that to his mother.

"It's not what you think."

"You make me sick!" Timothy blurted.

"How dare you do this to mom, again!" Peter angrily shouted.

"How did ya'll know about...about me and...Ms. Smith?" Frank asked.

"The whole church knew," Peter shouted. "Yet, we didn't want to believe it was true. I guess you were a hypocrite back then...too. Just like all churchgoers!"

"My mistakes don't make all churchgoers bad people." Frank defended. "I messed up."

"Seems like you keep doing that!" Peter blasted. "You don't deserve our mother! She's too good for you!"

"She is too good for me," Frank spoke through his pain. "But I love her and I want to be with her for the rest of my life," tears collided down his face. "I had an affair with Ms. Smith for one month. It was crazy. It was wrong. I hurt your mother…and you guys, but it does not change the truth. I am not having an affair with Ms. Smith now."

"Tell that to the Preacher! You all are a bunch of hypocrites! Maybe he'll believe you, but not me!" Peter walked off.

"Peter, come back here! Come back here, now! I'm still your father!"

"In name only," Peter turned and then got on the elevator. He wouldn't let them see him cry. The moment the elevator door closed, Peter slid to the floor and wept. When the door opened, he closed it and rode it several times, before finally getting off. Not knowing what to do or where to go, the sign to the chapel beckoned him. As he walked toward it, desiring to find any comfort he could, he stopped in his tracks. *I will not be a hypocrite like my dad.* He pivoted and exited the hospital. Even though he wanted to be there for his mother, Peter couldn't stand being near his father right now. No telling what he might do. Because every ounce of his being wanted to strike his dad with his fist.

Frank was going after him when Daniel pulled his arm. "Let him cool off, Dad. It's a lot to deal with right now, for all of us. "

Frank plopped in the chair, covering his eyes with his hands. He felt so overwhelmed. He was a failure, failing those whom he loved the most. Frank was their father, the head of their household. He was supposed to protect them from harm, from hurt—not be the reason for their suffering. He would never erase from his memory the common look in all of his sons' eyes. He had lost their respect.

"You've preached to us to live out the Bible, to be epistles, read by man, so that others can see Christ in us. Well, all I see in you is a fake. A fraud. A liar. A cheater. Not ever wanting to believe what others said because you and mom went on pretending everything was great. It was all a lie. Your marriage. Your commitment to God and to mom. And then you have the audacity to have an affair with the same woman again." Timothy couldn't help himself. His faith already waivering, which only made Larry's case stronger. The Bible was outdated. God was evolving and making allowances just as He did with people getting divorced because He knew the world was wicked.

"You may not like me," Frank finally spoke, anger in his tone, "but you will not disrespectfully talk to me that way. Until you know the whole story, don't judge me and murder me without cause. I am the same man, who took care of you, loved you, raised you the best I knew how. Yes, I messed up. Yes, I cheated on your mother, years ago. However, I am not cheating again. I have not since and never will again," he calmed. "I made a stupid judgment call, in agreeing to meet Ms. Smith, because she convinced me that it was urgent and if I didn't I would regret it. I figured if I met with her, she would leave us alone."

"Well, was it urgent?" Timothy asked, not really wanting an answer. "Because I sure hope it was worth causing my mother to have a heart attack."

"Dad already feels bad," Daniel spoke up. "He loves mom,

and I believe him when he says he is not cheating."

Timothy shrugged his shoulders. "I don't know what I believe anymore!" he said, dropping his head and walking to the far end of the waiting area, wanting to distance himself from his family. He just wanted to be alone. He plopped himself in a chair and silently wept.

Watching him, Frank wanted to comfort him, but he knew Timothy would only reject his love. His family was in complete shambles. Peter and Timothy were walking away from the foundational principles of the Holy Bible. His indiscretions surely didn't draw them back to their faith. Daniel was torn between trying to be angry with his father and yet, loving him all the same. Sherry, she was suffering physically, emotionally and spiritually. Frank was the blame for her suffering. What would the family do when they found out he had a daughter?

*A daughter.* Though thankful for the three boys God had blessed them with, he and Sherry had always wanted a daughter. What was he going to do about Farah? She was his flesh and blood. For the sake of his family, could he just let her go to strangers, even though she was a stranger to him, as well? Knowing somewhere out there he had a daughter, who didn't even know him, how was he going to just stay out of her life? How?

Just when Frank thought things couldn't get any worse, in walks the doctor with more bad news.

"Mr. Reed, your wife is stable and out of recovery. The surgery went well, but unfortunately, she slipped into a coma. She also has acquired Hemiplegia. This is a type of paralysis which has caused your wife to become paralyzed on her right side."

The news shattered the three men, Timothy, Daniel, and

Frank, as they stood closely, listening to the heartbreaking news.

"Is it permanent?" Frank asked.

"Both conditions will require monitoring her closely. We will have to wait to see how her body will respond to recovery after such a major surgery and with medications. Based on how things are now, her prognosis is promising."

"That's good," Daniel, sighed. "God is a Healer!"

The doctor smiled. "She's in intensive care right now, but only one of you can see her, I'm afraid. She really needs to rest."

Daniel looked to Timothy, who looked to their father, "You go…Dad," Timothy extended an olive branch. "Please tell her that we love her."

Too choked up to speak, Frank just embraced Timothy, giving him a bear hug, while Daniel joined in. "I love you, both," Frank sniffled.

"Love you, Dad," Daniel spoke first.

"I love you, Dad," Timothy said, his eyes watery. "No matter what."

"Thanks." Frank walked away, his shoulders sagging, still feeling the weight of the world upon his shoulders. *I will lose my boys when they find out about Farah.*

Though he was wrong in so many ways, God had forgiven him. However, Frank found himself in the same place that he was before. He could not forgive himself for the pain he was causing his entire family. Once again, he had opened the door for the enemy to come in and wreak havoc upon his family, leaving oppression on the family's doorstep and in their hearts.

# CHAPTER 13

## *Discord among the brothers*

Still in a comma a week later, Sherry's condition hadn't changed. She wasn't worse, but she wasn't better either. Sleeping in the uncomfortable recliner, Frank stayed by his wife's bedside all day. Gratefully, his manager Charles could oversee the business. If need be, Frank could work on his laptop, checking emails, making calls. His primary focus was on his wife. After all, he was to blame for her setback.

Frank hovered over Sherry, like a mother hen over her chicks. He bathed her face and combed her hair, braiding it daily. He prayed for her, read to her from the Bible and talked to her, believing that Sherry heard every word spoken or read. He massaged her legs and arms, doing therapy on her limbs as the therapist instructed.

Undeniably, Frank would change places with his wife in heartbeat. Endeavoring to be strong for Sherry and his boys, Frank fought hard not to succumb to tears or any outward sign of fear. Albeit internally, Frank felt as if he was treading on tumultuous waters. He could either sink or swim. He chose to swim, among the tempestuous tides. If Sherry couldn't fight for herself, then he would do all within his power to fight for her—and his family.

Speaking of family, Frank was at his wit's end with the boys. Every day a new battle between Timothy and Peter erupted. The love-hate relationship was a horrible strain on everyone. If it weren't for Sherry's illness, Timothy and Peter would avoid each other altogether. Standing in the middle, Daniel did everything he could to be the peacemaker. Yet, nothing worked. The rift between Timothy and Peter was tearing the family apart even the more. Both brothers would rather be right than seeking reconciliation. There was such deep animosity toward each other. The brotherly union appeared thoroughly severed. It would take a miracle for them to bond again.

Saturday, evening, while reading passages in the Bible to Sherry, Peter entered in with a foul mood. He had just gotten into another argument with Imani. Since finding out he would be a father, Peter's anger had stepped up several notches. He wasn't ready to be a father. He didn't want to be a father, especially not now with things being so chaotic with him, his family, and his relationship with Imani. Peter was so confused about everything. Since denouncing his faith, he felt lost. Once putting everything into the church, and his youth group, Peter had no outlet. He felt empty. Imani used to make him happy. He saw her as pure gold, but now she was tarnished. She didn't measure up, no matter what she said or did. Truthfully, he was taking everything out on her and on…Timothy.

Timothy walked in, not alone.

"What's *Tooty Fruity* doing here?" Peter pounced the moment Larry entered in Timothy's shadow.

"Why do you have to be such a jerk?" Larry spoke before Timothy could say anything.

"Don't speak to me!" Peter shouted. "You're nothing! You have no business here!"

"Shhh!" Frank put his finger to his mouth as if he were talking to children.

"Your kind is not needed here," Peter ignored his father.

"He's with me," Timothy inserted, "and if you don't like it you can leave!"

"I'm not leaving! She's my mother, not his!" Peter pointed. "And mom doesn't approve of his kind!"

"He's a human being, Peter."

"He's an abomination!" Peter countered.

"What do you care? You don't believe in God anymore, nor His Word."

"At least I'm not being a hypocrite!"

"Here we go again!"

"Shut up!" Frank demanded. "Shut up right now! Your mother would be so disappointed in the way you two are at each other's throat," he calmed. "Now, you might not like each other right now, but I be darn if I'm going to allow you to bring confusion in here when your mother is fighting for her life. This sure doesn't help her recovery."

"Sorry Dad," Timothy replied.

"I'm sorry for...arguing...here," Peter stated. "But, Timothy shouldn't have brought...that here!"

"Jerk!" Timothy stated under his breath.

"I'm leaving. I'll wait for you in the car, Timmy." Larry hightailed it out the room.

"Good ridden! I hope you never come back!"

"Just because you're miserable doesn't mean you have to make everybody around you miserable," Timothy felt torn. "Mom, I love you. I'll come again later," he leaned over and kissed her cheek. "See you, Dad!"

"Wait," Frank walked outside the room with him.

"I don't know how you and Peter are going to settle your differences, but you have to, for your mother's sake. She needs her family to be united."

"Dad, you saw Peter. He was behaving like such a jerk. Larry didn't deserve that."

"Son, don't take this the wrong way," Frank put his hand on Timothy's shoulder. "But right now it's not about you or Larry or Peter. It's about your mother. Right now, it's not sensible to bring Larry around. Your mother had a hard time with this before and if she had awakened and saw him, I don't know what that would have done to her."

Timothy pondered his father's rationale before finally speaking. "What about love? Didn't you both teach us to love everybody no matter what?"

"You and Peter want to be right. You want your views validated, but your focus should be on praying for your mother and her getting better. Love is always expected and demonstrated as much as possible. However, you are flaunting everything we believe is spiritually wrong and expect everyone just to accept it…to accept Larry. As a human we accept him, but as your significant other, speaking for myself, I do not."

Timothy sighed, his shoulders dropping noticeably. "If you cannot accept Larry, then I guess I'm not welcome around the family anymore."

"So just like that you're going to walk away from those who have supported you, loved you unconditionally, been there for you, brought you into this world…for a life that is not pleasing to our God," Frank spoke evenly, purposing to remain calm and to speak in love. "We all have choices, Timothy. The Word of God declares that we must choose this day whom we will serve. Will it be God or will it be man? If you're choosing man's way, my heart breaks for you. However, I will always love you. I may not agree with your lifestyle, but I will always love you. As far as Larry is concerned, I love him. As your friend, he is welcomed, but as anything else outside of God's Word, I cannot condone or give you my blessings," Frank paused, sensing that his words were penetrating Timothy's defensive wall. "God loves you. God loves Larry, so much He sent His only Son to die for him. But just as God loves the sinner, He hates the sin. Sin separates us from God. If you choose to continue this path Timothy, living in sin, it will separate you from God. The choice is yours."

"Dad, I've done some searching myself. The Word says that nothing can separate us from God."

"No, the Word says nothing can separate us from the love of God." Frank corrected. "God loves us no matter what."

"Well, we are not under the law anymore. The law has been done away with."

"Jesus fulfilled the law, son and now it's not written on tablets, but in our hearts. Besides, it's not the law that separates us from God…it's sin."

"Homosexuality is not even listed in the Bible. You cannot find the word anywhere."

"Son, the word is not listed because the English word came after the Bible was written. However, if you leave the word out, the Word still says in Romans, chapter one, verses 26 & 27 that men committed shameful acts with other men. It was an abomination in OT and is the same in the NT. God and His Word didn't change, people are trying to change it…to fit their mold, their beliefs, their ways," his father stated. "Timothy, it was wrong for me to commit adultery. God hated my sin. What I did is no better or no less than your sins. Sin is sin.

I'm not looking down on you at all. I have no right. That's the pot calling the kettle black. Only, I have confessed my sins and desire to sin no more. We all have to work out our own salvation with fear and trembling."

Timothy sighed, adding one final refutation. "Sodom and Gomorrah were not destroyed because of homosexuality but because of the attempt of gang rape. Also, Ezekiel 16:49 declares that Sodom was destroyed because of her pride, an abundance of idleness and didn't help the poor and needy."

"Really?" Frank took out his phone and pulled up his Bible Ap. He silently read the 49th verse and then felt led to read the 50th as well. "That's true, Timothy. However, if you read the next verse it says: 'and they were haughty and committed abomination before Me, therefore I took them away as I saw fit.' That word abomination is the same word listed in Leviticus."

Timothy was surprised. *Pastor Dave only mentioned verse 49.*

"Timothy, I'm glad you're seeking the Truth. You'll find it," Frank smiled.

"See you later, Dad," Timothy embraced him. "Please keep me posted with Mom. I'm headed back out of town and I'm not sure when I'll be back."

"I'll be praying for you."

Timothy walked away, more confused than ever.

Timely, Peter came out. "Dad, I'm sorry for causing a scene, but it grates my nerve how Timothy flaunts his gay life on us, like its normal."

"And why do you look at the speck in your brother's eye, but do not consider the plank in your own eye? Or how can you say to your brother, 'Let me remove the speck from your eye,' and look, a plank *is* in your own eye? Hypocrite. First, remove the plank from your own eye, and then you will see clearly to remove the speck from your brother's eye." Frank quoted the familiar passage in Matthew, chapter seven.

"So, you're approving of Timothy and Larry?" Peter frowned.

"No," Frank replied. "Just as I am not approving of you and your lifestyle, shacking up and worse than that, walking away from God. However, I still love you and I love Timothy. As I told Timothy, right now it's not about us. It's about your mother. We shouldn't be arguing and carrying on. We should be focusing on her."

"And what about you, dad? You're no saint. You were having lunch with Monica Smith. You brought all this on mom." Peter continued to point fingers. He went straight for the jugular, angry, bitter, and mean-spirited. None of these characteristics fit the old Peter.

"All that anger inside of you is nothing but poison," Frank eyed his son with empathy. "You're killing yourself and hurting those around you. Yes, I was wrong, which I have owned up to my wrongdoings. Perhaps you need to go home and take a good look in the mirror and really glimpse the bitter man staring back at you and realize you're not perfect either." Frank patted his shoulder and reached for the doorknob. "I'm praying for you," he said before going inside.

Frank leaned over and caressed his wife's cheeks. "I'm sorry Honey. I have made a mess of our family and I don't know how to fix it. It's all because of me that you're lying here," he sniffed, "and all because of me that our boys are fighting each other, and loathing me. I am so sorry. I love you so much. I was an idiot! Stupid! Evil! I hate the man I was back then. I promise you, if you awaken, I will spend the rest of my days proving my love to you and our family. I need you, Sherry. I cannot mend our family without you. Please come back to me," he kissed her cheek, his tears touching her face. "Please come back to me."

Sitting in the chair next to the bed, Frank leaned back, closed his eyes and silently prayed. He needed a miracle. Nothing short of a miracle could help the mess he was in. His prayer was temporary interrupted by several text messages from the thorn in his flesh.

Call me Frank.

I'm sorry about Sherry, but we really must talk.

I am leaving in ten days. I must know what you're going to do.

Frank, you cannot ignore me.

Frank, I need to know what you want me to do about your daughter, Farah.

Okay, Frank if I don't hear from you by Friday, then I am signing her over to Children's Foster Home.

Finally, Frank text her back.
My wife is fighting for her life. I cannot handle this right now. Please give me some time.

Monique texted back...
I am sorry for what Sherry and your family are going through. I really am. But, there is no time Frank. If you cannot decide, I will.

Frank covered his face with his hands and just let loose. Every pint-up emotion plummeted out like a raging flood. Frank was oppressed beyond measure. He didn't know what to do? He couldn't talk to Sherry about her. He feared if she ever found out, not only would that destroy her, but also it would destroy their marriage. Yet, Frank was tired. Tired of the secrets. Tired of living a lie. He had to come clean. He had to at least tell the boys about it. They deserved to know they had a sister, even if he couldn't bring her into their home or into their lives.

Frank sent a group text to his sons.

I need to see you all at the house tomorrow, Sunday. Come around noon. No excuses. Be there. Dad

# CHAPTER 14

## Coming Clean

Before going into the dining room, Frank spent several hours in prayer, seeking God's guidance on how to handle this family meeting with his boys. He needed to be empowered by the Greater One to handle what was about to happen. Having on the full armor of God: the helmet of Salvation, so nothing said or done could mess with his mind or play with his emotions. The breastplate of righteousness, though he sinned, Frank was now in right standing with God. The shield of faith to quench the fiery darts thrown at him by his own children. The belt of truth, he would speak the truth in love, knowing he had Jesus—the Way, the Truth and the Life wrapped around him. Feet shod with the Gospel of peace, Frank would be the peacemaker today. Lastly, the Sword of the Spirit, the Word of God, Frank had the living and powerful Word of God to help in his hour of need.

Frank was ready for battle, recognizing the battle was not his, but it belonged to the Lord. Though he would surely have scars, he would come out the victor and not the victim—in the end.

Entering the dining room, Peter, Timothy, and Daniel were already seated. Looking serious, unsure and somewhat fearful, the sons all eyed their father, wondering what horrible news he was about to reveal.

"Good afternoon sons," Frank formally greeted. "I'm glad you all made it."

"Did we have a choice?" Peter blurted, miffed about everything.

"You did. You are all grown. I cannot make you do anything. All I can do is ask," he smiled. "And right now I am asking you all to have open minds. Listen to everything that I have to say without interrupting. Finally, do not leave this table until I have concluded our family meeting. Can everyone come to an agreement on what I'm asking?"

"As long as you're not preaching to us." Once again, Peter spoke up. "No sermons."

"I will not preach. However, I will openly speak my heart. Moreover, we always began family meetings with prayer and scripture. That has not changed and will not change."

"I'm in agreement, Dad," Daniel stated.

"Me too," Timothy followed.

"I guess I'm in agreement," Peter shrugged his shoulders, not really wanting to agree to anything.

"Good." Frank smiled. "Listen, no interrupting and no walking away," he reiterated.

"Let us pray," Frank began. "Almighty Father, we come to You, first giving thanks for this day. Thank You for allowing us to be together, once again. I ask Father that You be with us as we have this family meeting. May our hearts remain in love, one for another. Let nothing be said or done that brings disgrace to You or causes permanent separation from each other. Guide my words, as I speak and let the hearers, my sons, be merciful and gracious. Touch Sherry right now. Heal her from the top of her head to the soles of her feet. We bind up paralysis and believe that she will awaken on this very day. We believe that she will suffer no inward or outward effects from the heart attack. Make her whole again and make our family whole again in Jesus' name, amen."

"Amen." Daniel and Timothy uttered. Peter said nothing, still wearing the sour expression as if it were a well-worn garment.

"I'm going to read a portion of Psalms 127 and then conclude with a verse from Matthew, chapter seven," Frank began. "Unless the Lord builds the house, they labor in vain who build it. Behold, children are a heritage from the Lord, the fruit of the womb is a reward. Like arrows in the hand of a warrior, so are the children of one's youth. Happy is the man who has his quiver full of them; they shall not be ashamed," Frank paused turning to Matthew in His Bible. "A wise man who built his house on the rock, and the rain descended, the floods came, and the winds blew, and beat on the house and it did not fall, for it was founded on the rock…a foolish man who built his house on the sand, and the rain descended, the floods came and the winds blew and beat on that house, and it fell. And great was its fall."

Frank closed his bible and looked directly at each one of his sons. He was a blessed man, no doubt. Though all were different, he loved them greatly. His quiver was full and he was happy, despite the rains, the winds and the floods that were trying to destroy their home—their very lives.

"This Reed Home has weathered many storms. We have endured many battles. Withstood many struggles and we have always come out stronger as a family unit. A house that is built on sand cannot stand. However, a house built on Christ the

Solid Rock, cannot fall. It will withstand the severe storms. It cannot fail. It always prevails. If it is built on Christ Jesus it will last and not pass…like people or things. Such as my love for you all. It will outlast anything or anyone that comes against us.

"God values families. Children are a blessing, a heritage from the Lord. The enemy seeks to separate families. Making the Lord the foundation of our family ensures that our home is stable, secure, and a shelter in the good and bad times. It's not that we are perfect, but the Perfect Builder upholds us, keeps us, shields us, protects us and loves us through it all.

"We are at a pivotal place in our family. We have to decide is our family worth it? Will we hate each other or love each to life…not to death? Will we choose to be right or choose to do right by our family and by our God? Will we forget the truth and so easily accept a lie. The Bible says, 'False Christs and false prophets will appear and perform signs and wonders that would deceive even the elect.'"

Timothy stiffened, ready to defend his beliefs. He wasn't the only one at the table who had sinned, who had missed the mark and yet, he felt the brunt of it resting on his shoulders.

"We are living in the days when Christians are falling by the wayside. Believing a lie rather than the Truth. Giving into peer pressure, giving into temptation and sadly, walking away from God," Frank paused, allowing his gentle, soft words to marinate a few moments. All eyes were intently on him, even Peter watched with earnest. "We cannot afford to allow the enemy to divide and conquer us, to tear our family apart. On the flip side, we can choose to be there for one another, even if we don't agree with one another's choices. I will not, nor will your mother, participate in sin. However, we will love each one of you, with all of our hearts. Nothing and no one can separate our love for you. It's unconditional and everlasting, just as God's love is for you.

"With that being said, I have something to tell you that will upset you all, I'm sure. For it is upsetting to me, as well. I remind you to listen, not to interrupt and not to walk away." Frank cleared his throat. "As you all know over two years ago, I messed up and had a brief affair, not even a month, with Ms. Smith."

Tension occupied the room in the highest. Other than Frank speaking, an awkward silence infiltrated the room. Frank continued. "Well, the reason I met up with Ms. Smith was because she insisted that if I didn't I would regret it. I feared she would try something stupid to endanger my wife or my family, maybe not in actions but in words, so I met with her. Cutting to the chase, she informed me that out of the two times that I slept with her, a daughter was conceived. Her name is Farah."

Timothy and Daniel gasped simultaneously. Peter clutched his fists so tight that he was making imprints in his skin. Every ounce of his being wanted to get up and run. He stood to do just that, when Frank cautioned, "You promised you would not leave! Sit down, Peter! Now!" He gave a stern look.

Reluctantly, Peter complied.

"I know this is a shock to you all, but let me finish." Frank took in a deep breath, seeking God's strength to continue. "Ms. Smith informed me that Farah, who is eighteen months old, has been raised by her parents, who are both sickly now and cannot raise her anymore. Being that Ms. Smith doesn't want children, never has and never will, she is going to put Farah up for adoption. Ms. Smith is moving to Germany for a job.

She already has contacted a children's home that will take the child in until she is adopted." Taking in another painful breath, Frank continued. "I have decided that I will not bring Farah into our family. Sherry and you all have suffered enough and don't need to be reminded daily of my infidelity."

"Can I say something now, Dad?" Daniel inquired.

"Yes, but remember the meeting is not concluded until I say-so."

"Well, Dad, I have forgiven you for what you did. I hate that you hurt, mom. However, God reminded me the other day, that Saul had hurt so many of His children, but God forgave him and changed his name to Paul and used him to change the lives of so many people. Why? Because God loved him. So I choose to love you, Dad."

Frank's eyes watered as he listened to the voice of his youngest extend mercy and love to him. "Thank you, Daniel."

"I personally want Farah to be a part of our family," Daniel added. "She's family."

"Yes, she's our sister," Timothy agreed. "I'd like to meet her. I've always wanted a sister."

"Me too!" Daniel chimed. "I am not the baby anymore."

"Half-sister!" Peter corrected. "She's a half-breed!"

"Doesn't matter," Timothy stated. "She is still our sister and I want to know her."

"Don't hate her," Daniel addressed Peter. "She didn't do anything wrong. She's an innocent child. Hate the sin, but not the sinner." Daniel repeated one of his father's favorite idioms.

The familiar words struck a chord with Timothy. Looking to his father, he recalled those same words spoken by his father in the hospital. Frank smiled.

"What about Momma?" Peter was so mad. "She just had a

heart attack. How do you think she is going to feel about this illegitimate child? It could kill her! Surely, you're not going to tell her?" Peter gazed at his father with contempt.

"I will not deceive her, Peter," Frank replied. "As much as it will hurt her, she deserves the truth."

"The truth that you're a hypocrite! A deadbeat dad to a child who is almost two years old!"

"You can voice your opinions, but you will not disrespect me by calling me names." Frank spoke sternly, giving him a look to let Peter know he was treading on very thin ice.

"I'm only speaking the truth!"

"You're speaking hatred!" Frank countered.

"You brought it out of me!"

"No, Peter, hatred is all in you, eating away at the core of your soul," Frank calmed down. "You're angry at me, sure I get it. But why are you so angry at the world? At God? What did He do to you that would cause you to hate Him?"

"I don't hate God!" he said quickly.

"You sure act like it," Frank replied. "Nevertheless, you can be mad at me, but this anger is killing you."

"Are you finished?" Peter yelled.

"Almost," Frank replied, taking out three small envelopes with handwritten letters inside and handed them to his sons. "Please find a quiet place and read these. Allow the Holy Spirit to speak to you. What I have written was written in love. Don't be defensive, but be willing to hear my heart. That's all I am asking of you.

"Your mother was and is a strong woman. However, with the family structure being so shaky right now this added stress doesn't help her heart condition. It makes battling lupus nearly impossible. We have to find a way to pull together, in spite of our differences. We cannot turn on each other, but need to turn to each other. We may not agree about everything, but our love should withstand it all because we have a solid foundation. This Reed family was built on God, on Jesus Christ and the Holy Spirit. This family is built on Love. The Word of God states that love prevails. It covers. It never ends. So, let's remember that.

"Knowing that we would all mess up, God sent His only Son, Jesus to die for us. While we were yet sinners, Christ died for us. Can you extend that same mercy to me? Maybe not today, but I pray in time, you all will.

"Does anyone have anything else to say before we conclude this meeting?" Frank looked to his children. Daniel was smiling. Timothy, also smiled, pondering everything as usual. Whereas Peter was frowning. He couldn't wait to get out of their home.

"Whatever you decide, I'll support you, Dad. But, I would like to meet my sister," Daniel affirmed.

"I support you, Dad," Timothy echoed. "I, too, would like to meet Farah."

"I want nothing to do with her!" Peter grunted. "Nothing at all!"

"You have that right, Peter," Frank was disappointed. "However, Daniel and Timothy, I will try to make it happen that you can meet Farah, but I will not bring her into our home. I cannot hurt Sherry anymore."

"I understand," Timothy said.

Daniel nodded.

"Before I close in prayer. Christmas is seven days away. You mother loves Christmas. I pray that she will be home by then and if so, I want for us to come together...for her sake."

"Who is cooking?" Daniel asked. "You know you cannot cook Christmas dinner, Dad…no offense."

"I was thinking of having it catered, for the most part, and asking Mom to do the turkey."

"Can Larry come?" Timothy asked.

"No!" Peter answered for him.

"Peter!" Frank signaled. "Timothy, I have nothing against Larry as a human being. He is welcome to my house, as your friend, but not as your lover. Also, think of your mother. Is this good for her or not? With that being said, I will let you decide."

"Well, then I guess Tooty-Fruity will be here because Timothy is selfish! He'll put his wants before anyone else's needs." Peter scoffed.

"Selfish! You're the selfish one!" Defensively, Timothy sparred. "What about bringing your tattoo friend here! You know how rude she is with mother, but you don't care!"

"Look at you!" Peter berated. "You want to flaunt your relationship in front of mom and know that it will break her heart?"

"Like you haven't already done that! You walked away from God!"

"At least I said it, but you're trying to live a double life! God on one hand and sleeping with the enemy on the other! At least I'm not a hypocrite!"

"Enough!" Frank's hands came down hard on the table. "See what I mean! Your mother wants her family back together. That's the greatest Christmas gift you could ever give her… whether you believe in Christmas or not." Frank looked at Peter. "Peace, love, and joy in our home. Can you forget about yourselves for one minute and think about your mother."

No one said anything.

"Father bless our home, bless our children, bless my marriage, bless our family and friends and bless Sherry. Go with us. Be with us. Never leave or forsake us. For we need You more than anything or anyone. In Jesus' name. Amen." Frank concluded, pushing his chair from the table, he swiftly embraced all of his sons, even unenthusiastic Peter and then he left the room. There was nothing else to be said or done. It was all in God's hands now.

# CHAPTER 15

# The whole truth and nothing but the truth!

While Frank had a family meeting with their sons, God was working a miracle in the county hospital. Sherry was beginning to shows sign of life. Subtle movements in her fingers and toes. Fighting her way back, her body was responding.

Her eyes fluttered several times. Finally, ever so slowly, her eyelids opened. Sherry's breath caught, nearly traumatized by what she saw. Sherry beheld the woman who broke her heart. The woman whom she trusted, who ate of her bread, sat at her table, and then turned around and slept with her husband. *How dare she stand over me! How dare she come near me! How dare…*

Shaking her head, as if to shake her from her dreams, Sherry was confused. Though her right side moved slowly, it was evident she was no longer experiencing paralysis. However, she was too weak to sit up. To weak to lift her hand to strike the one who betrayed her. *Forgive me, Lord.*

"What are you doing here?" Sherry spoke quietly, although she was yelling on the inside. "Where is Frank…my sons?'

"I don't know," Monique answered. "I'm so glad you're

alive."

"Are you really?" Sherry didn't believe her. "Surely you want me dead, so you can have my Frank! My entire family!" Sherry' strength was leaving her, as she almost went into a panic attack.

"Please don't say anything. Let me get the nurse." Monique was about to leave.

"No!" she mustered up all of her strength to speak. "Give me a minute." Sherry took in several deep breaths, before continuing. "Why are you here? How do you even have the nerve to show your face after sneaking around with my Frank, again?"

"It's not like that, Sherry," Monique felt bad. After all, she deliberately put her hand over Frank's hand when she saw Sherry enter the restaurant. "Frank loves you. Always have and always will."

"Apparently, not enough because he cheated with you and is still cheating."

"I didn't come here to upset you, Sherry."

"Then why did you come?" Sherry rebuffed. "I awaken and I see you. How would that not upset me? Where is my family? They should have been here."

"Do you want me to call them?"

"No, I want you to tell me why you are here and then leave!"

"Okay," Monique contemplated on how to begin. "I felt guilty that you had a heart attack. I felt guilty for what I did to you years ago. You didn't deserve it and well, believe it or not, I still love you."

"I don't believe you ever loved me," Sherry uttered. "Because if you did you never would have betrayed me. Love would have kept you from sleeping with my husband."

"I loved you and I envied you," Monique confessed. "You had what I wanted."

"Frank?" Sherry frowned.

Monique nodded. "I was in love with Frank before you two started dating. We actually went out a few times, but Frank only saw me as a friend. When he met you, I was history."

"I didn't know that," Sherry replied. "Frank didn't tell me."

"He didn't know how I felt back then."

"But you were married to Andrew and he loved you so much. You broke his heart."

"I did," Sherry nodded. "And I'm sorry that I did that to him…to you. Truthfully, I never really loved Andrew. He gave me a home and security. In time I grew to care for him."

"It doesn't matter. What you did was wrong," she paused. "I cannot blame you, alone. It takes two to tango. Frank was equally wrong."

"Not really." Monique looked away, gathering the courage to tell the whole truth and nothing but the truth. "I invited Frank over to talk about Andrew and our problems. You know Frank loved Andrew and was willing to do anything to help us. It was a farce though. I had immoral intentions. Anyhow, Frank came. We talked. Then I…uh…I purposely got Frank drunk."

"Frank doesn't drink." Sherry frowned.

"You and he had such a terrible spat. You had been rejecting him and well, we talked and I offered wine to him. He refused at first, but you know me, I'm persistent, I get what I want," she faked a laugh. "I gave him wine, and then added vodka and the next thing you know, Frank was intoxicated. I seduced him…and well, you know what happened."

Sherry was sickened. How could Monique, a professed

Christian behave so wickedly? She thought she knew Monique, but obviously, she didn't know her at all. "Frank said it happened two times."

Monique nodded. "I threatened him. I told him that I would tell you if he didn't come see me. Well, Frank was so drunk he really didn't know what happened, so I fabricated everything. Anyhow, I manipulated him to have sex with me one last time and promised I would never tell you. He didn't want to...but Frank was so intoxicated...let's say...I took advantage of him. I thought if I could...well...it didn't work. Frank loved you, not me."

Suddenly, Sherry felt sorry for the woman, who appeared to have it all. Beauty, great career, huge home, wealth, and good health. She looked good on the outside, but an empty shell on the inside. Frank didn't stand a chance with her. Monique was the predator. Frank was her prey.

"Then why were you meeting for lunch?"

"I don't think it's my place to tell you," Monique answered. "Just know that it wasn't Frank's idea. He wanted nothing to do with me."

"I want you to tell me," Sherry insisted. "I think you owe it to me."

Thinking it over, Monique didn't know what to do. She knew the news would hurt Sherry even more and she didn't want to cause her to have another heart attack.

"I deserve to hear the truth from you."

"I have a daughter," Monique stated.

"What! A daughter! I thought you couldn't have children."

"No, I said I didn't want children."

"Okay. What does this have to do with you meeting Frank?" Sherry couldn't put two and two together.

"My daughter is also Frank's daughter."

Sherry panted for air.

"See, I knew I shouldn't have said anything!" Monique watched Sherry's face pale as her breathing became abnormal. "I'm getting the nurse!" she ran to the door.

"No!"

"You're crazy! I'm not going to be the cause of you dying!"

"No!"

Uncertain, legs trembling, Monique turned around and faced one determined woman.

From somewhere, Sherry had found the strength to sit straight up. "Where is she?"

Unhurriedly, coming to Sherry's side, feeling lower than ever, Monique answered. "My daughter, Farah is here in town, being raised by my mother or at least she is for now."

"What do you mean?"

"My mother is too ill to continue caring for her and so is my father. That's why I reached out to Frank. I wanted him to know about her and at least give him the chance…"

"Chance to what?"

"I don't want to raise Farah. *Me* and children don't mix." Monique made her feeling known again. "So, I thought that perhaps Frank wanted her and if not, I am putting her in a children's home to be placed for adoption."

"Frank has a daughter." Sherry leaned back, closing her eyes for a minute as tears collided down her cheeks. "We always wanted a little girl."

"I'm sorry," Monique meant it. "Don't worry, Frank doesn't want her either. He doesn't want anything to come between you and him. So, you won't have to worry about Farah. The children's home believes that they have found a good family to take her."

"Frank told you he didn't want her," Sherry's eyes opened.

She nodded, pulling out her phone and then showed Sherry the text message.

We created an innocent child in sin. Consequently, we reap what we sow. Although I desire to take this little precious child into my life, I will not hurt my wife or my family any further. My heart is permanently tormented because I cannot raise Farah, see her grow up, watch her graduate or get married. That's my punishment. My prayer is for her to be happy, blessed, and joyful and to know Jesus Christ. I relinquish all rights to her for my family's sake and hoping my wife will forgive me and have me from this day forward. Please do not contact me ever again. Frank.

Sherry's heart went out to her husband. She knew this was extremely hard for him. Frank was an upright man, who loved family. He couldn't easily walk away from a child that was his. *This has to be killing him inside.*

"Thank you for showing me that," Sherry said through her tears. "But Frank will not relinquish his rights. I won't let him."

"No disrespect, but it's not up to you," Monique said cautiously. "Frank doesn't want her."

"Frank doesn't want to hurt me," Sherry amended, "but Frank wants…Farah and if I have anything to do with it, he'll get her."

"Are you sure about this?"

"Very sure," Sherry wiped her eyes. "When can he get her?"

"Any time before the New Year. I'm leaving to go to Germany to be a reporter for the US."

"Your dream job," Sherry remembered. "I'm happy for you."

"Really?"

Sherry nodded, praying for inner strength to do what she needed to do for some time now. "And I forgive you." Saying the words was easier than Sherry thought. Even more surprising, she meant them. Being near death had a way of making one see clearly —Life is just too short.

"Oh, thank you, Sherry. I truly regret hurting you and losing our friendship."

"I forgive you, Monique, but right now...I still don't like you." Sherry said honestly. "For Farah's sake, I can at least be cordial to you."

"Farah doesn't know that I'm her mother and I want to keep it that way. My mother adopted her, so she can always know that she is adopted, but I don't want her to ever know about me. Ever!"

"Your choice."

"Thank you."

"Well, I plan on being out of here by Christmas. I think Farah would be a great Christmas present for Frank, don't you?"

"I'm not sure what I think," Monique was skeptical. "How are you going to feel raising another woman's child? My child?"

"I honestly, don't know, but I will at least try."

"You're a better woman than me," Monique chuckled. "But we already know that."

"Just wait for Frank's text. I'll talk to him and then plans can be made for Farah to live with Frank."

Monique noticed that she said Frank and not "us" but she said nothing.

After receiving a call from the hospital that his wife had awakened, Frank rushed to the hospital. He didn't call the boys yet, figuring he would find out her health status before saying anything to them. As Frank entered the hospital room, Sherry noticed that he looked tired, as if he hadn't slept in days, which he hadn't, save a few catnaps here and there. His shoulders slightly slumped, he footsteps measured, Sherry knew Frank was guarded. Once, standing near his wife, Frank was inundated with an array of emotions. His eyes watered. Cautiously, he took her hand. To his delight, Sherry didn't let go. Instead, she squeezed it lightly.

He touched her soft, thin cheek with the other hand and said, "Honey, I'm so glad you came back to me...to us," he bent over and kissed her forehead. Thankfully, the right side of Sherry's face was normal and there was no paralysis. "Our boys need there momma. I don't care how old they are, they need you. You have a way of keeping us all together. I know I have hurt you, again, but I promise it's not what you think. Although, I feel like right now things are going to change again for us." Frank thought of his daughter, the child he was willing to give up for the sake of his family. *Lord, how will Sherry forgive me for this when she couldn't forgive me for the affair?*

**Cast it all on Me. I care about you. I care about Sherry.**

Frank laid his head on her bosom and wept, fearing he was about to lose it all after coming clean to his wife. "I'm so sorry, Sherry. I need you. I don't want to lose you. I love you, so much. You are my everything. Please don't leave me! Please!" he came totally unglued.

Sherry had never witnessed such heartbreak in her husband. His pain was now hers. She needed to release Frank from the guilt she wanted him to feel. She needed to let go of all the bitterness and anger she had been holding inside. Once again, she prayed for inner strength to do the right thing.

"I forgive you, Frank," she whispered, gently running her fingers through his thick hair, which needed trimming.

"Huh?" Frank pulled himself up, wiping his eyes in total shock.

"I forgive you," she forced a smile. "I know why you met up with Monique."

His heart dropped to his toes. He could hardly breathe as he stared in disbelief at his wife, unable to speak. Unable to move.

"Monique visited me earlier."

"Oh my word!" he shrieked. "I'm so sorry. I don't..."

"Shhh," she stopped him. "I'm glad she did. Now I know the whole truth."

"What did she tell you, Sherry?"

"She told me how she pursued you, using my illness as a weapon. How she seduced you, for all practical purposes, when you were at your lowest. We were struggling. I rejected you in the bedroom for months," Sherry admitted.

"But that's not your fault," he was quick to stop her for blaming herself for his wrongdoings. "You're not to blame for any of this."

"Yes, Frank, I played a role in it," she nodded. "I shut you out of my life. I was mean to you and nagged you. Though I am not condoning what you did because you hurt me dearly. I realize that Monique would have never been able to seduce you if I had been doing my part to keep our marriage happy and healthy," she paused. "She told me you slept with her twice..."

"Two times too many," Frank took a deep breath. "I was so wrong."

"Yes, you were and so was she. She admitted the first time,

she purposely got you highly intoxicated, and she was sure you didn't know what was going on. So she used that incident, holding it over your head, making you feel guilty and lured you once again."

"I'm a grown man, Sherry. Even though I hate to admit it, I knew what I was doing. I knew it was wrong. I was just caught up in the moment…just stupid."

"Thanks for admitting that Frank."

There were a few moments of silence before Frank spoke. "Did she say anything else?"

"Yes, she told me that you have a daughter named, Farah, who is eighteen months old."

Fresh tears spilled over. Burdens weighted on him like a ton of bricks. "I'm sorry, Sherry. I didn't know. I promise you, that I didn't know."

"I believe you. She said as much."

"And I promise you that I will not bring my indiscretions into our home. I've already told Monique that she can sign the papers for Farah to be adopted."

Sherry witnessed both, sincerity and pain in her husband's eyes. She knew this was the most difficult thing he had ever had to do. For they both had wanted a daughter so badly but were grateful for the three sons God had given them.

"I wouldn't ask you to do that, Frank."

"You're not asking," he leaned over. "I want to save our marriage, Sherry. I'll do anything to do that. I'll do anything to win you back."

"I would never forgive myself if I allowed someone else to take your daughter away from you," she swallowed. "Call Monique and tell her that you want to raise her."

Confusion filled him. "I will not raise her without you,

Sherry. I will not!"

"Frank, I'm not sure what is going to happen to us," she began, "but I know you have a responsibility to Farah, just as you have a responsibility to our sons. She's your blood. You must raise her."

"What about us?" his lips quivered.

"I don't know Frank. I need to time to sort this out."

"I understand."

"For now, I think it is best that you move in with your mother…with Farah and we'll see what happens next."

"Please don't put me out," he begged. 'I'll stay in the guestroom…with Farrah. I won't ask you to do anything for her. I'll take her to daycare and tend to her needs. You won't have to lift a finger to do anything for her."

"I don't think that's a good idea. What about Daniel?"

"I've spoken with the children and told them I was going to allow her to be adopted. Daniel wasn't too happy about it. He wanted me to bring her home."

"Sounds like Daniel," Sherry smiled. "What about Peter and Timothy?'

"Timothy wanted to meet her, but, I'm not sure about how he feels about her living in our home. Well, Peter wants nothing to do with her."

"Sounds like Timothy and Peter. I'll think about it. Dr. Hills says I can go home Tuesday. He believes that my recovery is nothing short of a miracle."

"For sure. Did he tell you that you were experiencing paralysis on your right side?"

"Yes, he did. God is a healer. I give Him all the glory and honor for doing what no other doctor could do…make me whole."

"Amen." Frank wanted nothing more than to just lean over and smack his wife right on this lips with a tender kiss. Oh, how joyful he felt that she was alive.

"Let me sleep on this, Frank and I'll give you an answer tomorrow or at least by Tuesday." She closed her eyes, feeling weary.

"Sherry," he called her name sweetly.

"Yes," her eyes opened again.

"Will you pray about it?"

She nodded, tears spilling over.

"I love you with all my heart."

She closed her eyes.

# CHAPTER 16

## God's Plan

Daniel sat at his desk in his room and read the letter from his father.

Daniel,

I first want to apologize again for the pain I have caused you and our family. You have always said I was your hero. Sadly, I have not lived up to that eminence. Disappointing you has been one of my greatest regrets. I endeavor to prove myself as a loyal father and faithful husband again, for our entire family. Yet, don't put me on a pedestal. Humanly, I cannot live up to it. In this flesh dwells no good thing. Save that position for Christ Jesus, only.

I want you to consider my words, pray about them and mediate on them. Receive them in the love that they were written. I know that you love Molly. We all do. She is beautiful inside and out. However, are you joining the army and marrying Molly so quickly, so you can provide for her, give Molly better medical help and possible the surgery that she needs? All your life you have been a caretaker, taking care of your mother, while I was working countless hours. Peter was always doing something with sports and Timothy was either studying or hanging out with friends. You stayed home as much as possible, making sure your mother's needs were met. I apologize, son, for putting so much of your mother's healthcare on you. You have now made it your priority to take care of Molly. You are so devoted to her, which is admirable and I know you truly love her. However, you have always desired to be a band teacher. You woke up singing as a baby. As a toddler, you enjoyed all instruments and still do. Your passion is music. Don't sign up for the military just so you can take care of others. Sign up for it because you believe God wants you to. Several colleges have offered you full scholarships. You can still marry Molly, but later, when you have pursued your dreams of going to college and majoring in band. Live life and enjoy it. Escape all the responsibilities for a moment and take care of you. Like your mother, you take care of everyone else. It is time that you take care of you. Do what your heart is telling you. I am proud of you, Daniel. I am taking over the role of taking care of your mother and this family. Let Molly parents continue to help her. Molly loves you. She'll wait for you. You have been captive in your heart, not free to do what you desire to do. Be free son! You're like a bird in a cage, having the ability to fly into the unknown, but can only go as far as the cage will allow. Son, the door of opportunity is open...fly son...fly as high as you can fly. Then when you're finished, come back to us...come back to Molly. It's your time to soar on the wings of purpose and freedom.

"Man makes plans, but God orders his steps." Proverbs 16:9. Son, let God order your steps and not you step out of His order." Love Dad

Daniel rested his elbows on his desk, lowering his head

into his hands. His father's words struck a deep cord within. For if he were honest with himself, Daniel wanted nothing to do with military life. He only wanted Molly to receive the best healthcare possible and now it just wasn't affordable. He loved her that much to sacrifice his hopes and dreams. Molly deserved his best and the best appeared to be the military. Or was it?

Daniel had been wrestling in his spirit since he decided to join the army. He never had peace, just relentless turmoil. Daniel just wanted the people he cared about to be happy. So even if he wasn't feeling it, he'd put on a happy face. Do whatever necessary for his loved ones to experience goodness. He'd take one for the team—even if that meant joining the army.

*What am I to do Lord?*

**Follow Me. I have plans to prosper you and not to harm you.**

*Molly needs better healthcare and surgery.*

**Trust Me.**

*She'll be so hurt if I go to college now. We have made plans already.*

**My plans will be established.**

Daniel knew what he had to do. *Lord, give me the strength to do it.*

Timothy was in a *funk*. Ever since his meeting with his dad, Timothy felt empty, void of life or enthusiasm. He used to laugh more and make people laugh. His life had changed. Was it really for the better? Why wasn't he happy?

He had forgiven his dad, but everything just seemed off kilter. Things had changed so drastically in his life, Timothy felt unprepared for any more changes. Plus, his mother. Although she was out of a coma, he felt like he had hurt her so much by choosing his lifestyle over his upbringing. He didn't know what was right anymore. He was so confused.

Oppression covered him. He couldn't escape its wrath. He was endowed from head to toe with its effects. Feelings doomed, Timothy opened his father's letter.

Timothy,

First, I want you to know that I love you, unconditionally. Your mother and I love you beyond words. We have always been so proud of you. Please receive my words, written in love and not judgment. You are special to God. Special people must go through special experiences. When you study the book of Job, you realize that Job wasn't perfect. He wasn't a perfect father nor a perfect husband. He had flaws. Yet despite the flaws, God bragged about Job. He saw underneath the surface of a man who was loyal, faithful, devoted and sold-out to Him. Timothy, God sees the same in you. He sees what others cannot see. He sees beneath the surface. You say a Leopard cannot change its spots. I agree. You were not created to be a Leopard because your heritage is of the Lion of Judah! Jeremiah 13:23 reads: "Can the Ethiopian change his skin or the leopard its spots? Then may you also do good who are accustomed to doing evil." You must choose to do good and not evil. The Israelites had become so accustomed to doing evil that they had lost their ability to change. God never ever rejects His people, those who return to Him. When you know to do right and do wrong, it is a sin. Timothy, deep down you know what is right. You weren't born this way. Just as an alcoholic wasn't born a drunk, even if he'd seen it all his life. Regardless, if his mother or father were drunks. It's always a choice. You say it is more than that. It is what you feel. You know son, Eve could have walked away from that apple. She didn't have to have it. There were other fruits. There were other things to enjoy. She had everything... but not that one thing. She had a strong desire...a strong feeling... a strong yearning for it. The devil tempted her... with his words. Don't let anyone's words tempt you away from the Truth.

You are not happy Timothy. I see it in your face, in the way you walk, in the way you talk. You can pretend everything is good, but I know all is not well. I'm not going to quote Scriptures because you know them (Leviticus 18:22, Romans 1:26-27, Mark 10:6-9, Jude 1:7, Ezekiel 16:49-50).

When a father sees his son, headed in the direction of a forest fire, he does everything in his power to stop him. That's what I am doing Timothy. I love you and I do not want to see you get hurt. God loves you. That will never change. However, He will not turn a blind eye to sin. You can overcome this, just as I can overcome infidelity. None of us are perfect. We all have sinned and fallen short. There is no little or big sin. Sin is sin. Just as I have returned and submitted to God, and resisted the devil, I pray for you to do the same. Timothy, submit it all to God, resist the enemy, and he will flee. We are fervently praying for you and believe it or not, we are praying for Larry. He, too, needs Jesus in all His fullness. Timothy, look to Him, the Author and Finisher of your faith. Remember, God is not the author of confusion, but of peace. The devil brings confusion. He complicates things and makes you question what you know to be the truth because He desires to divide and conquer. He sees you as a quest to win. Don't let him!

When God created you, He fearfully and wonderfully made you. You are His masterpiece. However, the evil one desires for us to get off course, by giving into feelings and unnatural things. We all have issues, son. We all have things we must face. We all have to resist things. None of us are excluded from temptation. Jesus was tempted by the devil and yet, he resisted. In this flesh dwells no good thing, but we must consciously choose to do what pleases the Father, even to our own hurt.

We're all here for you, Timothy. I love you! Dad

Every word spoken pricked the core of his soul. It wasn't anything new, but the timing was perfect. Timothy wanted out of the misery of his heart. Of the constant warfare, between his spirit, soul, and mind. The ongoing turmoil. Quickly, he searched out the scriptures his dad had mentioned —even though he had read them numerous times.

Not only did God say it was an abomination in the Old Testament, but homosexual was wrong in the New Testament, leading people down the path of eternal destruction. Many times, he had read these Scriptures. Still, the fleshly urges, the desires to be with someone of the same sex, called his name, like crack calling a drug addict. This was his weakness —his thorn. Why couldn't God remove this from him? Oh, how Timothy prayed that God would take it away. The desires. The pulling of his heartstrings toward a man? This wasn't the life he wanted. To possibly be separated from God, as he was separated from his family. How would he ever make things right again? To choose his family over Larry? To choose God…over his own will, which seemingly he couldn't control anymore.

*Lord, I am confused. I don't know what to do?*

"Hey, what you're doing?" Timely, Larry walked in.

"Studying the Word of God.

"What are you studying?

"Studying how homosexuality is an abomination to God and…"

"Not again!" Timothy shouted. "How many times am I going to tell you, God loves us all and He knows we are but dust? He knows that we are this way and still loves us."

"God wiped out Sodom and Gomorrah for such sinfulness. You cannot deny it."

"That's Old Testament. It's all brainwash! Remember, what Pastor Dave said…Sodom was wiped out because of pride… and not taking care of the poor…stuff like that."

"Yes, but he left out the following verse, which said also because of the abomination they committed."

"We're not under the law, Timmy," Larry countered.

"It's not the law that separates us, Larry. It's sin."

"You're still being brainwashed!"

"The New Testament says the same thing," Timothy stated. "It's a sin. Just like adultery. Just like murder. Just like theft… Wrongdoers. These are the ones who will not enter into heaven. Larry, I don't want to die and go to hell."

"What about David and Jonathan. They loved each other, more than loving a woman."

"That's friendship, Larry. I felt the same way about you,

and somehow we perverted this friendship. I just don't know anymore."

"Perverted it!" Larry dropped to his knees. "I love you, Timmy. You mean the world to me and there is nothing perverted about what I feel for you. You're my heart. God brought us together. Please stop trying to find a reason why this is too good to be true."

"It is, Larry." Timothy stood up. "It is too good to be true."

"Timmy, we are good people."

"Yes, but good people die and go to hell. It's not good works, it's God's grace that saves us." Timothy walked away.

"Timmy, please don't leave. You cannot leave me! I love you!"

Turning to him, with tears cascading down the sides of his face, Timothy spoke raspingly. "I will always care about you, Larry, but I need time to think...alone. I need to seek God for myself. I don't need to hear what Pastor Dave has to say, or what you have to say...because it's contrary to what the Bible says. I just need space. I am going to check into a hotel for a few days. Please don't call me. I will call you when I'm ready to talk."

"But Timmy!" Larry rushed to him, trying to embrace him.

"Don't!" he held up his hand. "Give me space. That's all I ask."

Larry watched in horror as Timmy walked out of the room, and possibly out of his life. Larry feared he would never see Timmy again. His heart was shattered into many pieces, like broken glass.

Peter tossed his letter in the trashcan in his bedroom, refusing to read anything from his father. Peter was grumpy, angry and bitter. Mad at both his Heavenly and earthly father. Mad at Imani. Mad at Elaine. Mad at Timothy. Even mad at his mother for getting sick again, for having a heart attack. The only person he wasn't mad at was Daniel. Perfect Daniel…did nothing wrong. Daniel went out of his way making everybody happy, even if it caused him unhappiness.

Peter wished he were home alone. He didn't want to deal with Imani. She irked him. The fact that she was pregnant didn't help matters because he knew deep down that Imani had purposely trapped him into this situation.

"Hi Babe," she greeted him. "How was your day at work?"

"Like always. Busy." Peter turned his face away when she tried to kiss him on the lips.

Feeling hurt, Imani replied, "I'm tired of you punishing me."

"I'm not punishing you."

"Yes, you are. I get it you don't want this baby. Fine. I'll take care of it. I'll have an abortion. Anything to get you back."

He stilled. Peter felt as if she had just slapped him hard in the face. He was so angry that he swore. Something he hadn't done since high school. "Don't you ever say anything like that!" He jumped up like an angry bear. "If you even think of killing my…"

"Hold up!" Imani interrupted, literally trembling in her boots by his brusque demeanor. "I wouldn't do it if you are against it."

"You better not!" he threatened.

"I thought you didn't want the baby."

"I don't, but I would never kill an innocent baby!"

"Peter, what is it? What can I do to make you happy again? I just want you back, Peter. I love you so much, and I'll do anything for you."

"We'll talk about this later," he stormed away.

"Peter! Please don't walk away. I need you."

He stopped. He wanted to be free of Imani! Truthfully, he didn't feel strongly for her anymore. In all honestly, Peter never felt what she felt for him. Initially, Imani was intriguing. She doted on him. She gave him what he needed at the time— physical attention. Imani was attentive to his every need. She helped take his mind off all the bad stuff, including his breakup with Elaine. She was the distraction he needed at the time.

Peter had only loved one woman—Elaine. Imani was a rebound, a way for him to escape his pain, temporarily. Now, the pain was more prominent and Imani could no longer fill or cover the hole in his heart.

"Imani, my focus is on my mother. I cannot handle anything else right now."

"I'm sorry about your mother, Peter, I am." Imani went to him. "But I'm fighting for us."

Once again, his head was throbbing. His blood pressure had been off the charts lately. He just wanted to just blink his eyes and witness everything disappear, including Imani.

There was a time when he couldn't wait to see her. It was all fun, exciting, and sort of rebellious, at first. He knew his mother and father didn't approve of Imani because of her warped beliefs, which made her all the more appealing. Now, knowing his mother spent many days and nights praying for him, fearing the worst because of his relationship with Imani,

Peter felt deep regret. Especially, since she was right—it was lust and not love.

"We'll talk later."

"Are you coming back?" she feared.

"I don't know."

# CHAPTER 17

## Where do we go from here?

Returning home from the hospital, Sherry decided that Frank could remain home. Facing death, she realized that life was too short to continue going around the same mountain of mistrust and un-forgiveness another day. The fact that she loved Frank, despite his shortcomings, overrode her desire to be independent. All too soon, Daniel would leave for basic training. The thought terrified her. She didn't want to be alone.

Sherry was glad to be out of the hospital. Thankful that God had spared her life. Grateful to have the support of her family, including Frank. Still, at times, Sherry felt as if she had fallen in a long, narrow dark hole, with no way of escape. She experienced moods of oppression and felt like she was a wounded prey cornered and trapped by some unseen force. Was there some oppressive cloud hovering over her family? Everyone was a mess, including herself. Things had to change.

"Good morning," Frank entered the room. "How are you feeling?"

"My legs hurt just a little, but I'm fine, Frank."

"Did you sleep well?" he sat on the bed.

She nodded. "What about you?"

"I miss sleeping with you," Frank boldly stated, his eyes

fixed on hers.

"Frank…"

"Shhh," he put his finger to her lips. "I'm not pushing anything, my Love. I am just glad to be home. For wherever you are is where I want to be." Frank massaged her legs. His eyes didn't leave her face. Though Sherry had just awakened and her hair was disheveled, all over the place, not in her typical neat braid, she still made his heart accelerate.

Frank's simple touch sent a surge of fire not just in her leg, but also, all over her body, making her feel sensitive. Sherry gazed at her husband. He sure was handsome with his salt and pepper hair. His face showed some signs of aging, but Frank appeared at least fifteen years younger than his age. He had the smoothest chocolate skin, with not a spot or blemish visible and hardly any noticeable wrinkles. Undeniably, Sherry was still smitten by Frank. He still made her heart leap and her body respond to his presence.

"Have you heard from Peter or Timothy about Christmas?"

"Timothy is going to try to come."

"He's not bringing Larry is he?"

"I asked him not to."

"And Peter?"

"Peter doesn't celebrate Christmas, so he doesn't want to be hypocritical," Frank sighed. After numerous tries of just asking him to come for his mother's sake, Frank conceded to his son's wishes. However, he kept the matter in prayer.

"It's that Imani! She has our son all confused. If only he would have stayed with sweet Elaine. She was good for Peter. They seemed so happy."

"Whatever happened between them sure shocked everybody. Pastor Law asked me recently did I ever find out what happened to them. I don't think he likes the guy his daughter is dating now."

"Me either," Sherry frowned. "He's the bad-boy type if you ask me."

Frank chuckled.

"Why are you laughing?"

"That's what they said about Peter."

She chuckled. "I guess you're right there."

He smiled, though a wistful look was in his eyes. "Where do we go from here, Sherry? The day after Christmas, two days away...Farah is coming to live with me...us."

She took a long, deep breath before responding. "As I told you at the hospital, I've decided to work on our marriage. I have forgiven you for the past. Although a child was conceived through sin, she is not to blame. Children are a blessing. Yes, it hurts, but I choose to move on from it."

He didn't think it possible, but he loved her even more.

"But, I'll need some time, Frank. I can't just jump back into our marriage...this child...baby steps."

"For sure," he squeezed her hand. Magnetically, he was attracted to his wife. She was drawing him, without even trying. Love for this woman permeated ever cell in his body. How could he ever make her feel the same way about him again?

"So, what's the final plans for Christmas dinner," Sherry swiftly changed the subject.

"Mom wants to do all the cooking, even though I insisted that I had a caterer already lined up."

"Your mother loves cooking. Let her do it."

Frank was once again taken back. There was definitely no love-lost between Sherry and his mother, especially since his mother took every opportunity to put Sherry down. "This is a shocker. I figured you didn't want my mother anywhere near your kitchen…especially after Thanksgiving dinner."

"Martha is lonely, Frank and I think I finally get it. She's been lashing out at me because she misses your father and you. She blames me because she thinks I keep you from her when it's just the opposite. You're so busy and tired that even when I insist you go, you think calling her is enough. But it's not Frank. I miss my boys," she became teary-eyed, "especially now with our family in such disarray. I want them to always feel welcome…including their perspective wives."

"Does that include Imani?" Frank eyes stretched.

"Well, if Peter loves her, then I guess we will have to find a way to love her as well…Love her to Christ Jesus."

"Amen," he grasped her hand. Sherry tried to slip her hand out of his, but he clutched it tighter. "Just like our boys. We've already loved them to Christ, loved them while they were in Christ and now we have to love them back to Christ."

"I remember that sermon from Pastor Law."

"Love covers a multitude of sin," Frank quoted. "My prayer is that your love for God and your love for me will in time cover my wrongs so that we can be happy again."

Tears once again pooled her eyes, and tenderly she reached up and placed the palm of her hand on his cheek. "I desire to be happy again."

"I want to be the one who makes you happy."

"I have to find it here first," Sherry pointed to her heart. "I have work to do in me, Frank."

"What can I do, Sherry, to make it easier for you…better for you? Anything, Sherry and I will do it." Frank was desperate to please her.

"You're doing it now, Frank. Just being here and being patient."

"I am deeply in love with you, Sherry. More now than ever."

"Can you please run my bathwater," Sherry broke eye contact, abruptly changing the subject. "I want to at least sit in the den and look at the Christmas tree. You mentioned that you and Daniel decorated it."

"Yes," he chuckled. "We sure had a time. We needed your expertise. Putting decorations on a tree looks easier than it really is. You make it look so easy and so beautiful. I'm afraid you're going to be disappointed."

"The fact that you both put the tree up and decorated it, is all that matters to me."

Frank leaned over and placed a light kiss on her lips. "I'll go run your water."

Watching him leave, Sherry released a pint up sigh. She wanted her marriage to work, she really did. How was she going to give her heart freely to the man who stomped all over it before? How was she going to raise the child of Frank's mistress, her ex-friend, Monique? How was she going to move forward when reminders of the past would always be there to haunt her?

While Frank had gone to work a few hours, Sherry was in the den, stretched out on the recliner, enjoying the Christmas decorations and soft Christmas music playing. She had read her daily Bible devotions and was now reading an inspirational novel.

"Hey mom," Daniel kissed his mother's forehead. "You look refreshed and cozy."

"I'm feeling better," she smiled. "Thanks for helping your dad with the tree."

"I think we did a good job!" Daniel looked at the tree with admiration. "Sure can't compare to yours, but it was done in love. We had fun."

"That's good to hear."

"I was just talking with Timothy and he says he is coming for Christmas and he's coming alone."

"Wonderful!" she clasped her hands. "I just want my family together for Christmas. Did he sound alright?"

"He seemed like something was troubling him. I didn't want to push him. I just let him know that I am praying for him."

"That's good. I'll pray for him…and Larry."

"Yes, Larry needs our prayers. Peter still won't answer my calls. He's so pigheaded. He knows you're home, you would think he would at least call and check up on you."

"I know Peter is worried about me," Sherry began. "He doesn't handle crisis well."

"He doesn't handle anything well if you ask me."

"Oh, Peter has a big heart and he loves us all. It's just that he has a hard time showing it. But at the end of the day, he'll lay his life on the line for his family. He'll come around."

"I hope so. We used to be close. I miss my big brother."

"We just *gotta* keep praying for him."

"So, Mom, I want to talk to you about Molly," Daniel sat.

"Sure." Sherry's heartbeat was pumping fast with every second that past as she waited for her son to communicate. She feared more bad news.

"I love Molly," he began.

"Of course you do. Anyone can see that."

"But…"

Sherry waited impatiently.

Clearing his throat several times, Daniel released the secrets of his heart. Several times, he had to pause, his emotions surfacing. "I want to take care of her. I want her to have the best medical care and the military is the only solution I can come up with." Another long pause. "But, I don't want to go into the military," he finally owned up to it.

"Really?" Sherry was shocked. "I thought you wanted to follow in your father's footsteps."

He shook his head.

"Does Frank know?"

"Yes. He wrote me a letter…"

"A letter," Sherry didn't know what to make of all of this.

"Yes, before you became conscious again, dad called a meeting and told us about his past wrongs and about Farah. He gave us all a handwritten letter. Anyhow, in my letter dad wrote that he didn't want me to join the military for the wrong reasons and he knew I always wanted to go to college and major in Band/Music. And he's right."

"Frank wrote that."

He nodded. "And he also stated about me trying to take care of Molly and you and everybody, but that I needed to take care of me."

"Wise words," her eyes misted. "Frank is a very wise man."

"So, the thing is…I have been accepted into Newton University on a full scholarship."

"Oh, Daniel!" she exclaimed. "I'm so proud of you! Come

here and let me hug you!"

He obliged. Sherry smothered him with love, hugs and kisses.

"You have to follow your heart, Daniel," she released him. "Molly will understand and she'll wait on you."

"I don't want to lose her, Mom. I'll be gone for four years at least."

"You'll be home for holidays, breaks and some weekends. If you both love each other, then love will keep you together. As long as you communicate and still make each other a priority, your relationship will survive the separation." She spoke. "It may not be easy, but it will be worth it."

"What about her medical care? There is this surgery that can help her mobility and even possibly give her movement in her lower limbs."

"We'll just believe God for it. He's her Source, not you, Daniel. Molly has always been independent. She wouldn't want you to give up your dreams for her."

"Do you think she will be upset about us not marrying now?"

"She'll be hurt, but she'll get over it, in time. Daniel, you have to be honest with her…soon."

"I'm going to wait until after Christmas."

"That's a good idea."

"I just don't want to hurt her or lose her."

"You won't. Pray about this and ask God for the right words and the right time to do it."

"That's all I have been doing."

"Prayer works."

"I see it working with you and dad," he boldly said.

"Oh, do you?"

"Dad messed up, Mom, but he loves you deeply. When he thought you were going to die, he was so lost without you. He didn't leave your bedside, not one moment. He refused to and when he did it was for the family meeting…to make sure things would be in order whenever you awakened."

Hearing Frank's endearment stirred her within, arousing a longing that she couldn't ignore. "I married Frank till death do us part and I intend on keeping my commitment."

"It has to be more than a commitment, Mom. It has to be because you love him."

"You're a wise man, Daniel."

"Like dad."

"Like your, Dad," she smiled.

When Frank came home, Sherry was in the kitchen preparing a light dinner for the men of the house.

"Do I smell spaghetti?"

"You do." Sherry turned and faced Frank with spaghetti sauce on the side of her lip and cheek.

"You shouldn't be cooking." Frank openly admired his wife, meticulously scanning her from head to toe. Her hair wasn't in its customary braid, but hanging loosely. The burnt orange housedress was alluring, gracefully accenting her every curve. Their eyes locked from across the room.

Frank's approval caused her heart to visibly pound out of her chest, pounding like drums as he approached her. After all these years, he still had such an electrifying effect on her. He moved the core of her soul.

"I thought you were cooking it and not wearing it," a wide lopsided grin spread across his thin lips as he contemplated his next move. Now standing right in front of her, Frank gently wiped the side of her cheek. Helplessly, he didn't use his hands to wipe the sauce off the side of her lips. Instead, unable to contain his emotion his mouth lowered onto hers, "The sauce tastes good," he moaned.

Unbashful, Sherry wrapped her arms around his neck as the kiss deepened. In just a few seconds, the sky lit up like the fourth of July in her dull heart.

With his arms clipped around her waist, he held onto Sherry, even when her lips left his. Their eyes were fastened on the other. Their hearts chimed in harmony. She saw love in his eyes, while he felt it in his soul. There was an exhilarating connection.

"I better finish cooking," she stirred, attempting to get out of his embrace.

He still held onto her tightly, never wanting to let her go. "Let me finish. You go sit down and rest."

"I'm not an invalid, Frank," she felt uncomfortable and yet, comfortable at the same time.

"No, by no means are you an invalid," his eyes twinkled with mischief. "You haven't kissed me like that in forever. What a kiss!"

Her cheek inflamed. "Well, I can't remember you kissing me like that in a long time, either."

"I plan on making up for that," he leaned over.

"Stop Frank!" Sherry finally swiveled away from him and turned back to the stove. "Go change. Dinner will be ready in twenty minutes. Please tell Daniel."

"Sure thing!" Frank winked, walking away feeling lighter

than ever.

"Oh, and Frank," she called after him. "Thanks for the letter you wrote to Daniel. It helped him to make the right decision."

"Good! Let's pray it will do the same for our other two sons."

"You're a wise man, Frank. I have no doubt your words will help them to see the truth."

Her approval meant everything to him. "Thanks, Sherry."

"Go change!" she dismissed him with a smile.

# CHAPTER 18

## Christmas

Christmas morning Sherry awakened early to an empty bed, once again. She was lonely for her husband, yet, afraid to allow him not only into her bed again, but fully into her heart. Since being home, she enjoyed Frank's flirtations, but she knew he wanted so much more. He wanted an intimate relationship with her.

Sherry hadn't been intimate with her husband since the betrayal. Two years was a long time to be celibate, married and living under the same roof with the one who could erase all loneliness away. Sherry had denied her husband intimacy repeatedly, due to her illness or feeling menopausal, not wanting anything to do with sex. All excuses. Frank had needs and she didn't meet them—time and time again.

She practically drove Frank to Monique, handed him the keys and told him to come back when his needs were met. Just as she blamed Frank, she blamed herself.

What is the saying? What you did to get him, you must do to keep him. Well, she botched that up.

Closing her eyes, Sherry silently poured her heart out to God. *Lord, help me to move on. Help me to give all of myself to Frank, withholding nothing, even if it means being vulnerable to pain. I want my marriage to work. I miss what we used to have. I miss Frank and I miss waking up to him every morning.*

*I miss Frank holding me and kissing me before he leaves for work. I miss him calling in the day just to check on me or to just because he wanted to hear my voice. I miss him watching hallmark movies with me, even if he really thinks they are corny. I miss walking in the park and holding hands.*

*Lord, I want it all back! My marriage. My kids. My peace. My joy. My happiness. My spiritual closeness with You. I want it all back!* Sherry emptied her soul, fresh tears of peace trickling down her face.

"Merry Ch...." Frank entered. "What's wrong?"

"Nothing!" she covered her face.

"Oh, Baby, it's going to be all right. Are you in pain? Do I need to call Dr. Hills?"

"No," she dropped her hands and looked to Frank. "I want our old life back!" she sniffed.

"Oh, Sherry!" Frank embraced her. "That's all I want for Christmas." He pulled away, gently wiping her tears away. "But, I selfishly want it to be even better than before."

She nodded. "You can move back in the bedroom."

"Are you sure?"

"Very sure."

Frank gave into the impulse to taste his wife's lips on this glorious Christmas morn. His lips met hers in a tender caress, soft and light as a feather, making Sherry's toes curl under the cover.

Frank melted like butter in this sweet moment of passion. Christmas morn represented the Birth of Christ and now, the rebirth of his marriage. *Thank You, Jesus!*

Sherry felt mellow and peaceful, as she pulled away. "I

need to make Christmas breakfast."

"We decided to do something different." Frank pecked her nose.

"Different," she shook her head. "I think we should stick with tradition."

"Tradition is that you get up and *slave* over a hot stove to prepare a big breakfast, then turnaround and prepare a big meal for Christmas dinner," Frank stated. "We've appreciated you spoiling us, but now we're going to spoil you."

"But I'm not even cooking this year."

"Knowing you, you'll have your hand in something today," Frank smiled.

Right on time, Daniel entered the room carrying a breakfast tray with a small poinsettia on it. "Merry Christmas, Mom! We have prepared a delicious breakfast of cinnamon toast, turkey sausage, scrambled eggs and apple juice for you."

"Oh, how wonderful!" Sherry felt blessed, looking at the constant men in her life. Although their family hung by a thread, Frank and Daniel never wavered in taking care of her. Even when she didn't make it easy for either of them. "What about you, two?"

"We sort of ate while we were cooking," Frank chuckled.

"Yeah, Mom. It was hard to cook and not eat," Daniel echoed. "I don't know how you do it?"

"Practice. I'd be as big as a house if I ate while cooking. I've already gained a few pounds here and there."

"You're perfect," Frank winked. "I love you just the way you are," he inclined slightly to peck her lips.

"Ugh, you two forgot you have a kid in the room."

"So, now you're a kid," Frank jibed. "Make up your mind. Do you want to be a man or kid?"

"Both!"

"You'll always be my baby boy," Sherry held out her arms to him. Gladly, Daniel succumbed to her loving embrace. What a great Christmas morning miracle. To behold his parents being affectionate and loving towards each other.

*Thank You, God, for hearing and answering my prayer! Now bring my two brothers back into the family and loving each other.*

Traditionally the mistletoe hung over the doorpost between the kitchen and family room. Several times, Frank purposely caught Sherry under the mistletoe and brazenly kissed her, no matter who was around.

Martha scoffed a few times, unpleased at the open display of their renewed commitment. While Daniel and Molly, who arrived early to spend the day with his family, enjoyed seeing their love blossoming again.

Timothy came around noon and caught his parents kissing. "When did you two get back together?" he inquired, pleasantly shocked.

"Technically, we never really separated," Frank answered, while still snuggling close to his wife. Timothy almost laughed at his mother's beat red cheeks. She was glowing.

"It's so good to have you home." Immediately, Sherry hugged her middle child. "You've made my day!"

"I think I'm a little too late for that," Timothy grinned. "Seems like dad has already got that covered."

"Ah…" she kissed his cheek. "Daniel and Molly are in the

den. I'm going to go help Martha in the kitchen. Frank try to behave yourself."

"Do I have to?" he attempted to grab her.

"Go get a room!" Timothy teased.

"Sounds like a good idea," Frank drew closer.

"Stop Frank! I have things to do."

"How about we do them together."

"When did you become a big tease?" she laughed.

"Always have been. You just forgot." Frank winked, patted her on the butt before Sherry left the room.

"Well, I see you two have kissed a made up," Martha mumbled, as she stirred her homemade giblet gravy for the dressing.

Sherry stiffened, bracing herself for the hostilities of Frank's mother.

"How do you feel about him bringing an illegitimate child into your home?"

"I don't see...Farah as illegitimate. She is just a child who needs to be loved."

"Humph! So you think you *going to* just love her like that? Knowing full well her mother was your best friend, who slept..."

"Martha!" Sherry abruptly cut her off. "I know all the gory details and it still doesn't change the fact that I love your son, very much. I have always loved him. I just don't understand why you cannot accept that or me. Why are you always trying to hurt me?"

"I'm not hurting you." she scoffed.

"Yes, you are." Sherry stood her ground. "There is nothing I would ever do to come between you and Frank. He loves you. You're his mother," she paused. "And I love you, Martha."

Martha stopped stirring, her hands visibly shaking as she turned to Sherry, tears of old spilling down her worn face. "Frank has hurt you, but you still want to be with him."

She nodded, her eyes matching Martha's watery eyes.

"I hurt you, and you still love me."

She nodded, taking her mother-in-law's hands in hers. "Very much so."

"I don't want to hurt you anymore," Martha sobbed, falling into Sherry's arms. "I don't want to hurt anymore either."

"Oh, Mother Martha, only God can heal your hurt, like He is doing for me. You just got to move out of the way and let Him take over." She held her tightly. "I know how it feels to be lonely. I had Frank here and still rejected him. However, you didn't have anyone, including us, but I promise we're going to be closer. You're always welcome here…and we'll visit you more. I promise."

Martha stood tall, eye-to-eye, with the woman who had her son's heart. "I would like that very much."

"Good! That's our Christmas present to each other. We *be* a real family."

"Good! Now let's stop all this mushy stuff and finish cooking."

Unbeknown to his mother or wife, Frank stood at the doorway; his eyes were wet with tears. He had witnessed another one of God's miracles today. His mom and Sherry had buried the hatchet and were now embracing each other with love.

*A Christmas miracle!*

Martha, with the help of Sherry, had outdone herself in the kitchen. The buffet table was filled with many delicious foods. Roasted turkey, baked ham, lemon pepper tenderloin, dressing, collard greens, string beans, yellow seasoned rice, potato salad, macaroni and cheese, corn on the cob, broccoli casserole, sweet potato pies, coconut pies, red velvet cake and pecan pie. This was a feast to behold.

Sitting at the head of the table, Frank looked around, feeling overwhelming blessed to have his mother, still alive and feisty as ever, sitting beside him. Molly and Daniel sat next to her. To his right, Timothy sat, with two vacant chairs next to him. His beautiful wife sat at the other end of the table, smiling outwardly, but he knew she was heartbroken that Peter's chair was empty.

Just as Frank was about to pray, his wife's prayer was answered.

"Sorry, I'm late!" Peter entered. "Traffic is crazy!"

"Oh, Peter!" Sherry leaped up and greeted him with a mother's love. "You made my day!"

"I thought I already made your day!" Timothy jeered.

"Hush up!" she playfully squatted him. "You have all made my day!"

"Starting with dad," Daniel added his two-cent worth.

Again, her cheeks became rosy.

"Stop teasing your mother," Frank grinned. "Although I love seeing her flush. It only heightens her natural beauty."

"Frank…"

"What have I missed?" Peter looked to his parents, who were both glowing. "Are you two back together?"

"Technically…" Frank responded.

"Technically they were never separated," Timothy,

answered for him.

Peter rolled his eyes at Timothy. "What about the child?"

"None of that today." Sherry uttered. "We're only going to focus on having a joyous, happy, wonderful, loving, family Christmas!"

"I don't celebrate Christmas." Peter couldn't help himself.

"Always the negative one." Timothy rebuffed. "Can't you think of somebody other than yourself?"

"Shut up! I'm not even talking to you tinker bell!"

"You're a mean brute with a heart to match! Oh, I forgot you don't have a heart. You're like the tin man in the *Wizard of Oz*."

"You need to get your head out of the sand long enough to see that you're a disgrace to our family!"

"Well you…."

"Shush!" Mother Martha stood, looking to her son, who was also standing. "Please let me say something, Frank." He nodded and reluctantly sat down. "Today is the Lord's day!" she looked to Peter. "Rather you celebrate our Savior's birth today or not…it is still His day. We are family and family shouldn't treat each other so disrespectfully."

The boys looked at their grandmother as if she had gone bonkers. Wasn't that the pot calling the kettle black?

"I know I have treated your mother unkindly and been downright disrespectful to her, but I made my peace with her today and with God. So, you two," she pointed to Timothy and Peter, "need to make peace with each other. Life is too short to go around carrying all that poison in your hearts. It's going to kill you one way or the other. Now, I've said what I need to say." Martha sat down. "Go ahead and pray Frank, so we can eat."

"Yes mother," he smiled, looking at his wife, who seemed fragile as if she would break at any moment.

"Let's join hands," Frank requested, waiting before finally, Peter and Timothy joined hands, even if was by the fingertips.

"Father God we thank You so much for allowing us all to come together to recognize the birth of Jesus Christ, our Lord, and Savior…"

Purposely Peter cleared his throat a few times.

Frank ignored him and continued. "…Who came into this world, so that we could live forever with You, God. You unselfishly gave the greatest gift to humanity and that's Jesus Christ, because of Your love for us. Help us to show that same love to each other. Forgive us for our wrongs and help us to forgive those who have wronged us. Seal our love for one another by Your Holy Spirit, causing our family unit to be healthy, happy, strong, and revived. The enemy has oppressed us Lord, but Your Word says that Jesus went about doing good and healing all those who were oppressed of the devil. Heal us. Heal our hearts. Heal our family. Heal our hurts. Heal us and make us whole, individually and collectively. Now, Father please bless this food we are about to receive for nourishment and strength to our physical bodies. Bless the hands that prepared it and bless us to be a blessing to one another and to the world, in Jesus' name, amen."

"Amen," everyone replied except Peter.

Initially, there was still tension in the air as everyone ate. There definitely was a rift between Peter and Timothy. Peter refused to give an inch, angry with his brother for associating himself with the gay lifestyle. Timothy refused to be bullied by his brother, wanting Peter to accept him for who he was and love him regardless. Daniel shifted anxiously in his chair, as Molly talked on and on about the wedding plans. Slyly, he looked to his mother, wanting her to fix everything with a magic wand.

After dinner, Peter said he had to go be with Imani. Really, Peter didn't want to stay for opening presents. Before nightfall, Timothy left taking his grandmother home and Daniel went to spend time with Molly and her family, which left Frank and Sherry alone.

While Frank turned on the Christmas lights and picked up the wrapping papers in the den, Sherry cleaned up the kitchen. Thankfully, Martha had done most of it. Although Sherry wanted today to be perfect, the obvious rift between Timothy and Peter put a slight damper on things. Yet, Sherry purposed to focus on the silver lining in the clouds and not the clouds. *Thank You, God, for bringing us all together again!*

As Sherry worked tirelessly, Frank watched her from the doorway. Sherry's long hair was hanging down her back. She had flat ironed it earlier, solely to please Frank. Seeing his wife, looking so delicious in her red fitted dress, Frank wanted nothing more than to swoop his arms around her and carry her to the bedroom. What if she rejected him again? Frank felt his manhood couldn't take another rejection, at least not so soon. Even today, after all the kisses under the mistletoe and the obvious flirting going on between them, he still felt uncertain. Things seemed perfect and then Sherry would erect the wall again. Just like a few minutes ago, she freely kissed him, but he felt her trembling in his arms as if she feared him.

Unable to stifle the urge, Frank came from behind, kissed the nape of Sherry's neck, and wrapped his arms around her. Her heart was pounding like bongo drums. His lips continued to peck her teasingly on the neck, sending her emotions haywire, all over the place. Lastly, Sherry turned to him.

He tenderly kissed her on the lips. She enjoyed the sweet kiss and then felt annoyed that it didn't last longer. There he stood, just gazing at her. Sherry wanted more. She needed more. Didn't he know that? Didn't he want the same?

He kissed her again, this time longer and stronger. Every inch of him desired more. The kiss intensified. Her heart rate climaxed. His chest rose up and down, sounds of ecstasy escaping his lips, moaning and groaning coming from both of them.

Frank paused and gazed at her, his eyes glistening with passion and desire. Hers matched his. Frank searched for any ray of hope, some indication that his wife loved him and wanted him. Sherry's breath caught. She was intoxicated by the sweetness of it all. Her knees went limped and instantly with a swoop, Frank picked her up and carried her to their bedroom. He kicked the door closed with his foot and as the Bible would say…Frank knew his wife on Christmas Night.

# CHAPTER 19

At the breakfast table, Frank, Sherry, and Daniel shared a simple meal of waffles and bacon. While Daniel excitedly talked about his plans for Howard and the variety of activities the college offered, Frank stole a few glances Sherry's way. He couldn't help himself. Sherry was stunning, glowing. Last night did something for them both. Refreshing and reviving their marriage, taking it to a level it had never known. Frank desired Sherry more than the air he was breathing.

Color seared her cheeks. Sherry felt like a lovesick teenager. The way Frank was looking at her as if she was a banana split with a cherry on top, *his Sherry*, she felt giddy inside. Not in the middle-aged, motherly, wifely way, but as the love of his life way. Audaciously, Sherry was allowing her long locks to hang without being braided. She knew her husband liked it this way. Sherry wanted to please Frank.

"What you think, Dad?" Daniel looked to his father.

Frank's focus was totally on his wife, he didn't hear a thing. "Dad!"

"Huh!" Frank had the look of being caught. "Sorry, son. What were you saying?"

"Forget it," he chuckled. "You two are in a world of your

own." Daniel scooted his chair back and took his plate to the sink. "I'm going to my room and I suggest you two do the same."

"Danny, don't leave," Sherry smiled. "We're having breakfast."

"No, I'm having breakfast, while you two are making googly-eyes at one another. It's sweet, but I'm just going to call Molly and plan our day."

"I was hoping you would be here," Frank interposed, "when...um, Farah arrives."

Suddenly, Sherry's spirits dropped. She knew the day had arrived, but she wasn't ready for it. She wasn't ready for Farah. Would she ever be ready?

Frank gazed at her. She feigned a smile that never reached her eyes. *Lord, please don't let us take a step back from this.*

"What time is she coming?" Daniel asked.

"Around noon."

"I'll stick around until then." Before going to his room, Daniel kissed his mother's cheek, knowing this had to be hard on her even though she was putting her best face forward.

"I think I'll go rest until then." Sherry pushed her chair back and went to the kitchen to wash the dishes.

"Let me help." Frank came from behind.

"No, Frank," she said sharply. "I can do it."

"Sherry, look at me."

She shook her head.

"Please," he tried to nudge her around, but she refused. "Sherry, please look at me."

Slowly, turning to him, his heart ached as he beheld fresh tears. Gently, he wiped them away. "Honey, please don't cry. I know this isn't easy for you. I told you that Farah could be adopted. I am good with that. Really, I am," he meant every word. "We've come so far, and I don't want to go back to the way it used to be. I love you."

"I know," she sniffed. "It's just that we wanted a girl so bad." Sherry nestled her head in his chest. "It's going to be harder than I thought, but she's your child…"

"I'm calling Monique right now." Frank relinquished his wife and took his cell phone out of his pants pocket.

"No!" Sherry snatched the phone from him. "I'm a big girl, Frank. I can handle this. I'm just confused, afraid…"

"Afraid of what?" Frank wrapped his arms around her, pulling her closer and tighter.

"That somehow she will come between us."

"Only if we let her and I'm not going to let her. I told you, she's my responsibility. I'll take Farah to daycare and pick her up. I'll make sure she's fed and does what little kids do. You won't have to lift a finger, Sherry."

"And you really think that will work?" She looked up at him. "That's crazy, Frank. She'll live here and be a stranger to me…in our house. That will cause separation for sure. She'll get all your attention and none from me."

"I don't know what you want me to do, Sherry. You don't want her to be adopted, but you don't really want to play a role in her life, or do you?"

"I'm confused," she shrugged, pulling away. "I'm going to rest until she comes." Sherry left.

Feeling crushed, Frank cleaned the kitchen and silently prayed for God to intervene. *Please, God, I cannot do this by myself. I need Your help!*

♥♥♥

Meanwhile, Timothy was doing some soul-searching. Every Scripture his father had written to him, he studied, even looking up the Hebrew or Greek meaning of certain words. The conversation he had at the hospital, still vibrated in his soul. He couldn't forget it. For four hours straight, he studied, trying to find the answer to why he felt this strong drawing toward the opposite sex. Why did he feel this way? Why wasn't he attracted to women? Why couldn't he just snap his fingers and everything be the way it used to be?

*God, I would have never chosen this path for myself. Yet, here I am. I don't want to be this way. I want to be normal, like Daniel. I want to live up to my parents' expectations. I want to follow Your Word. But, I'm confused.*

**God is not the author of confusion but of peace.**

*If homosexuality was an abomination to God in the Old Testament, wouldn't it be the same today? God doesn't change. His Word is everlasting. Yet, Romans declares God gave them up to vile passion. For even the women exchanged the natural use for what is against nature. Likewise also the men, leaving the natural use of the woman, burned in their lust for one another, men with men committing what is shameful and receiving in themselves the penalty of their error, which was due.*

"God show me what to do!"

Timothy's phone vibrated. Assuming it was Larry, he ignored it.

"I want to live right. I try hard. I feel like Paul. For the good that I will to do, I do not do; but the evil I will not to do, that I do. Help me! I uh…uh…know the Truth, but…"

His phone vibrated again. Once again, he Timothy ignored it.

"It's hard. Larry keeps calling me and well, I miss him."

One again his phone vibrated.

Frustration, Timothy answered. "Larry, stop calling me!"

"Timothy, its Anna…Anna from church."

He was floored. He hadn't seen Anna in about four years. She had moved away right after high school. "Anna Knight."

"Yes, the one and only!" She was chipper. "I bet I surprised you."

"That's an understatement," Timothy paced the room. Anna was his high school crush in the 9th and 10th grade, but she was too popular for him. Anna was the cheerleader that every guy wanted, but only Eddie, the popular football quarterback had won her heart.

"I am in town and ran into Daniel and he gave me your number."

"Oh…" Timothy felt like a quack for not saying more, his tongue literally sticking to the roof of his mouth.

"I was hoping we could get together?"

"Huh?"

She chuckled. "Yeah, I've moved back and was hoping to catch up with some old friends. You were such a gentleman in high school, so smart and funny. I wasn't surprised that you went to Newton University. It's the best! But you should be out for winter break, right?"

"Yes."

"So are you home?"

"No."

"That's too bad. I really wanted to see you."

"Well, um," he cleared his throat, feeling like such a dud. "I was planning on coming home for New Years and staying a few days."

"Great! How about we get together on New Year's Day? Maybe, that evening?"

"Sure. Text me your address."

"I will. You can pick me up about seven."

"Then it's a date. See you at seven."

"I'm looking forward to it, Timothy."

"Me too."

"Good! You take care."

"You too."

"Wow! Anna Knight called me," Timothy said aloud. Stunned. Happily surprised. "She was the most beautiful girl in Western High School and we're going on a date."

His phone vibrated.

"Anna!" He thought she forgot something.

"No, it's Larry!"

"Oh…Larry."

"Who is Anna?" Larry fretted.

"Someone from high school."

"And you're talking to her? What is going on Timothy? I thought you needed time to clear your head and come back to your senses. I didn't think you would be talking to old girlfriends. I don't like it!"

"Anna is not an old girlfriend. She's just a friend."

"Come home, Timothy."

"I'm not getting into this again with you. I need time, remember? I'll call you when I'm ready."

"But…"

"Goodbye, Larry!"

"Have you made an appointment with a doctor yet?" Peter asked Imani.

"No," she shrugged. "There is plenty of time."

"Prenatal care is important, Imani. I don't understand why you keep putting it off."

"And I don't understand, why you care!" she lashed back. "You don't even want the baby! You refuse to talk about it. You act as if I don't exist! You're mad all the time..." she kept going. "You treat me like you don't even like me."

"None of that has anything to do with you being a responsible mother." he refused to argue with her. "Just make the appointment and let me know when it is so I can make sure I'm off to go with you."

"You're going with me." Imani was surprised, knowing full well that she still wasn't pregnant. Peter hadn't slept with her since she told him she was carrying his child. No matter how hard Imani tried to seduce Peter, he wouldn't sleep with her. Relentlessly, Imani practically threw herself on him. To no avail, would Peter give her the time of day.

"Yes. I am not a deadbeat, dad. I'll take care of my responsibilities."

"But..."

"But what, Imani?" he stared at her.

"Nothing," she turned away. "I'm glad you're going."

Peter felt bad. He had been giving her the cold shoulder treatment, but he couldn't help it. He didn't love her and he found it hard being near her anymore. The lust had worn off. They were two different people. He was so mixed up inside, he felt drained. There was nothing left for him to give Imani or anyone, including this baby. He had no one to turn to. Not his parents. Not his brothers. Not even God. He had closed the door and didn't have the strength or the willpower to open it again. For what?

Peter didn't know what he believed in anymore. Or Who he believed in for that matter. Yet, his heart longed for more. Longed to be filled with something that only God had given him before. Peace.

The doorbell rang promptly at noon. Daniel trotted downstairs, eager to see his baby sister. Sherry followed behind him, while Frank paced back and forth near the door.

Taking his wife hand in his, he whispered, "You are the love of my life. I will not let anything or anyone come between us. I am nothing without you, Sherry. Absolutely nothing!"

"Thank you, Frank. We'll get through this."

"You promise."

"I promise. Now open the door."

The doorbell chimed again.

Before opening the door, Frank bent slightly and kissed his wife passionately. So passionately, it left her feeling lightheaded and lighthearted simultaneously.

Clearing his throat, Daniel uttered, "Do you want me to get the door since you two are busy?"

"Shush!" Sherry was embarrassed. "Your dad is full of surprises, isn't he?"

"He sure is." Daniel grinned. "And I like it."

"Speak for yourself," Sherry said.

"And there is more where that came from," he winked at his wife, grabbed her hand and opened the door.

Sherry gasped as she beheld the beautiful little girl who was the identical image of her father. Hazel eyes, curly black hair, and chubby high cheeks. Farah was beautiful.

Monique put the child down. Frank knelt, his eyes glistening with water. "Hello, Farah."

Monique gazed at Sherry, who was doing everything in her power to hold it together. "Hello, Sherry."

"Monique."

"My goodness dad," Daniel came from behind. "She looks just like me." which meant she looked like her dad.

"She does," Frank choked. Scooping her up in his arms, Frank embraced her. "I'm your daddy."

Farah stared at him shyly.

"Come in," Sherry invited Monique.

"No, thank you," she said politely. "Her things are in the car."

"I'll get them," Daniel followed Monique to her car.

Frank carried Farah to the couch and placed her on his lap. He motioned for Sherry to sit by him, but she shook her head, sitting on the loveseat instead. She was still shocked by the resemblance of the child to Frank. There was no denying Farah was his. She looked nothing like Monique, and Sherry was secretly grateful for that.

"This is going to be your new home and we are going to be your parents." Farah still stared at him. She wasn't frightened, but curious for sure. Frank was overwhelmed with joy. This beautiful little girl was his daughter and he instantly loved her. He wanted to protect her and to care for her. However, when Frank looked at his wife, her eyes were wide, resembling a deer in headlights, he panicked. What would this love for his daughter cost him?

# CHAPTER 20

## New Year's Eve

Tension occupied every corner of the Reed's household. Sherry stayed in the background, giving Frank the chance to really bond with his daughter, whom he obviously adored. She was such a sweet child. Farah was sharing, caring, laughing, playing, and enjoying her Mickey/Minnie Mouse room, which used to be the guestroom, Frank's old room.

The family had developed a routine in three days. Frank got up and dressed Farah, fed her, and took her to daycare, while he worked. Then he would pick her up, come home and play with her, while Sherry prepared dinner. Then the family, Daniel, Farah, Frank, and Sherry would sit down at the table and talk about the day. Sherry usually said little. Daniel chatted and played with his sister. Daniel loved Farah and she was attached to him, as well. Frank did his best to engage his wife in conversation. However, Sherry remained aloof. Inwardly, Frank worried about her. Sherry was in remission with lupus, but she was withdrawing from him again. They slept in the same bed, but she avoided intimacy, once again.

Sherry was standoffish, not wanting to intrude, not knowing how to act or what to do. Everything had stopped. She felt out of place in her own home, like an outsider looking in. Then there was this silent absence of her boys. She hadn't heard from Timothy or Peter since Christmas. Though Daniel appeared upbeat, she knew he was still troubled about his relationship with Molly. He still hadn't spoken with her about Newton University.

"I'm going to talk with Molly tonight," Daniel blurted at the table. "It's New Year's Eve. I cannot go into a New Year with old secrets."

"It's about time," Frank said, trying to feed Farah some mash potatoes. Farah wanted nothing to eat, which concerned Frank. "She's not eating today. Ms. Smith, Farah's daycare owner, said she didn't have an appetite all day. I hope she's not getting sick."

Frank looked to Sherry, who said nothing.

"What do you think, Mom?"

"Think about what?"

"About me talking to Molly tonight."

"I agree. She needs to know."

"Are you alright, Mom?" Daniel knew something was different with his parents. They hadn't been acting like lovebirds. Instead, his mother stayed in her room, while his dad spent most of his free time with Farah. Things were getting back to the old way when their marriage was in trouble. Daniel feared Farah coming to live with them maybe wasn't the best idea, though he adored his baby sister.

"I'm fine. Just a little tired," she pushed her chair back. "I am going to rest before the Eve's service."

"Maybe we all should rest before tonight," Frank suggested. "I'll go put Farah down and then I'll join you."

"I'd like to be alone, Frank," she said softly. "I need to prepare for tonight with the songs and also, I just want to spend some time in prayer. You understand, don't you?"

He nodded, but Frank knew it was more to it than that. Sherry didn't want to be with him. "Okay." He touched her hand and squeezed it. "I love you, Sherry."

She nodded and walked away.

"Things are back to the way they used to be." Daniel uttered. "And I hate it. Mom is not sick, but she looks sick."

"I know," Frank sighed. "And I don't know what to do to help her."

"Nope! But God does!" Daniel cheered. "He's going to work everything out for our family and next year is going to be a better year. I just know it!"

"I pray so!" Frank said.

"You see, God doesn't separate us from Him," Pastor Dave was concluding his New Year Eve's Service. "It is humans that try to separate us from God. Why? Just because we're different. What makes us different? Is it our color? Our race? Our social status? Our weight size or shoe size? We are all different in some way. However, the Christian community will say we are wrong because we believe God created us all equal—male and female, white and black —all different colors, including heterosexuals and homosexuals. In God's eyes, we are all one. God loves everybody."

*He loves the sinner, but hates the sin!* Timothy remembered his father's quote, as he squirmed a little in the seat, trying to scoot over from Larry who was sitting entirely too close for comfort.

"Well church, it's time to count down the New Year. Everybody, please stand. Ten, nine, eight…"

Timothy counted with everyone else. "Five, four, three, two, one! Happy…"

"…New Year!" Larry grabbed him and kissed Timothy right there in church.

"What are you doing?" Timothy jerked away. "We're in church."

"So, look around you," Larry yelled. "Everyone is embracing and stuff."

"Embracing yeah, but kissing, no."

"So what! It's a New Year…New beginnings for us!" Larry hoped. "It's going to be a better year, Timmy."

Timothy was shaking his head, heated about the fact that Larry would kiss him in God's house.

"Let's go home," Larry held out his hand.

"Shacking up is a sin, Larry. You do know that, don't you? It's wrong for heterosexuals as well as homosexuals?"

"Then marry me!" Larry blurted.

"I'm only twenty-one. I haven't even graduated from college."

"We can get married in June or July. A summer wedding would be nice."

"Are you crazy?"

"Yes! Crazy in love with you!"

"I can't do this!" Timothy pushed past Larry and headed for the door.

"When can you do it then, Timmy?" Larry caught up with him. "Stop running away. Face life head on. Face me. Just be a man!"

Timothy turned and gazed at him. "I am a man! That's

the problem!" And with that, Timothy spun on his heels and practically ran out the door.

"Timmy come back! Come back!"

Meanwhile, Daniel was taking Molly home from their New Year Eve's service.

"You've been so quietly, Daniel. I've been trying to plan the wedding, but you act like it's the last thing you want to do. What's going on Daniel?"

He pulled into her driveway and turned the ignition off. Daniel turned to her and reached for her hands, "I love you, Molly. I love you so much."

"You're scaring me, Daniel. Just say it. Say what you've been wanting to say for some time now, but couldn't."

"No matter what, you have to know that I will always love you. Nothing will change that."

"Daniel!"

"Daniel!"

"Molly, I want to show you something." Daniel took an envelope out of the glove compartment and handed it to Molly.

Her expressions changed while reading the acceptance letter from Newton University. Daniel was eager for her to say something, but he waited silently.

Finally, Molly looked up from reading the letter. "You got a full-scholarship to Newton. That's awesome!" her words didn't match her eyes.

He seized her hands. "Can you believe it?"

"It's what you have always wanted," her voice cracked, her

eyes misted.

"What I've always wanted was you." Daniel wiped the tears ebbing down her cheeks.

"So, we're not getting married." Molly pressed her lips tightly together, doing everything in her power to keep her composure.

"Yes, we're getting married," he quickly replied. "Just after I graduate from college, so that you can still get medical care from your parents."

"Medical care," she derided. "It's the worst. I can't have the surgery…" It just hit her—like a lightning bolt.

Guilt consumed him. "Somehow, you will. We will raise the money."

"We've tried that."

"I didn't accept Newton's offer," he said. "I don't have to go. We can keep our plans and I just join the army."

Molly wanted to see things from Daniel's perspective. He would resent her later if she didn't encourage him to fulfill his lifelong dream of becoming a band director. What an awesome achievement to receive both an academic and band scholarship. Though Molly wanted desperately to marry her high school sweetheart, she somehow knew it was for the best to postpone their wedding plans. Everything was so rushed and so centered on her surgery. Often they talked about it and it seemed like marriage and military were the next steps. However, deep down Molly knew Daniel was settling. He was born with the sound of music in his bones.

"No." she finally mumbled. "You must go to Newton. You deserve this, Daniel. No one gives more than you do. This is an opportunity for you to be on the receiving end for a change."

Daniel loved her more for that. "Molly, I want only you.

No university, no distance, no person or thing will ever change that. I'm doing this not just for me, but also for us. It's my calling."

She nodded.

"We're still engaged. It's just a long engagement. We'll be together as often as I can make it home. Please say you will wait on me."

"I'll wait for you, Daniel, forever." she said without hesitancy.

He leaned over and kissed her cheeks, kissing her tears away and then claimed her lips with his.

Imani had an unwanted visitor—her monthly came on. "What am I going to do? Peter will know I am lying if I don't take care of this. Knowing Peter would be home soon because he promised to take her to a friend's New Year Eve party, she had to put on a performance of a lifetime, in hopes of bamboozling Peter to believe she miscarried. Hopefully, he would feel empathy and be the compassionate man he used to be. Things would go back to the way they were before. It was a longshot, but Imani held onto her waning optimism.

A few hours later, Peter returned. Dreading going to a party, especially with Imani and her wild friends, Peter figured he owed Imani a night out, especially since he was planning on breaking things off soon. He should have never gotten involved with Imani in the first place. His running away from his problems resulting in more problems. It was time for Peter to face the music. Face his demons. In addition, even face

Elaine. He owed it to himself and he owed it to Elaine.

Peter needed to dig deep within to find the courage to face God. Like his namesake in the Bible, he too had denied God, openly and privately. It was time to make things right.

"Imani!" he called.

No answer.

"Imani," he called again, walking to the bedroom. Opening the closed door, he immediately saw Imani curled up in a fetal position on the bed, crying.

"What's wrong now?"

She sobbed louder.

"Imani," he sat down on the bed. "Tell me. Are you sick?"

"I loss our baby!" she was crying uncontrollably.

Something powerful and dreadful punched him in the gut. He couldn't breathe. He couldn't speak. He couldn't move. His heart was frozen in anguish, barely beating. *Lord, not again!*

She turned over and looked at him. "Did you hear me? I had a miscarriage."

Like a zombie, Peter stared into space. Everything around him was fuzzy. It felt as if his chest was being squeezed in a narrow bottle, sealed with a lid, making it impossible to inhale or exhale.

"It's your fault!" she said flippantly! "You didn't want our baby and it was stressing me out! Now she's dead! You should be happy!" Imani didn't mean to go this route, but since she wasn't getting any sympathy or compassion, she lashed out, pushing Peter to the edge.

This was the straw that broke the camel's back. Peter couldn't take it. He was a broken man. Oppressed by failure, defeat, and death.

Peter jumped up and ran out the room as if he was being

chased by something…by guilt…by accusations…by the blood of another innocent baby.

*It's all my fault! Two babies died on my watch!*

"Peter! You get back here! You're not leaving me here to deal with this alone! Peter!" Imani yelled after him.

Too late. Peter was gone.

"What have I done?" Imani wept.

# CHAPTER 21

## Making Peace

Frank found himself in a pickle on New Year's Day morning.

Charles, his manager, called saying that they were in jeopardy of losing a major account. He needed Frank to come in and see if together they could figure out a way to fix it.

Not wanting to leave Farah, who still had a slight fever, nor Sherry, who seemed to be slipping further into an oppressive state, Frank didn't know what to do. He couldn't afford losing one of their biggest clients, but his family needed him.

Glancing over at his daughter, Frank was thankful that Farah was finally sleeping in her toddler bed. Since the time she first contracted the virus, he'd been sleeping in her room.

Saying a quick prayer, Frank got out of bed and tiptoed out the room.

Entering his wife's room, he was glad Sherry was awake. "Happy New Year!" he drew near and kissed her on the cheek.

"Happy New Year."

"Sherry, Charles called and…" he related the crisis to her. "I really need to go in for a few hours to straighten things out, but Farah is still sick. I know she's not your responsibility, but since daycare is closed today I really need your help."

"Frank…I'm not up for babysitting today," she sighed.

"Please, Sherry. I wouldn't ask if there was any other way."

Sherry looked to her husband, who was practically begging her to lend a hand. Dark circles framed his eyes. He looked deadbeat. If only, she could push past her stoic resolve to punish Frank, even though she denied doing such a thing. Frank asked very little of her, the least she could do is to help him with his child. She was the one to insist Farah stay with them. Deeply, Sherry was ashamed of her behavior toward this innocent child, especially since she wasn't feeling well.

"Please Sherry. I promise…"

"Alright," she pulled the covers back. "But don't work long. I have to cook. We're still having New Year's Dinner here. Is your mother coming?"

"I'll pick her up on the way back."

"What about Timothy and Peter?"

"Timothy, yes. I called Peter several times to ask, but he hasn't responded."

"Why does he always have to be so pigheaded?" Sherry pushed past Frank.

He caught her hand and spun her around to face him. "He got it honestly, don't you think?"

She wanted to be mad at him, but she couldn't. Sherry knew it was the truth. "I guess he did," she smiled.

"I love this pink gown." Frank touched it, his eyes speaking volumes. "It's one of my favorites."

"You better get dress and go to work," she chided. "We have a lot to do before dinner."

"Thank you, Sherry. I know this isn't easy for you."

"It's not easy for any of us, Frank," she said through her hoarseness.

"I love you."

"I know, Frank." Sherry walked away.

While Frank was at work and Farah still slept, Sherry was in the kitchen preparing dinner. Listening to the gospel station, she was uplifted by encouraging songs that seemed to feed her thirsty soul. Conviction about the way she had been acting toward Farah and Frank cut like a two-edge sword into her heart. She couldn't have it both ways. She couldn't be mad at Frank for bringing Farah here when she insisted the child live with them. She couldn't walk in love as God commanded and then be secretly harboring a grudge, taking it out on an innocent child. She couldn't forgive one minute, then throw it back in Frank's face and treat him like a criminal.

***As far as the east is from the west, so far has He removed our transgressions from us.***

"Forgive me Father for not showing mercy toward my husband or to Farah. Help me to love her as You would want me to love her," Sherry's heart cried in sincerity. "And Father, wherever my boys are right now, let them know that we love them unconditionally and that You love them…protect them… keep them from the hands of the enemy. Wrap Your loving arms around them, shelter them and draw them back to You. They belong to You. The devil cannot have them! I declare Acts 16:31 over my household…my family, in Jesus' name, amen!"

Sherry's spirit was rejuvenated. While humming, the sound of a crying child made Sherry drop the knife as she dashed to Farah's room. It had been a long time since something or someone had made her sprint like that.

Farah was sitting up, bawling when Sherry sprinted in the room.

"Da-da," Farah repeated.

"Daddy is a work," she replied on bended knees. "It's alright princess," Sherry's heart ached, as she felt her head. She was burning up. Retrieving the thermometer, Sherry took Farah's temperature.

*101.4. Hmm.*

"Come on," she picked her up. "Let's get some apple juice and take your medicine."

Still sobbing, Farah finally rested her head on Sherry's shoulder. "Ma-Ma."

Sherry melted like butter. Any resentment, any anger, any bitterness she had felt before vanished like vapor. Love soothed her heart. Instantly, Sherry loved her. It felt so good having a baby in her arms again, a little beautiful girl at that. Suddenly, it didn't matter how she was born. All that matter was that Farah was now hers, to love and to take care of.

"It's going to be alright, Princess," Sherry coddled her, rocking her in the rocking chair that Frank had brought down from the attic and placed in the family room. "Hush little baby girl," she sang, "Everything is going to be alright. You have angels all around you…all day and all night."

Daniel entered the room.

Placing her finger to her lips, Sherry cautioned him to be quiet.

It did his heart good to see his mother holding his little sister. Straightway, Daniel knew that everything would be all right. Love had found its way in his mother's heart for Farah, just as it did for him. Who couldn't love such an adorable, sweet, precious child?

Almost dinnertime, Frank entered the kitchen with his mother, as Sherry was finishing up in the kitchen. Farah had just gone to sleep again, her temperature normal.

"Hello Darling," Frank timidly approached his wife as she was setting the table.

"Let me help with that," Martha took the napkins from Sherry. "You look tired." She touched Sherry's cheek. "Go take a load off, I'll handle the rest."

"Are you sure?" Sherry smiled, so glad to be at peace with her mother-in-law.

"Very sure. Frank go take care of your wife."

Frank beamed, looking at his mother. He was so glad to witness this side of his mother again. The loving, genuine, nurturing side. "Sure thing. Come on, Sherry." Frank lifted her up in his arms and proceeded to carry her to their room.

"Put me down, Frank," she said nicely.

Reluctantly, he complied. "You look like you're going to fall flat on your face. Was it that bad watching Farah?" Franked worried, a knot in the base of his throat lodged itself.

Teardrops cascaded down her cheeks.

"I'm sorry." Frank's words were soft, but his posture was stiff and rigid as guilt abided within.

"Don't be," Sherry placed her hand on his chest. "She's a princess, Frank. Your princess and my princess."

He placed his hand over hers, unable to speak, yet moved with hope.

"I love her," she gazed intensely at him. "As if she were my very own."

"Oh Sherry!" he hugged her closely to his chest. Her confession enthralled him. Those three words were like water in a blistering hot desert. "I'm so glad! Thank You, Lord!"

"Yes, Thank You, Lord!" she nestled comfortably in his loving embrace. Looking up to him, Sherry admired the handsome man standing before her, holding her securely in his arms. His eyes crinkled when he smiled at her, showing crow's feet, which made him appear mature and yet thoughtful at the same time. With age, Frank had become more dashingly handsome. Aging looked good on him, *real* good. "I love you, Frank."

"I love you, Sherry," he peered at her, pinning her with his intense gaze. Then Frank kissed his wife fervently. His *schoolboy* kiss was so passionate and fiery it made Sherry's ten toes tingle.

"Umm," Daniel cleared his throat as he entered the hallway with Molly. "Do you two need a room?"

"Hush!" Sherry's cheeks flamed. "I'll go check on Farah right quick."

"Let us both go check on her," he grabbed his wife's hand. "I need to change anyway."

"Okay," she beamed.

"Oh, hi Molly!" Sherry greeted swiftly. "You're family, so just make yourself comfortable. Dinner will be ready shortly."

"Yes Ma'am," she grinned. "I see your parents have kissed and made up."

"Literally!" Daniel laughed.

"What's so funny?" Timothy arrived.

"Our parents. Caught them making kissy face again. It's embarrassing."

"Yes, but it sure is better than them arguing or not speaking to each other."

"You're right about that."

"Is Peter coming?" Timothy asked.

"I doubt it. He won't answer his phone."

"Selfish! Mom begged him to come. You'd think he would do it for her."

"I know," Daniel shrugged. "I had a bad dream about him last night. Too terrible to repeat. I just pray that nothing bad happens to him."

"That's strange," Timothy sat down. "I had a bad dream about him last night, as well."

"Both of you," Molly chimed in. "Maybe we all should pray for him."

"We'll wait for mom and dad to come down and ask them to pray, as well."

"Do any of you have his girlfriend's number? Maybe we can call her," Molly suggested.

"No," Daniel answered. "But I know his address. He texted it to me awhile back."

"Give it to me," Timothy asked. "Maybe I'll go check on him, later, if he doesn't show up."

"Not a bad idea."

"And Father God bless Peter," Frank added after blessing the food, "wherever he is and in whatever he is doing. Protect him. Keep him from harms' way. Cover him with the precious blood of Jesus Christ. Permeate his angry heart with your agape love. Give him a new heart and put a new spirit within him, removing the heart of stone. Let him feel You. Let him hear You, so clearly. Let him sense Your Presence. Let him see

You, again. Spirit draw Peter back to You. Draw him Father God. He needs You, in Jesus' name, amen."

"Amen," in unison they replied.

Looking around the table, Frank was a blessed man. His wife was glowing, beaming like the young girl he fell in love with almost twenty-five years ago. She was holding the gift that God had recently given him, Farah. His mother was healthy and seemingly, happy. Martha had finally found her way back from the sorrow she carried after losing her husband several years back. Daniel and Molly were giggling, like two young people in love. Then there was Timothy. Something was different about him today since to Christmastime. He seemed more at peace. *Lord, deliver Timothy from the hands of the enemy. Let Him know what true love is, like the love I have for Sherry. In addition, the love Daniel and Molly share. Oh, and let Peter experience it again, as he did with Elaine.*

"So how is the wedding planning coming?" Martha innocently asked, not knowing that things had changed.

"Oh," Daniel responded, but Molly grabbed his hand.

"We're going to wait," Molly stated. "Daniel has been accepted into Newton University on a full-scholarship for the band and his academics." She looked to Daniel, her eyes sparkling with admiration. "I'm so proud of him. Anyhow, we're going to wait until Daniel graduates and then we'll have a big, beautiful wedding."

"Yes, we will," he caressed her cheek. "And we'll see each other as much as possible."

"Call, text, email and even write love letters," Molly added.

"Plenty of love letters," Daniel promised.

"Okay, we get it." Mother Martha interrupted, chuckling. "You two are made for each other."

"Definitely," Timothy added. "Proud of you, brother. I knew you weren't cut out for service. You're too much of a music nut for that."

"Yes, I guess so," Daniel stated.

"God will work out the surgery, Molly," Martha spoke. "He is in control, not man. We try to fix things our way, but make a mess of things. Ask Sarah. She foolishly gave Hagar to her husband so he could have a child. When all she had to do was wait on God. Just like my Frank and Sherry," she glanced at both of them. "They begged God for a little girl…and look… now they have Farah. See, God had a plan for all of us before we were born. In His plan, Daniel he gave you music…a love for music, like David. Now, He's further equipping you through college, free of charge, to master your gifts. And Timothy, you may have strayed off the path a little, but I believe you know how to get back on it. It's the narrow way, not the wide path that so many follow. As for Peter, I believe God will reach him before it's too late. The gates of hell cannot and will not prevail against him," Martha concluded.

"Thanks, Mother," Frank reached over and squeezed her hand.

"Yes, thanks, Martha," Sherry added. "Such powerful words of comfort."

"Yes, grandmother," Timothy spoke, his upper lip twitching, a sign of his emotions getting the best of him. "I aim to walk the straight and narrow path from now on." Timothy understood that he had a long way to go in dealing with this major issue in his life. Nevertheless, he believed God would help him and deliver him completely. *One day at a time Jesus!*

Sherry gasped, covering her mouth as tears creased her eyes. "Praise Jesus!"

For a few moments, everyone at the table embraced Timothy, showering him with love. Still perplexed about what Timothy fully meant about walking the straight and narrow path. The family's hope was renewed, soaring on eagles wings.

*Prayer works! Train up a child in the way he should go, and when he is old he will not depart from it.*

# CHAPTER 22

## Deliverance

"So where are we going?" Timothy asked Anna as he cranked his car.

"To church!"

"What?" he frowned.

She laughed. "There is a special After New Years' Service tonight and I have to be there."

"Why?"

"I want to start the New Year off right…in church."

"Okay," his eyebrow lifted. Looking at Anna, he couldn't believe how beautiful she was. She hadn't changed at all. She was still witty and still drop-dead gorgeous!

"Wow! Church!" he wasn't sure how he felt. Partly, Timothy wanted to go, but feared the gut-wrenching feeling of condemnation.

"I thought you were a church-boy, Timothy. I remember you always talking about the church in school and demonstrating sainthood in high school. Don't tell me you're not a Christian anymore."

He swallowed, looking straight ahead now, feeling his conscious pricking him in the depths of his soul. "Let's just say, I took a detour and now, I'm edging my way back on the right road."

"Really?" Anna would have bet her life on the fact that nothing would have ever taken Timothy off course. He loved the Lord. "Well, I'm glad we're going to church. We both need our spirits refreshed and revived."

"I'm glad to be with you, Anna."

"I'm glad too, Timothy," she touched his hand. "This is going to be a great year, Timothy. I just know it!"

Her optimism was contagious, spilling over to Timothy's hungry heart.

Though the church was filled to capacity, Timothy felt right at home. The atmosphere was bursting with exuberance and energy! There was a great expectation in the air and Timothy felt it and needed it more than anything.

As the worship service was going on, Timothy glanced over at Anna, who was practically leaping in the air, enjoying the robust fast-pace tempo of the song. She was in a world all of her own, enjoying Jesus! Timothy grinned. He wanted what she had. Peace. Joy. Victory!

*Lord fill me!*

Even at the close of praise and worship, it took the Pastor a moment to delve into the Word of God. There was such a sweet, sweet spirit in the sanctuary.

"In this New Year, we have to purpose to do things God's way and not man's way," he said in the middle of his sermon. "We cannot expect God to bless us when we are a mess. Living messy lives. Living unclean lives. Living in sin and doing things that cause the Father to weep. We serve a merciful God and He wants us all to get it right. He is longsuffering toward us but not eternal suffering. We cannot have one foot in the church and the other foot in the world at the same time. You have to make a choice. Sin or Righteousness? God or satan?

"Listen, we all struggle with something. The enemy is always lurking trying to get us to do something we know we shouldn't do. We all have issues. Apostle Paul had issues. He had a thorn in his flesh he couldn't get rid of. Some of us have thorns that we will die with, but God's grace is sufficient. He will strengthen us at our weakest to overcome things that seem impossible. Addictions. Sin. Lust. Lying. Stealing. Adultery. Sexual sins. We have all sinned and fallen short of God's glory. However, do we continue in sin? Certainly not!

"God loves us, but He sure hates sin. He wants us to get it right. That's why He has thrown each of us a lifeline, called grace. Does grace run out? I think if you ask the children of Israel they would say yes because many died in their sins in the wilderness. I believe if you ask the rich beggar who died and saw Lazarus the beggar, he would say, *'yes, grace runs out.'* If you ask, Ananias and Sapphira, they both would agree that grace runs out. For some it's long and for others, it could be just like that," he snapped his fingers. "It's God's grace, only He knows when your well of grace will run dry.

"There is no big sin or little sin. Sin is sin! Your sin might be lying or another might be cheating or murder. Still, when God sees it, all He sees is sin and sin cannot enter into the Kingdom of heaven.

"We cannot follow man, but follow God. Follow His word without compromise. It's not based on feelings but on faith.

Paul says in Romans seventh, starting at the eighteenth

verse: *18 For I know that in me (that is, in my flesh) nothing good dwells; for to will is present with me, but how* to perform what is good I do not find. *19 For the good that I will to do,* I do not do; but the evil I will *not to do,* that I practice. *20 Now if I do what I will not to do,* it is no longer I who do it, but sin that dwells in me.

"So what Paul was saying is that the more I try to do right I end up doing wrong. He knew he couldn't depend on His flesh. He couldn't even depend on man. He had to depend solely on Jesus and what the Word said.

"Paul concluded in verse 24-25: *O wretched man that I am! Who will deliver me from this body of death? I thank God—through Jesus Christ our Lord!*

"To do right, to live right and to be right, we need Jesus Christ. He's a Deliverer. We all sin. We all mess up. We all have habits that aren't good. We all fall prey to the enemy's tricks and traps. The only remedy is found in Jesus Christ.

"So, I beseech you my fellow brethren, follow Jesus. Follow in His footsteps. Follow His direction and His commands found in the Holy Word. Don't deviate from it. Don't add or subtract from it. If the Word says it, then it is settled in heaven. If God says it, then it is true. Don't let man tempt you from following God. Follow Jesus. The Word tells us that we must enter by the narrow gate, for wide is the gate and broad is the way that leads to destruction and there are many who go that way. However, the narrow is the gate and difficult is the way, which leads to life, and only a few find it. It's a choice, saints. God's way or the world's way, which is controlled by satan?"

"Let's all take a moment to repent and turn from our wicked ways right now. Let's go into the New Year...right...and in right-standing with God. Choose Christ Jesus. Choose to do what is right. The altar is open now for those needing prayer and for me to touch agree with you on whatever concerns you. If you need deliverance, God Almighty is here to deliver you. Don't leave the same way you came. Make this year a year of victory and jubilee. Kick those addictions, habits, and lifestyles of sin to the curb for good. I'm not saying it's going to be easy, but what I am saying is that with God all things are possible! He will never leave you or forsake you. He will help you and sustain you. He will deliver you. Come…"

With a surrendered heart, Timothy quickly answered the call. He knew what he had to do and he knew Who he needed… Jesus! With open arms, Jesus received Timothy. Forgiving his sins, removing his transgression as far as the east is from the west and remembers them no more.

Timothy looked over and saw Anna, with tears streaming down her cheeks, at the altar with him. It did his heart good, to know that he wasn't the only one not perfect. He wasn't the only one who had messed up, missed the mark. There were many who surrounded him at the altar, seeking God's deliverance and His forgiveness.

When God delivers, He sets you free. Whom the Son sets free is free indeed. No more chains. Nor more oppression from the enemy. No more confusion. As dew settles in the morning, peace had settled over Timothy in the evening.

Timothy walked away from the altar a changed man with a clean slate. The old lifestyle of sin was replaced with a fresh desire to live for the Lord. The old had passed away and now behold all things had become new.

Timothy was a new man with a new purpose.

"What a service!" Anna exclaimed, holding hands with Timothy as the twosome walked her neighborhood, enjoying the Christmas lights that were still shining brightly all over the community.

"Sure was," he looked at her. "I'm so glad you invited me."

"Me too," she grinned.

"I feel so..." he searched for the right word, "joyful. I haven't felt that way in a long time."

"God gives joy unspeakable and full of glory," she chimed. "I remember when I was so messed up, Timothy. I was sleeping around, drinking and partying all the time," she began. "Living a life that I knew was wrong. I just wanted to fit in with my college friends, you know."

He nodded.

"For a while, it was fun and then, it got old. I was forever trying to fill the void in my heart and nothing and no one could do it. My parents were praying, and I know that because of their prayers I returned to my faith."

"What made you stop?"

"I just woke up one day and just felt like I couldn't go another day like this. Nothing dramatic, just an inkling that I needed to change. The Spirit of God just wouldn't let me rest. There was a constant battle between my spirit and my mind, as if I was in warfare. I was miserable, even though I tried to convince myself that I was happy. I was far from it."

"I understand that," Timothy squeezed her hand. "You can only fake happiness for so long, until faking it becomes impossible. You can't even fool yourself anymore."

"Can I ask you something?" she stopped walking.

"Sure."

"How did a squeaky clean guy like you stray away from

God? I mean, you were sold out, you and your brothers."

Timothy chuckled. "We are all a mess now, except Daniel."

"That's had to believe."

Shoulders drooping, head hanging low, no pep in his steps whatsoever, he finally spoke. "You know how the guys used to pick on me saying I was sweet and stuff like that?"

Anna nodded. "They were just jealous because you were so smart and handsome."

"Well, somehow, I started believing that."

"Huh?" Her eyes stretched in disbelief, dropping his hand as if it was hot as fire.

Guilt and shame stabbed his heart, leaving it throbbing with disappointment. He hated seeing the look of pity, mixed with disappointment in her eyes. "Hanging with guys...who were also...dealing with my issues, if you know what I mean. They accepted me for me...and eventually, I accepted them."

His wounded look shook Anna out of her shockwave. She knew he was hurting enough already. "Not you, Timothy. How is that possible?"

"It's possible," he spoke softly, embarrassed by it all. "I was lost, Anna. I didn't think I was lost because I was still in church...praying, seeking God, but...I was only fooling myself. I was living in two worlds. I left my parents and started *shacking* up with someone."

"Not a guy."

He nodded.

"Wow!" she walked again. Never in a million years would she have believed such a thing about Timothy. She would have staked her life on it.

They walked awhile before either spoke again.

"Thanks for trusting me to share something so personal,"

Anna took his hand again.

"I'm ashamed of who I became Anna. I know it's not going to be easy, but I want God to restore me and use me for His glory."

"Oh, Timothy, He will. I'm certain of that."

"I'm tainted goods, Anna. Nobody would ever want me now?"

His words stirred her to tears. Anna stood on her tiptoes and kissed his cheek. "You're wrong about that, Timothy. Every single girl in church tonight was looking at you."

"You're crazy."

"Breaking their necks to see who the handsome guy was that I brought to church."

He gazed at her deeply. Her large dark eyes were mesmerizing. Shoot, everything about Anna was mesmerizing. "Did you know that I used to have a huge crush on you?"

"When?"

"All through high school, but you were dating Eddie."

"Really? I didn't know."

"How could you? You only had eyes for Eddie."

"Thank God I didn't stay with him," she giggled. "He's in jail."

"I had heard that."

"This has been a wonderful night," she stopped walking. "I hate for it to end."

"Me too." Timothy's outward smile reflected his inward joy.

# CHAPTER 23

## Finding Peter

Timothy stayed with his parents for the weekend, planning on leaving this Monday morning. He enjoyed bonding with his siblings and his parents. Already, Farah had stolen his heart. Timothy adored her. He and Daniel battled for her attention and Farah just ate it up. They were spoiling her but in a good way.

Frank and Sherry were both enjoying having a toddler in the house, even if it meant more work. They were building precious memories with the newest member of their family, which brought them closer together. Thankfully, Farah slept most of the night, not interrupting their sleep. She was also good at sleeping by herself, in her own toddler bed. Albeit, frequently Frank and Sherry both tiptoed in, peaking in on her while she slept. She had won them all over. She was a bona fide member of the Reed family and everyone was happy about it.

Nonetheless, still an oppressive, dark cloud still hung over the family. It had been over a week since anyone had heard from Peter, which was worrying Sherry. This just wasn't like Peter. Even if he didn't want to be bothered he'd send a text to check in and always signed off with an "*I love ya!*"

"Frank, I think we need to contact Imani," Sherry said

while watching Frank get dressed for work. Farah was still sleeping and wasn't going to daycare for a few days. Sherry wanted to bond with her more.

"I think Daniel has her number. I'll ask him before leaving," he sighed. "You're right. A week of being MIA from the family is long enough. He could at least return my text or something. I know he's mad…"

"Mad at who?" Sherry interrupted, "me, Timothy, you, God? Who is he not mad *at*? It doesn't matter, we're still family."

"You're right. I think it's more than that. Peter has been angry for a while now. After he broke up with Elaine, anger and bitterness became his dutiful companions. His renouncing of Christianity is Peter reacting rebelliously. Something deeper is going on."

"He's too old to be rebelling. It's time for Peter to just grow up. Be the man he says he is and stop blaming everybody."

"That's just it," he turned to his wife. "I think Peter is dealing with a deeper issue. The rebellion is just an outward expression of something he's dealing with inwardly. Now, it's becoming too unbearable. He doesn't know where to go, what to do, or who to turn to. He's just lost."

"Well, that's what happens when you walk away from Christ Jesus," she shook her head. "Peter had such a strong relationship with the Lord. It doesn't make sense. I cannot blame it all on Imani. I mean, Peter is grown and he is the one who has chosen to date her. No one made him."

Frank nodded. "Although, Imani has her way of persuasion about her."

"Jezebel!"

"Sherry!"

"Well, she is. Jezebel wanted to kill all the prophets. She just wants to kill our son."

"That's a little harsh, don't you think?"

"Maybe…"

He leaned over and kissed her. "We just need to keep them both in our prayers. We don't want Imani to perish either."

"No. I'll pray harder."

"That's my *Luv*. I'm going to skip breakfast since we stayed in bed later than usual."

"Sorry, I made you late," her face flushed.

"It was well worth it," he winked. "As a matter of fact, I'll skip breakfast every morning if you reward me with something sweeter and…"

"Go to work Frank!"

"Are you sure you want to keep Farah? She can go to daycare."

"Positive."

"I love you."

"Love you!" She blew a kiss, something she used to do all the time.

"I'll let you know about Imani later. Hope Daniel is still here."

"I think he's still in the kitchen."

"Okay, rest while you can. Farah will be up before you know it."

"I will."

Frank was glad to see both Daniel and Timothy in the kitchen. *At least their relationship is still strong. Lord, bring Peter back into the fold. Unite him with his family, especially his brothers.*

"Thought you would be gone by now," Frank fist bump Timothy.

"I'm heading out in a few."

"Is Farah still sleep?" Daniel asked. "I wanted to see her before I left for school."

"She's knocked out," Frank answered. "She'll be here when you get home."

"Funny Dad. I better go before I'm tardy." Daniel grabbed his book bag. "Is Mom okay? She's usually up fixing breakfast."

"Yes, just tired. We men can take care of ourselves. Sherry needs a break."

"I know, but she insists on spoiling us," Daniel said before turning to his brother. "See you next weekend."

"Next weekend?" Frank looked to Timothy. "Did I miss something?"

"He's got a hot date!" Daniel dashed out the room before Timothy could say something.

"Hot date, huh?" he frowned. Frank secretly prayed it wasn't with a male.

"It's not a hot date," Timothy colored slightly. "Just meeting an old friend, Anna. We're going to a Gamecock basketball game. She has season tickets."

"Ah..." his father grinned from ear to ear. "That's nice."

"Don't go reading anything into it and don't tell mom," Timothy pleaded. "She'll have us married with ten children in no time at all."

"What happened to Larry?"

"Nothing happened to Larry," he shrugged his shoulders. "Something happened to me. I uh, rededicated my life to Christ and I uh…want to live fully for Him, without comprising His Word or my upbringing."

Inwardly Frank was doing somersaults. His hope flickered during the family dinner on New Year's Day. However, Frank wasn't sure if the prodigal son had fully returned to his Heavenly Father. "Praise Jesus! I like that you've come to this conclusion."

"Dad, I haven't had peace since I walked away from everything I was taught. But your letter triggered my search for truth…again. Thank you, Dad."

"Praise You, Jesus!" Frank repeated, grabbing his son in a tight bear hug. "You have to tell your mother."

"I will before leaving. I have to get on the road soon."

"Can you do me a favor first?"

Timothy waited.

"I need you to swing by Peter's home before going home. He's on your way."

"Peter is thirty minutes in the other direction, Dad. I really don't have time and I don't feel like dealing with his nasty attitude."

"Something is wrong with Peter," Frank said with deep concern. "It's not like him to ignore our calls like this. Your mother is worried sick, and you know that's not good for her."

"Peter can take care of himself."

"Not this time. He needs us."

"It's not like I'm a skip and hop from home, Dad. I will call him, though. Peter is just being his standoffish self."

"Now, who is being the selfish one? Something is going on with him. Something happened to make him change so drastically. Aren't' you curious to find out what it is?"

"Like he'll ever tell us. He's a closed book."

"He's suffering.

"Dad, we're all suffering! We're one messed up family! So, you and mom are back together…for now! What happens when she gets tired of raising your mis…"

"You're treading lightly. I have made my mistakes and so have you. God has forgiven me and…"

"I'm sorry, Dad," Timothy interrupted. "I didn't mean it."

Frank nodded. "I'm glad you've rededicated your life back to Christ. However, you might want to rededicate your heart, as well. I remember you being such a loving person. Willing to help anyone. You'd give your last to make sure others didn't do without. You would put others above yourself. Right now, your brother needs you. It's your choice. Text to let me know you made it home. Love you, son." Frank hugged him one last time and left.

Halfheartedly, Timothy took a detour to his brother's apartment. His dad's words struck a chord of benevolence within. He had become so defensive, so wary of others because of their judgmental attitudes, especially Peter. Timothy didn't want to be like that anymore. He wanted his old self back, the loving kind-hearted person he used to be, but a little more selfless. *I want a servant's heart.*

Timothy knocked several times before the door finally opened.

"What are you doing here?" Imani irately hailed.

"Hello to you, too," Timothy gritted his teeth, not up for dealing with Imani or Peter's insolences. "I'm looking for Peter."

"Join the crowd."

"He isn't home?"

"He hasn't been here since New Year's Eve."

"Do you know where he is?"

"No, but even if I did, I wouldn't tell you. You're the last person he would want to see."

Timothy took in a deep, long breath, trying to remain calm and Christ-like. "My parents are worried about him and so am I. He hasn't returned any of their calls."

"Well, I've been trying to reach him, too," she sighed. "We had an argument…again. Anyhow, I think he's angry about the miscarriage."

"You were pregnant."

She nodded, somewhat for feeling guilty, but not guilty enough to come clean.

"Wow!" Timothy was stunned. He couldn't picture Peter with a child. "I wonder where he could be."

She shrugged her shoulders.

"Well if he calls, please tell him to call his parents. It's really important. Please."

"I guess I can do that," she didn't sound pleased.

Driving away, Timothy felt distressed. Something was amiss. He needed to find his brother. Impulsively, he called his job. After speaking with his boss, Timothy requested another day off.

"Lord where is Peter? Show me where he is and how to help him." Timothy prayed. Driving the opposite way, headed back home, Timothy continued to pray.

"The cabin!" A light-bulb flipped on in his brain. "He has to be a grandfather's cabin. He loved that place." Timothy was certain he'd find his brother there. In their younger days, their grandfather's cabin was where they spent most of their summers. It was something about being away from everything and nestled in the heart of the forest that brought about a peace for the siblings, especially Peter. They would explore the woods and enjoyed playing outside with each other. Their grandfather would tell them stories about growing up. Peter hung onto his grandfather's every word as if it were the gospel. Those were the times when life was good, less taxing, and family was a priority.

Less than an hour away, Timothy pushed the speeding limits, feeling the urgency to get to Peter. Praying in the spirit, Timothy sought the Lord's help and strength.

# CHAPTER 24

## Avoid the Deer

Sequestered in his family's cabin for over a week, Peter was wasting away, literally. Barely eating anything, but drinking plenty of beer, wine, vodka, and anything that would help him not feel anything. Never one to drink alcoholic beverages, Peter wanted to drown himself in his sorrows. He wanted to free himself from the guilt plaguing him. The pain was suffocating him. The shame consuming his manhood.

Holding his father's letter in his hand, Peter struggled within to find the will to read it. Would it help him? Would it send him even deeper into oppression? Would it heighten the remorse he already felt?

Shutting himself off from the world, his family, his friends and even Imani, Peter just wanted to die! He didn't want to go on. He felt as if there was nothing to live for anymore. There was no fight left in him. Peter had walked away from everything that once mattered to him—his faith, his God, his church, and his family —Elaine—his one true love. Sadly, Peter felt he deserved none of them.

Peter's world had turned completely upside down. He was carrying burdens too heavy for him to bear alone. The blistering wounds of guilt were severe. His anguish was great.

His joy had been snuffed out for a long time. His heart writhed in inexpressible pain. Confusion overwhelmed him. Peter was ashamed of his sinful ways. Losing two unborn babies left a bitter taste in his mouth. The combination of all the guilt, shame, pain, and regret had reached its peak, taking a toll on Peter, mentally, physically and spiritually.

Shoving the letter in his jean pocket, Peter looked at his phone, which was vibrating. Another call from Imani. *Why does she keep calling me? Why can't she just all leave me alone?!*

Like a whirlwind, calamity overtook Peter. He was distressed and overwhelmed. This cyclone of oppression was on every side, hedging behind him and in front of him. There was no escaping it. Peter felt doomed. His heart was sick. His vision was blurred by grief and uninterrupted tears of agony. He was being tormented by the enemy and felt helpless to stop it. For Peter had walked away from the One who could rescue him.

Once again, stumbling over to the nightstand, Peter took out the handgun that he had purchased a few weeks ago. Wanting to shut out the voices in his head and the guilt calling out his name, he put the gun to his head. This wasn't the first time he had done so. However, this was the first time he was determined to go through it. Sobs shook him. He wasn't in his right frame of mind, barely conscious. Peter was at the end of his rope. He wanted out.

"I can't take it anymore! God, if You really are out there, give me a reason to live!" he desperately cried out. "If You're really listening…take the pain away! Help me!"

Suddenly, a pounding on the door startled Peter. He waited, still holding the gun to his head. Again pounding.

*Is that You, God?*

Half-lucid, Peter's heart was pounding. No one knew he was at the cabin. It had been boarded up for years. *Who could that be?* He remained where he was.

Again pounding!

*God is that you?*

Pounding.

Frazzled, Peter put the handgun back in the nightstand and forced himself upward. Lingering, he staggered to the door.

"Open up, Peter! I know you're in there!"

*Timothy! What the heck is he doing here?* Of all people, Peter wasn't up for seeing his brother.

"I'm not leaving!" Timothy continued to pound on the door. "Open up!"

Yanking the door opened, Peter barked loudly at his brother. "What the heck are you doing here?"

"Good to see you too, brother," Timothy replied sarcastically, immediately noticing his brother's bloodshot eyes and hearing his slurred speech.

"Why are you here?" He asked again.

"Because despite your thickheaded, stiff-necked, judgmental and downright rude behavior at times, I still love you," Timothy said. "You are my brother and I will always love you." For a split second, his sincere words penetrated Peter's gruff exterior. "We may have our differences, but whatever you're going through, I'm here for you…we all are. We want to help you."

"You can't!"

"Let me try!"

"You can't. Now please just leave me alone. I don't want you here."

"So, what's your plan? Come here and just sit and die."

"Something like that."

"So you're planning on doing something stupid."

"Guess it's a curse!" Peter scoffed. "Just like you doing something stupid with Larry. Is he waiting in the car?"

"No. Larry isn't here. Larry was a mistake."

Peter looked at him long and hard before thinking up a comeback. "I'd say he was a mistake!"

"Don't judge me until you take the bolt out of your own eye!"

"Just leave! I don't feel like this! Do whatever you want with your life. I don't care. Just leave me alone!"

"I'm not leaving you like this."

"Go away!" Peter tried to push the door closed as best he could. In his condition, he was no match for his brother as Timothy barged past him.

"Mom and dad are worried about you," he began, "not to mention Imani."

"Imani!" Peter slammed the door. "Did you speak with her?"

He nodded. "I went to your place."

"How dare you!"

"Save the melodrama, Peter! Everyone is worried sick about you...including me!"

"Yeah, right!" Peter felt sick to his stomach. "Now that you see I'm okay, you can leave!"

"You're far from being okay! And you stink! When was the last time you took a shower?"

"Get out!" Peter screamed at his brother, wanting to knock that big chip off his shoulders.

"Combed your hair? Ate?" Timothy continued, feeling

sorry for his brother. He had never seen Peter appear so forlorn, so fragile. "And you reek of alcohol. So, now you're drinking?"

"Don't sound so sanctimonious, little brother," Peter scoffed. "You don't have room to judge me either."

"I'm not judging, I'm just stating the obvious," Timothy shrugged. "I didn't come here to fight with you. I came to let you know that we all care about you and we are here for you."

"Good! You've said your peace." Peter pointed to the door. "Now go!"

Timothy took a rigid stance, crossing his arms and eyed his brother. "So you're planning on doing something stupid." he brought it up again.

Peter swallowed. "What I do is none of your business!"

"Never figured you to be a quitter, brother."

"Never figured you to be a queer, but look at you!"

"I ought to just smack you right now," Timothy became so frustrated. "You judge me when you too have fallen short. You have impregnated a girl, out of wedlock. She miscarried and you hightailed like a jackrabbit, leaving her to suffer alone!"

Peter leaped up, nearly tripping, and barged toward his brother. They became physically aggressive. The brothers tussled on the floor. Fighting like cats and dogs. Unexpected, Timothy punched his brother right in the gut, after Peter struck him in the face. Already weakened, Peter felt his lungs constricted; he could hardly breathe.

Timothy leaped up. "Peter…I'm sorry."

"You're darn right you're sorry," Peter's voice was raspy, his eyes fiery red with anger.

"I know you're hurting…"

"You don't know anything!"

"I know you're upset about losing a child."

"A child!" he said with disdain. "I've lost two babies," his eyes moistened. "Elaine had an abortion," Peter revealed his deepest, darkest secret.

Timothy gasped, not seeing that coming. He had no idea that the two were sexually active. They both were so dedicated to God and worked so hard in the ministry. "Gee-whiz!"

"Now you know I'm not a saint! And neither are you! So don't look at me like that! Get out!"

"Stop being so bullheaded, Peter! Things happen. We all make mistakes, but God forgives. He's forgiven me."

"Well whoopee-do! God may forgive, but I will never forgive myself for my dead babies! Never!"

"It's not your fault," Timothy attempted to come closer.

"Don't!" Peter's stoic glance halted his advancement toward his brother.

"Let's talk about this," Timothy feared his brother was so unstable that he would surely do something crazy.

"You're the last person I want to talk to. If you want to help me, then help yourself right on out of this cabin!"

"Mom is beside herself, Peter. She doesn't need this kind of stress right now. At least call her," Timothy pleaded. "She loves you. We all do. You can get through this."

"Like you got through this phase with Larry! Well, my life is not a phase! It's a mess! I cannot just make it go away. I cannot bring my babies back," he sobbed. "I cannot stop the pain."

"But God can…"

"God!" he scoffed. "God left me a long time ago. I couldn't depend on Him then and I sure as heck can't depend on Him now!"

"God didn't leave you, Peter. You left Him."

"Shut up! You don't know anything!" Peter barged at him again. Timothy just grabbed him and held him tight. "Just let it out, brother. Let it all out." he coaxed, refusing to release him.

Struggling to free himself from his brother's embrace, like a maniac, Peter yelled, yanked, and jerked himself free, right to the floor. Humiliated, ashamed and wounded, he berated his brother. "You're a punk! A self-righteous punk! You'll always be a punk! Always be a *fagget*! Always be sweet like pumpkin pie! I hate you! I hate you! I hate you!" he blubbered, purposefully being heartless, to push his brother out of the cabin.

Shaken to the core, Timothy's heart broke. His brother had pushed him too far. "You go ahead and kill yourself and see if I care!" he bolted out the door, slamming the door so hard it nearly came off the hinges. He was raging mad, fury taking over. "Good riddance!"

Crumpled to the floor, Peter felt remorseful. He didn't mean to hurt his brother, but he was hurting so bad he inadvertently hurt Timothy. *Hurting people hurt others.* The agony of it all brought Peter to his knees.

"It's so dark, I cannot see. I ache inside. My spirit grieves. My heart breaks. What am I to do with all this pain, with all this sorrow, with all this oppression?"

Suddenly, the screeching sound of tires caused Peter to jump up and stagger out the door. The long driveway, which was about a mile long, Peter sprinted, fearing that his brother had something to do with the sound.

Timothy was so mad at his brother; he was speeding on the narrow driveway that led to the main road. Timothy was driving way too fast for conditions. It was raining hard. Then out of nowhere, a deer trotted in front of him. Trying to avoid hitting the deer, Timothy yanked his wheel to the right, while slamming on breaks. He lost control of the car. Timothy skidded across the grassy forest and plowed head-on into a large tree.

"Jesus!" Timothy shouted, as his body lunged forward full-force. Suddenly, everything went dark. Timothy was unconscious.

When Peter, at last, got to the car, he gasped loudly. Timothy's car looked like an accordion, squeezed and folded into the tree. The fallen tree limb had smashed through the front window. Timothy's head was a bloody mess. There was no way he could be alive. Peter feared the worst. He struggled to open the passenger's side, but couldn't. "Lord, please help me." He tried again. Reaching for his cell phone, Peter cursed when he realized the cell phone was dead.

"God help me! Please help me help Tim! It's all my fault! God take me instead! Please take me!"

Again, Peter tried to open the door, mustering all the strength he could. Then he heard Timothy's phone ringing from inside the car. *I must get to that phone.* Noticing an unusual size rock, Peter plunged it at the passenger's window repeatedly. The glass finally shattered. Unlocking the door, he grabbed the phone and called 911. Quickly, he related to the dispatcher his location and the severity of his brother's accident.

"I smell gas. I've got to get him out!" he tossed the phone on the ground, ignoring the operator. Peter had to pull his brother out. "Oh, God help me! I can't do this by myself. I need Your help!" he continued. Realizing that Timothy's legs were pinned, hindered Peter from pulling him out.

Timothy's body was covered with blood. *Purplish* bruises were already forming on his swollen face. Peter plucked and pulled as much glass as possible from Tim's face, neck, chest, and arms. Glass was everywhere. Peter put his head on his chest, listening for any signs of life. Timothy groaned.

Picking up the phone…Peter cursed again. "This phone is dead!" he felt defeated. "Lord, I need Your help."

Leaning over his brother, he held back his tears. Now was not the time to cry. Now was the time for him to be strong and brave for his brother. "Timothy, I don't know how I'm going to get you out of this car, but I am going to pull you out."

"Deer…" Timothy moaned.

"A deer…you saw a deer?"

He nodded.

"They are deer are all around here. You tried to avoid hitting one?"

He nodded again.

"Oh, Timothy…a deer. Always trying to save animals…people…me…" Peter swallowed hard. "Stay with me brother!"

"An---gel…"

"I'm not an angel, brother!" Peter uttered.

"An---gel…"

The smell of gas became stronger. Peter attempted to move him, but his brother screamed. Timothy's breathing was sporadical. His chest ached *something* fierce. He thought he was about to see his Maker.

"The Lord is my shepherd," he mumbled. "Forgive me…"

"Hang in there brother, I'm going to get you out of here!"

Timothy shook his head. "Going home!"

"No!" Peter shouted. "If you die, then I'm dying too! Fight, Timothy! Fight!" Peter was scared—really scared.

"Lord, don't take Timothy. Heal him. Please let the ambulance get here in time. Help me to get him out of this car before it explodes," Peter saw a spark. "Brother, this is going to hurt really badly, but *I've got* to pull you out of this car somehow."

"Home…"

"We're going home…to our childhood home! Hang in there!"

Peter did his best to yank his brother's body free. "God help me!" he kept praying. "I can't do this by myself!"

All of a sudden, Peter felt something grip his hands, empowering him with supernatural strength to free his brother's legs. It was like nothing he had never felt or could explain. It was as if they were being carried…away…from danger seen and unseen. There was strength….and peace…engulfing him. He wasn't alone. No sooner had Peter pulled his brother from the car and dragged him screaming, several yards away, he heard a boom!

The car exploded!

"My God!" Peter watched the car go up in flames. This was surreal. One minute more and…his brother would have died. "God, You are real!" He shouted. "Forgive me…for doubting, You! Thank You for sparing our lives."

The various wounds from Timothy's head caused a constant flow of blood spilling down the sides of his face, into his ears, and down his neck. It was hard to stay alert or coherent. Timothy was fighting to stay conscious, fighting to stay alive. Unable to handle the pain, Timothy blanked out. Timothy's head wound continued to gush blood like Kool-Aide. His face was so unrecognizable, swollen and marred. Peter gasped when he saw his brother's bone sticking out of his right leg, which was also bleeding profusely. Quickly, he took off his belt and tied it around his leg. "Come on ambulance."

Looking ahead, Peter shook his head several times, as he tried to clear his vision. Surely, he was seeing things. Must be from drinking. Was this an illusion or was he really seeing an angel standing guard over them? Such peace washed over him.

"You're going to survive, Timothy. God is with us."

Hearing the sounds of sirens, Peter released a loud sigh. "See! They are here, brother! You're going to be alright!"

The vision of the angel disappeared.

# CHAPTER 25

## Road to Healing

Peter was a wreck as he sat there in the hospital while his brother was in surgery. He prayed to God that they could save his leg and fix anything else that may have been wrong. The words he said to him in the cabin played repeatedly in his head. Timothy was fighting for his life because of him. He should not have spoken such things. He didn't mean it.

Another notch of guilt added to his belt. It would take his parents at least another hour to make it the hospital. The weight of the world was upon his shoulders. Would the pressure ever leave him? Peter's soul was dry, longing for water in a thirsty land. He yearned to feel the touch of his Heavenly Father again. Feeling overwhelmed, Peter went to the hospital's chapel. Sitting on the front row, Peter reached into his pocket and took out his father's crumpled letter. Unfolding it, he prayed for the words to soothe his battered heart.

Peter,

When you were born, I felt so inadequate as a father. I wanted to be the perfect dad, but then I realize one day there was no such thing as a perfect dad—not on this earth because even our righteousness is as filthy rags. However, because I serve a Perfect Father, He would help me to train you in the way you should go. I did my best. Though I have hurt you and our family, know that I am deeply sorrowful. Thankfully, I know that God has forgiven me. I pray that you, too, will find it in your heart to forgive me.

Remember, you are a Reed. Reeds love each other, support one another, undergird each other, help each other, encourage and pray for each other. However, lately, we have been at odds, fighting against each other. Particularly, you and Timothy. Even if you don't agree with him, you must love him. He is your brother. I said to him, you must not judge the speck in his eye when you have a bolt in yours. I say the same to you. We have all sinned and fallen short of the glory of God. Love should always love—unconditionally.

Son, you cannot control the world, only God can. Bad things happen to good people and good people do bad things. But we must be steadfast, unmovable, always abounding in the work of God...no matter what. You were resilient like that. But something happened. Now you are wearing depression and oppression like a cloak. It is heavy and it is weighing you down. Actually, it is weighing us all down. Our family has been plagued with oppression, but the devil is a liar! He is defeated. He cannot have my family. He cannot have you. Peter, there is a solution for this oppression. His name is Jesus. Acts 10:38...saying Jesus went about doing good and healing all those who were oppressed by the devil."

Son, turn it over to Jesus. Let him fix it. Don't blame God, embrace Him. Though He knows all and He allows the enemy to mess with us at times, there is a limit to what the enemy can do to us. Remember Job? God hedged him all around, but for a season, God allowed satan to take everything from Job.

He lost it all. Thankfully, the story didn't end that way and neither will yours. In the end, Job gained so much more. He not only recovered twice as much, Job knew God for himself. I believe that when you come through this, you will know— that you know—that you know that God is real. That God is for you. God is with you. God is in you. He will never leave or forsake you. He will always work things out for your good and for His glory.

Be free, Peter. That is my desire for you —to be free again in Jesus. To love hard. To laugh more. To live the life that God has chosen for you. You were on that path, but the deceiver found you at your weakest and you fell into his trap. He lured you and you followed.

You said that you don't believe in God anymore. That Jesus cannot be real because of all the "hell" on earth. I ask this question of you, son, 'Who woke you up this morning? Was it an alarm clock? Or was it the hand of God?' Your mother and I have trained you up in the way you should go and though you are older now and have taken a detour, I know in my heart that you will not depart from it permanently. You will return like the prodigal son. You, too, are in search of something. A search for peace? A search for answers. Seeking to discover your true self? You will come to your senses and return home. From afar off, God will see you and with open arms, receive you into His loving arms.

"A person who strays from home is like a bird that strays from its nest." Proverbs 27:8. The bird is lost. It can fly all over and still not have a nest or a home. When you leave the Truth, you're like that bird. Flying all around, with no place really to go. Lost. Homeless.

Apostle Peter denied Jesus three times, but later God used

Him mightily. Because it was with his lips and not with his heart. You too have spoken the words, but I know your heart says differently. Even after Peter had denied him, Jesus showed Himself to the disciples, including Peter and gave Peter the charge of feeding his sheep. There is much work for you to do in the kingdom...feed His sheep. First, you must forgive others and forgive yourself. Let the God of Perfection, perfect the things that concern you. Perfect love covers a multitude of sins. Let God's perfect love cover your sins as He has covered mine. Don't be deceived by false doctrines and false prophets.

1 John 4:2-3, 'By this you know the Spirit of God; every spirit that confesses that Jesus Christ has come in the flesh is of God, and every spirit that does not confess that Jesus Christ has come in the flesh is not of God. And this is the Spirit of the Antichrist, which you have heard was coming and is now already in the world. We are of God. He who knows God hears us; he who is not of God does not hear us. By this, we know the Spirit of Truth and the Spirit of Error.'

The Spirit of error has deceived you. He has blinded your eyes to the Truth. However, I believe God will remove the scales from your eyes and you will see more clearly than ever before that Jesus is real and that God loves you. You have been sifted, like wheat, but as Jesus said to Peter, I say to you: "But I have prayed for you that your faith should not fail, and when you have returned to Me, strengthen your brothers."

Your biological brothers need you, and so do the countless brothers that you have yet to meet need the gifting God has placed inside of you.

I have confidence in you, Peter. You will find your way

home and we will all rejoice and celebrate this glorious day. Look to Jesus! He is your present help in the time of need. Cast all of your cares upon Him and let Him care for you. There is nothing too hard for God to do. Believe that He is and that He rewards those who diligently seek Him.

It is a pleasure to be your dad. I wouldn't trade one moment of my life, raising you, watching your grow, watching you make mistakes and learn from them. You are not perfect, Peter, but God is. And He loves you. I'm always here for you.

Love, Dad.

Dropping to his knees, Peter wept bitterly. "Lord, heal my brother, Timothy. He needs a miracle. His body is broken and the doctors don't think they can save his right leg. Please don't let him lose his leg, because of me. If I hadn't run him away, Timothy wouldn't have been speeding out there in the woods. He would have seen that stupid deer in time. I said some mean things to him. Please, forgive me and give me the chance to make it right with him. I love him. I didn't even tell him that," he sniveled.

"Lord, forgive me. I have failed. I have walked away from You, blaming You for my wrongs. I messed up and I don't know how to make things right…but I know You do. Heal my hurting heart. And heal Elaine's. I know she is hurting, too. And help Imani know You for herself. I don't want to be away from You. Give me another chance. Please take me back, Lord. Forgive me, Lord! I want to come back home, to You!"

***Forgiven.***

Silence surrounded Peter. Then in a still voice, he heard, ***Peter, do you love Me more than anything?***

Peter whispered, *"Yes Lord."*

*Peter feed my lambs.*
*Peter, do you love Me?*
Yes, Lord.
*Feed My sheep.*
*Peter, do you love Me?*
Yes Lord, I really do love You.
*Feed My sheep!*
For the first time in a long time, Peter felt surpassing peace.

Returning to the waiting area, Peter had just sat down when he heard his name being called.

"Peter!" His father and mother were running to him, with Daniel on their heels. Molly and her parents were babysitting Farah.

"Oh, Peter!" His mother wrapped her arms around him, fresh tears spilling over. "Are you alright?"

He nodded, unable to speak.

"What's happening with Timothy?" his dad asked, he too hugging him.

"He's still in surgery."

"So glad you're alright, brother," Daniel hugged him. "I was worried about you."

"We all were," his mother said without condemnation.

"I'm sorry," Peter blubbered. "It's all my fault. Timothy's accident is because of me."

"So now you are in control of the deer, as well?" his father asked in a serious tone. "You have to stop blaming yourself for everything, Peter. God is in control, not you."

"But, we argued and I told him to get out…" Waterworks overtook him. Peter fell into his mother's arm. There was no better place for him to be. He needed the comfort of someone who loved him, flaws and all. "I said some awful things to him."

"Shhh," Sherry caressed his back, soothing him. "Your dad is right. It's not your fault. It was an accident. We all say stupid things at times. Timothy knows that you love him."

"I hope so. He can't die!" Peter cried aloud.

"He won't!" all three shouted simultaneously.

"He will not die, but live and declare the works of the Lord," Frank added.

Shortly afterwards, the doctor came out and revealed to the family that Timothy had pulled through surgery, but he had a long way to recover, fully. They were able to save his right leg, but he wasn't out of the woods yet. After they removed the cast, he would have to undergo physical therapy. Also, Timothy had a concussion, broken ribs and several minor injuries. The doctor explained that had the timing of anything been any longer it could have been too late. It was only by the grace of God that Timothy survived with all the blood that he had lost and the severity of his overall injuries.

Only two were allowed in ICU at a time, so Frank and Sherry went in first. Sherry clutched both hands over her mouth, stifling her anguish. Her eyes stretched wide with fear as she beheld her son. His face was so swollen, barely recognizable. Frank pulled her to himself, as they stood at their son's bedside.

"Thank God you're alive," Sherry leaned over and placed a soft kiss on his forehead.

Putting his hand on Timothy's arm, Frank prayed for his son. "By Jesus' stripes, you are healed. You will live and not die, and declare the works of the Lord. We plead the blood of Jesus over you right now, expecting total healing and rapid recovery. You will walk and go forth doing that which God has called you to do. Ministering angels are assigned to you right now, protecting you as they did earlier. In Jesus' name, amen."

"Amen." Sherry sniffled. The two stayed only a few moments longer so that Peter and Daniel could visit before visiting hours were over.

Fresh painful tears descended as Peter beheld his brother, looking so helpless and afflicted. Daniel blubbered, stunned by the sight of Timothy.

"We need you, brother," Daniel said aloud. "Pull through, quickly. We have to make up for time lost," he turned to Peter, who nodded. "No matter our differences, the Reed boys stick together ."

"No matter what," Peter agreed. "We love you, Timothy," Peter squeezed his hand and held it. His heart soared when he felt his brother squeezing back. "He's going to be okay!" he smiled.

"Mom, Dad, and you, too, Daniel, go on home," Peter addressed them in the waiting area. "I'm going to stay here tonight. If anything changes I'll call you."

"I'm not going anywhere," Sherry rebutted.

"Mom, you need your rest. Staying around here is not good for you," Peter replied. "Please, mom. No need for you getting sick or bringing about new pain."

"He's right," Frank looked at his wife. "You look like you're about to drop right now. Peter will keep us posted and we'll come back first thing in the morning."

Sherry felt torn. She didn't want to leave Timothy, but her body was shutting down, literally.

"I'm staying," Daniel chimed in. "I don't want to be separated from my brothers, not right now."

Peter smiled. "Me either," he playfully shoved his brother.

The brothers' camaraderie did their parents' hearts good. "Okay." Sherry relented. "I'll bring you both chicken biscuits in the morning."

"And strong coffee," Peter added.

"Of course." Sherry kissed his cheek, as tears ebbed down her own. "I'm so happy you're back with us, Peter. So happy."

"I'm sorry," Peter stated. "For everything."

"All is forgiven," Frank accepted heartily.

"I want to come home," Peter implored. "Just until I get back on my feet and find a new place to stay."

Sherry gasped, hugging her son, as Daniel did likewise. Lastly, Frank embraced him, his eyes glistening. "Welcome home, son! Welcome home!"

"Do you want to call Larry or do you want me to do the honors?" Peter asked Daniel.

"I'll call him," Daniel replied. "But promise me you will be civil to him when he visits."

"He may not come," Peter informed. "Timothy said something about he and Larry were a mistake. I assume that they aren't together anymore."

"Yeah, mom said he came back to his senses," Daniel laughed.

"Just like me!" Peter chuckled. "Two prodigal sons return home and to their faith. What a day!"

"Tell me about it!"

"Glad you kept your head on straight, Danny boy!"

"Don't call me that! I'm a man just like you."

"Don't rush it, brother. Life is hard out here in the real world. You have parents that support you, take care of you, pray for you and stand in the gap for you even when you don't know you need it." Peter paused, thinking about how blessed he was to have his parents and how he had often taken them for granted. "Enjoy your young years, Dann....Daniel. Before you know it, you'll be old like me and wonder what in the world have you been doing with your life?"

"Yeah old man, what have you been doing?" Daniel joshed.

"Making a mess of it," he sighed. "But, I'm believing God will redeem the time. It may not feel like it, but dad wrote that God would work it all out for my good and His glory. I believe it."

"I'm going to college instead of enlisting."

"Good! I was never on board with you not going to college. You're too smart for that. How does Molly feel about it?"

"She understands. Now she won't be able to have the surgery."

"That's why you were marrying her?"

"No!" Daniel quickly denied. "I love Molly and we're still going to marry. We're just going to wait until after I graduate."

"Good, because I like Molly. She's good people and it's obvious that you love her."

"With all my heart," Daniel meant it. "What about you? Are you going to go back to Imani?"

"Imani was a mistake. I used her to help me forget about Elaine," Peter admitted. "Truthfully, I am still in love with Elaine."

"Why did you breakup?"

"Stupidity!" Peter regretted

"Maybe you two can get back together."

"There are some things you just cannot undue, brother," he sighed.

"Yes, but there are some things you can."

# CHAPTER 26

## A New Chapter

During the night Timothy had been moved to a regular room, due to the surplus of other patients needing the ICU. His condition wasn't as critical anymore. After brushing his teeth and freshening up a little in the bathroom, Peter returned to his brother's bedside. It appeared that Timothy was still sleeping, but all too soon, his eyes opened and fixed on his brother.

With unseen bricks in his shoes, Peter couldn't move. For a split second, guilt weighted him down.

Timothy tried to sit up, but his head was throbbing. Groggily, he replied, "Come closer. I won't bite."

"Are you sure about that?" Peter forced a smile, while pain twisted in the pit of his stomach.

"I'm sure," his voice was feeble, excruciating pain shot through his ribs and ended at his toes.

"Do you need me to get the nurse?" Peter fretted.

"No, all I need is this," he squeezed the button that released morphine into his body. "It's a miracle drug for sure."

Peter chuckled. "Nothing like it."

Timothy grinned, trying not to laugh.

Standing over his brother, Peter's emotions got the best of him. He wanted to be strong for his brother, but his heart felt weak, witnessing his brother in so much pain.

"I'm so sorry, Timothy."

"Me too."

"You have no reason to be sorry."

"We both behaved like hooligans," Timothy reasoned. "I came to help you, but lashed out, hurting you more."

"I deserved it."

"No, you didn't," Timothy's voice was raspy. "We both deserve second chances."

Peter looked at his brother and nodded. "I'm so glad you survived."

"Me too. I have a lot of living to do," he paused. "I'm really sorry about you losing…your babies."

"It's a hard pill to swallow, brother, but I believe God will help me through it."

"What about Imani?"

"It's over," he stated. "I do have to face her and let her know that I'm here if she needs me."

"And Elaine?"

"That's another chapter. Though, I sure would like Elaine in it. I have never stop loving her. I was just hurt and confused. I took it out on her, wanting to hurt her like she hurt me by aborting our child."

"Elaine is good people. She'll forgive you."

"Yeah, but she's dating someone else."

"He's Trouble." Timothy injected. "I've seen him at church and well, let's just say that Elaine sure picked him from the *street*."

"That's harsh."

"I'm just telling it like it is."

"Enough about me. How are you feeling?"

"Like I've been hit by a truck, a car, and an airplane all at once."

"I bet. I'm just so glad you didn't lose your leg."

"Yeah doc said it was touch and go with my leg, but God had other plans.

"I called Larry."

"Why?" Timothy frowned. "We're not together."

"I know, but I thought it was the right thing to do. Just like I don't want to be in a relationship with Imani, I still want her to know Jesus."

"Larry doesn't want to change."

"Neither does Imani, but neither did I or Paul in the Bible. I just pray for both of them to have an encounter with Jesus that will change their lives forever."

"Can you do me a favor?"

"Sure, anything."

"Can you please call Anna?" he paused, catching his breath. Timothy suddenly felt sleepy and tired.

"The drugs are kicking in. You need your rest." Peter touched his brother's hand. "I'm not going anywhere. I'll be right here when you wake up."

"Call Anna for me? Her number is in my cell phone."

"Who is Anna?"

"She's the girl Timothy is dating now," Daniel entered the room. "Glad to see you in the land of the living, brother."

"Me too and I'm not dating her…we're just friends."

"For now," Daniel smirked.

"Anna?" Peter brows frowned. "Who is she and why do you want me to call her."

"I was supposed to call her when I got back to the apartment. I'm a little tied up, as you can see."

"So...Timothy has a girlfriend!" Peter teased.

"Hush up!"

"Look at him blushing," Daniel ragged more.

"You two are making me sicker than I was before you came," Timothy looked at his brothers, and said, "but I'm sure glad you're here." He closed his eyes and went to sleep.

Any friction between the brothers before the accident had dissipated like vapor. Nearly loosing Timothy had put everything back into perspective. Life was too short to let differences keep them a part. They loved each other and it took an accident to bring them all back to their senses. They were brothers and their blood was thicker than water, especially since their foundation was the blood of Jesus.

Entering the lobby, Larry nearly bumped into Peter. Larry braced himself for Peter's derogatory remarks.

Peter stared at the guy and felt pity for him. He, too, was lost, oppressed by the hands of the devil. Peter held out his hand to him. "Glad you came."

Stunned, Larry shook it. "Glad you called," he stuttered.

"Forgive me for my behavior at the game," Peter asked, wanting to make things right in his life. "It was wrong and ungodly."

"Sure," Larry swallowed. "Forgiven."

"Good!" Peter's smile widen. "Timothy is doing much better. He'll be glad to see you."

"I'm not so sure about that."

"Go see for yourself," Peter summoned and walked away.

He had to make other amends and it was no better time than the present.

Larry stood uncertain and uneasy. Seeing Timothy, lying in the hospital bed all banged up and broken, stirred Larry's soul with anguish. Larry wanted to comfort him, to hold him and to say words of endearment, but gazing at Timothy, it was as if he was seeing Timothy for the first time. The Timmy he knew before wasn't the man he glimpsed now. Though battered and bruised, something was obvious different about him.

Timothy had found himself. Found who he was and who he was not. There had been a line drawn in the sand that Timothy would never cross again. This was the Timothy that Larry didn't know. He had lost Timmy forever.

Larry's eyes became a fountain of water at the realization. Pain revealed itself in his face. He couldn't camouflage it. Timothy witnessed it firsthand, causing his chest to squeeze strongly, making his ribs hurt even more.

"Hey, Larry."

"Hi."

Silence filled the room. Neither said a word but just gazed at the other. It was awkward. Once sharing a close relationship, now it felt like two strangers meeting for the first time.

"Can you hand me the cup of ice water," Timothy asked. His mouth was dry. He needed something to drink, but even water couldn't quench the parchedness he felt inside.

Larry happily complied, assisting Timothy with sitting up enough to sip the water.

"Thanks."

"My pleasure," his tone was soft. "I'll do anything for you, Timmy. Anything!" his kind words were laced with hurt.

Timothy felt his pain. "How are you doing?"

"I've been better," Larry shrugged. "When Peter called me and told me what had happened, I felt like my world had been torn apart, once again…like I had lost you all over again," he gulped, trying to push down the torment lodged in his throat. "I miss you," he blubbered, unable to contain the tears.

Timothy's tongue stuck to the roof of his mouth. He could say nothing at first. *Lord, help me to say the right things to Larry. Speak through me.*

"Larry, when I was young, I felt like an outcast at times in my home. It wasn't anything that my family had done. It's just that my father and brothers were so manly and strong. Compared to them, I was weak and soft. They were all good at sports, even Daniel. I was lousy. Couldn't do anything but swim," he chuckled. "And I was lousy at that too, when compared to Daniel and Peter. All through my school years, my peers called me soft and said things to me that hurt deeply. I wanted to fit in but never did. One day my father said to me, right before I graduated, 'Son, it's okay to be different. Jesus was different. He didn't fit in with the in-crowd. Nah, he had some associates and then three true friends. Surround yourself with true friends and don't try to fit in. Make the world fit around you.' I remember those words and they matter more now than they did then.

"Larry, I'm different from my family. I am different from my college roommates. And I'm different from you."

"Opposites attract," Larry uttered.

"Yes, they do. It's not just that we're opposites. We are

different in our spiritual beliefs." Timothy was silent for a moment. He sucked in a deep breath, mustering the courage to own up to his convictions and face his truth. "I grew up believing homosexuality was wrong. Not just homosexuality, but fornication, adultery, and all immoral sexual acts were wrong…"

"The Bible is outdated," Larry interjected. "We are living in a different dispensation. This is the twenty-first century. Things have changed."

"God is the same yesterday, today and forevermore. He changes not. Heaven and earth will pass away, but His Word will never pass away," Timothy quoted. "Again, I grew up believing homosexuality was wrong and I still believe it. It's just as wrong as committing adultery and killing and lying. Sin is sin and I don't want anything to keep me from being in right-standing with God.

"We are traveling in two different directions, consciously choosing to follow different beliefs. It's a choice and I choose my faith and my beliefs. You have chosen your faith and your beliefs. I am not judging you. I'm not looking down on you. I don't hate you. I just have concluded that your lifestyles don't match the lifestyle I want to live. I was confused when I met you, tempted because my eyes weren't where they should be. I wasn't born gay. Neither do I believe that God wants me to be gay. Larry, you will always have a special place in my heart. I will always pray for you and want the best for you."

Tears trickled down Larry's cheeks. He had hoped that the accident would bring Timothy back to him. Yet, it seemed to solidify Timothy's resolve to break free of him and all that had to do with his lifestyle. "I want you to be happy."

"I want the same for you," Timothy's eyes moistened.

"Most importantly, I want you to know God, the true and living God, who sent Jesus Christ, His only Son to die for you and for me. I will never stop praying for your eyes to be opened to the Truth."

"Goodbye, Timothy," Larry squeezed his hand and walked away. Opening the door, there stood a female, carrying a big teddy bear and a bag of sour candy. *Timothy's favorite.* Larry knew in that instance that Timothy had truly moved on... without him.

"He's all yours," Larry whispered as he exited the room.

Stunned, Anna looked perplexed as she approached Timothy.

"Who was that?"

"My ex-roommate," Timothy answered honestly.

"Oh," Anna felt uncomfortable. "Sorry...I didn't mean to interrupt...anything."

"You didn't," Timothy held his hand out to her.

"Are you sure?"

He nodded. "I'm so glad to see you."

"I'm so glad you're alive," she touched his arm, rubbing it slightly. Timothy felt a bolt of electricity surge through his entire body, leaving its current of heat all over. Surely, he was burning up. He wanted to shed the covers and pour the pitcher of ice water all over himself.

"You look beautiful," he looked her over. Anna was naturally beautiful. He liked her shortcut hairstyle —her large dark brown eyes, naturally long lashes —high cheekbones and flawless brown skin. Anna's sweater and jeans fitted her in all the right places. No doubt, he was attracted to her, more now than he was in high school. She astounded him. It's amazing how Timothy was magnetically attracted to her when months ago, he was involved with a man. Timothy's thoughts drifted to something he read earlier in the Message Bible from James.

**Don't let anyone under pressure to give in to evil say, "God is trying to trip me up." God is impervious to evil, and puts evil in no one's way. The temptation to give in to evil comes from us and only us. We have no one to blame but the leering, seducing flare-up of our own lust. Lust gets pregnant, and has a baby: sin! Sin grows up to adulthood and becomes a real killer.**

"I was so worried about you," Anna invaded his thoughts. "Your face is a mess!" she teased.

"Don't I know it? You should have seen the car."

Gently, she touched his face, her heart going out to him. "I'm glad you survived. My heart would have truly been broken if you didn't."

Timothy looked at her with a look of desire. Anna's face flushed. He told her that he had always crushed on her, but now she was crushing on him…and he liked the way it felt.

"I brought your favorite candy and my big teddy bear to keep you company while you recuperate."

"Oh, you brought me a hand-me-down bear," he laughed.

"Yep! Andy is on loan to you until you get out. He'll be good company for you."

"I think I rather have Andy owner's company."

"Well, I can't be with you twenty-four-seven. Some of us do have lives you know, and can't lay in bed all day." She pecked his cheek.

"Don't tease me," he gazed at her.

"Stop being so fresh!" she giggled. "Right now you just need to get well so we can go out on another date."

"And another date and another date and another date,"

Timothy added.

"I like the sound of that," she beamed.

"Me too!"

# CHAPTER 27

## Moving on....

Peter stood outside his apartment, gathering the nerve to face Imani. His cowardly behavior of just leaving her, when she was hurting from losing their child, was heartless and cruel. Wanting to make amends, Peter knew what he had to do. Finally, he rang the doorbell.

"Oh, Peter! Why didn't you just use your key?" Immediately, Imani hugged him so tightly, he could barely breathe. "You're back! I knew you would come back!" she opened the door widely and pulled him inside. "I missed you so much." Imani sat down next to him, still holding his hand.

Peter gently pulled it away.

Imani flinched. "It's so good to have you home."

"Imani, this is not my home," he hated to burst her bubble. However, he needed to be truthful and own up to his wrongs. It was time to make things right and move on.

"Oh yes, it is." Imani shook her head in denial. "Things are going to go back to normal, now that a baby isn't involved."

Her words hurt, reminding him of the loss. Peter was dumbfounded how Imani had so quickly gotten over the miscarriage. She seemed almost elated. "I'm sorry about the miscarriage. I should have stayed by your side and been there to comfort you."

"It's in the past." She didn't want to talk about it. Unbeknown to Peter, Imani had been having nightmares about a dead baby. It bothered her that she had lied about it. Thus, Imani feared that in the future she would encounter such dreadful fate of losing a real child. Living a lie tortured Imani day and night.

Peter's head jerked. "Are you serious? Why are you so nonchalant about it now? You were distraught before, even blamed me."

"I was wrong to blame you, Babe." she reached for his hand again, but he refused. "It just wasn't our time," she paused. "And…I was wrong…" she whispered so low Peter barely heard her.

"Wrong about what?"

"I thought I had a miscarriage…but…I didn't," she stated, her eyes wistful.

"What!" Peter stood up.

"I made a mistake, Peter."

"You don't make a mistake about losing a baby!" Peter yelled.

"I thought I was pregnant…I did," she stuttered, "but…my monthly came on."

"You lied to me!"

"I didn't mean to," she cried. "I just wanted you to stay with me because I love you so much!"

"Love!" Peter turned his back to her. His mind went blank. Was he hearing what he wanted to hear or was she really saying she had never been pregnant? Imani only pretended in order to trap him. Peter pressed his lips so tightly together, as to seal them so he wouldn't say anything he'd regret later. He had enough regrets. This news was a hard pill to swallow, while at the same time he was relieved. He hadn't lost another child.

Then the passage in Proverbs Scripture came to mind that he read before coming over:

*The lips of an immoral woman are as sweet as honey, and her mouth is smoother than oil. But in the end, she is as bitter as poison, as dangerous as a double-edged sword. Her feet go down to death; her steps lead straight to the grave. For she cares nothing about the path of life. She staggers down a crooked trail and doesn't realize it.*

Turning toward her, Peter saw Imani for what she really was. Poison. She left a bitter taste in his mouth. Disdain for how he succumbed to her slippery smooth words. Sweetness concealed the poison underling her every word. Her every move was calculated and cold. He fell prey to her web of deceit. From his own evil desires and lust, Peter had yielded to temptation and found himself attached to such a person.

*But not anymore!*

With tears streaming down his face, Peter wiped the moisture from his eyes, unashamedly. These were freeing tears. Cleansing inwardly and outwardly. God was washing away all the guilty stains.

"I'm really sorry," she stated. "You didn't want a baby anyway."

"Not wanting a baby and losing a baby are two different things," he stated firmly. His muscles tensed as Peter stood before her. The old Peter would have lashed at her, cursed her or even potentially harmed her because he was just that angry inside. However, the new Peter knew this was one of those times he'd have to turn the other cheek. He drew a long, painstaking breath and uttered three powerful words. "I forgive you."

"Thank you, Peter. I'm sorry. I'm going to make it up to you, I promise." She pleaded for another chance. "Please don't leave me."

"Imani, it's over," he stated resolutely. "I am a Christian, a child of God. As His child, I forgive your deceitfulness, but I don't think that I can forget so quickly. You are not my favorite person right now... not even close. In fact, I am doing everything in power not to blow a gasket. You cannot imagine what you have put me through. I felt a load of guilt for losing a baby that never was. I blamed myself. I wanted to die." he threw his hands up, sucking in a deep breath. "But..."

"But Peter," Imani rushed to him, wrapping her arms around his waist tightly. "I love you."

"Imani, if you love me, then you'll let me go," His voice was stern. "Now!"

She dropped her hands in submission and with puppy-dog eyes, she gazed at him.

"I will pray for you, Imani," he said somewhat calmer. Peter felt deep pity for her. "That's all I have to offer you, right now. It's over."

Stepping back slowly, Imani bowed her head in surrender and walked away. Peter went to his former room, packed a few things up that he left behind and then left—for good.

A mixture of feelings flooded Peter's spirit as he stepped off the elevator to the fourth floor to see Larry. He was relieved and still heated that Imani had deceived him like that.

In a daze and not looking where he was going, Peter

collided with the last person he expected to see—yet, the one person he longed to see.

"Excuse…me…" Peter halted, speechless. Were his eyes deceiving him or was Elaine standing in front of him?

"Peter," she said softly, plastering a smile on her lips. "It's good to see you."

He nodded, still dumbstruck. Peter couldn't get one word out of his mouth.

"Dad is visiting with Timothy and…I was hoping to see you," she timidly admitted. "I'm glad Timothy is alright and… you're alright."

"God is faithful," Peter found his voice.

The intensity of his stare unnerved her. Even though Peter had been absent from her presence for many months, he hadn't been absent from her heart. Neither distance nor time had changed the truth that she still loved him. He had won her heart four years ago, and still held the key to it.

"How is Imani?" She broke eye contact with him, her nerves on edge.

"We're not together."

"Oh," she looked up at him. Elaine's beautiful smile alone warmed him right up.

"And how is …." Peter couldn't think of her boyfriend's name.

"We're not together."

"Oh," a flash of hope flickered in his eyes.

"It's so good to see you," she said again, reaching over and gently laying her hand on his arm. The warmth of their connection melted Peter's heart…slowly, but surely. "I'm so sorry, Peter. I regret what I did. It haunts me every day. I should have told you and somehow we could have handled it together," her eyes misted. "I was so wrong. I was scared and I…"

"I forgive you," the words rolled out of his mouth with no hesitancy. "The pressure of living up to your father and the church's expectation got the best of you. I understand. It got the best of me."

"If I could turn back the clock…I would have done things so differently. We would have been wonderful parents."

Peter swallowed several times, his emotions getting the best of him. "We made mistakes, Elaine. We should have waited until marriage, as we promised God and ourselves. Nevertheless, we cannot change the past. All we have is now and to purpose to live for Christ as best we know how."

"You're right."

"Now, I ask that you forgive me."

"For what?"

"For walking away. For giving up on you and giving up on us," he reached for her hands. "I was a fool Elaine, a real fool."

"So was I," she squeezed his hand as fresh tears spill down her cheeks.

"Don't cry," Peter wiped them away.

"Happy tears, Peter. Happy tears." Elaine wrapped her arms around Peter, hugging him so closely to her bosom. "I don't want to ever let you go, Peter."

"I'll never let you go, Elaine," he kissed her cheek, lifted her in the air, and gently twirled her around.

"Peter put me down," she chuckled. "We're in a hospital."

"Oh yeah," sheepishly he complied, his arms firmly around her waistline. Elaine nestled in his embrace, resting her head on his shoulders. It felt so right…the hug…the nestling… everything.

Peter kissed her timidly, as Elaine wrapped her arms around his neck, pulling him closer and kissed him back. His kiss left her breathless. Time stood still. All the time apart…the wrongs done to each other…the ill feelings of the past…disappeared. Their love was enduring, weathering the storms of the past. They were preparing to sail again into the unknown—together.

"It's about time!" Daniel shouted, pushing Molly in her wheelchair.

Peter turned to his brother, still holding onto Elaine, and said. "You got that right!"

With love radiating in his eyes, Peter gazed at Elaine and the heartache in his heart faded. He couldn't put the brake on his feelings for Elaine if he wanted to, which he didn't.

Dropping to his knees, spontaneously, Peter held her hand and his heart spoke. "Elaine Doris Law, I have wasted too much time running away from things and you. I do not want to waste one single moment…waiting for you. With all my heart, I love you more now than I thought possible. I know this seems crazy…but I don't care. I want to spend the rest of my life, taking care of you, holding you, kissing you, sheltering you, providing for you and walking side-by-side in our Christian walk, together. I want to be the father of your children and your best friend for life. Nothing would make me happier or more complete than marrying my soul mate. Elaine Doris Law will you complete me by marrying me?"

Again joyous tears flowed freely, as she nodded at first, unable to get the words out.

"Are you saying yes?"

"I'm saying yes!"

Peter leaped off his knees, lifted Elaine up, and twirled again her as if she were light as a feather. Once again, his lips claimed hers as they sealed their promise of marriage.

"What's going on here?" Reverend Law arrived with Frank and Sherry following.

"Peter asked Elaine to marry him," Daniel answered first.

"And Elaine said yes!" Molly finished.

"Praise God!" Sherry spoke first, hugging her son first. "Congratulations, Peter!" she held him tight. "God has answered my prayer."

"And mine!" Frank added.

"And mine!" Reverend Law echoed. "Glory be to God! He's an on-time God!"

"Yes, He is!" Sherry and Frank resonated.

# Epilogue

Five months later.

"Sometime we are oppressed by the devil because we have opened the door to sin," Reverend Law said in closing of his sermon. "You cannot invite the devil into your home and expect your life to be fine and everything good. No. He will wreak havoc. When you play with fire, you get burn. When sin is in the camp, all die. We know the story of Achan found in Joshua, chapter seven. Achan had accursed things in his tent. He had coveted something that didn't belong to him. He had sinned. God told Joshua, he couldn't stand before his enemies with sin in his camp. Therefore, the people stoned Achan and his family and burned them with fire. Church, you cannot play with sin. It opens up the door for the enemy to come in and oppress you. And not just you, but your entire family."

Everyone in the Reed family related to the message. On the second row sat, Peter and Elaine. Both had yielded to temptation, which brought about choices and consequences, causing the hand oppression to weigh heavily on them. Timothy held Anna's hand, thankful that she was with him. He, too, had caved into pressure and curiosity. Truly, curiosity can kill the cat. Steering off the righteous path that he had been taught, Timothy willfully went into the enemy's camp. He participated in its temptation, which left him in turmoil and in the state oppression. Thankfully, God had a way of escape for him. Then there was Daniel and Molly. Seemingly, Daniel had it all together, not a care in the world. When he too, wanting to play "god" did everything to make everyone around him happy, even willing to sacrifice his own happiness and dreams. Deciding before to go to service, when he knew that wasn't God plans for him, he became privately oppressed. Feeling the pressure of letting others down, snuffed out his real joy. Finally, there was Frank and Sherry, with sleeping Farah on her lap. Both had opened the door to sin in their homes. Frank, by having an affair, and Sherry by holding onto bitterness, and un-forgiveness. Oppression had hovered over their home and in their home for years, taking what didn't belong to it—joy, peace, love, happiness, and freedom.

Frank looked to his wife and squeezed her free hand. God had given them another chance to make things right, in their individual lives and in their marriage. His heart overflowed with love, displaying in his eyes as their gazes intensified. Only God could heal them and make their marriage better than before. For that's exactly what He had done.

"The children of Israel were oppressed by the Egyptians," Reverend Law continued. "On every end, they were being oppressed, in their homes, finances, physical bodies and even in their spirits. The Israelites cried out to God and He responded, 'I am the Lord. I will free you from oppression and will rescue you from slavery in Egypt. I will redeem you with a powerful arm and great acts of judgment…I will bring you into the land I swore to give to Abraham, Isaac, and Jacob. I will give it to you as your own possession,'" he read from Exodus, the fifth chapter. "As the Israelites cried out, realizing that they needed God, He answered. For their oppression, He was giving them a new possession…new land…new purpose…new victories. And so it is for each one of us today.

"When we cry out to God, asking Him to help us, to forgive us…He will remove that oppression and give us a new possession…new homes…new families…new purpose…new love…new victories…new hope…new life! We will no longer be captive and in captivity. We will be free and no longer oppressed!"

Before the benediction, the Pastor said, "As a reminder, we will not be having evening service today. At four o'clock this evening, Frank and Sherry Reed are going to renew their vows. The blessed couple is celebrating 25 years of marriage. They wanted to do it in front of their church family. After the renewals they want all of us to join them in the fellowship hall for the reception."

"Sister Sherry would you please close the service with a song," Reverend Law requested.

Thinking of no other song more befitting, Sherry went to the piano and played the familiar song of freedom. As she sang, such peace washed over her.

*It was God's amazing grace*
*That saved me,*
*Kept me*
*And never left me*
*I was oppressed, but now I have joy*
*I was blind, but now I see*
*I was brokenhearted, but now I am healed*
*I was captive, but now I am free*
*It was God's amazing grace*
*That saved me,*
*Kept me*
*And never left me.*

Yes, the family had come full circle. God had restored the Reed family, giving them double for all of their troubles and even adding a little sunshine into their lives, by way of little Farah Reed.

Frank's eyes watered as he beheld his wife coming down the aisle. He had never seen such a glorious vision. Wearing a chiffon gold gown, with beading wrapped around the waistline, revealed Sherry's slim and yet, curvy figure. Frank felt more like a newlywed today than he did 25 years ago. Renewing their vows was the perfect indication that they were in a better place...a happy joyous place. Their marriage had survived the trials, struggles, oppression, infidelity and so much more. Perfect love casts out fear and covers a multitude of sin. God restores! God heals! God renews! God frees!

Sherry fixed her eyes on her husband. Frank was dashingly debonair. Dressed in a black fitted tuxedo, with a gold bowtie to match her dress, Frank still made her heart do all kinds of funny things. He captivated her. He had won her heart all over again. Never had she felt so happy and so blessed.

As she reached the altar, she couldn't contain her happy tears. There standing next to her husband were her three boys, Peter, Timothy, and Daniel. To her left, were her future daughter in-laws...Elaine, Anna, and Molly. Looking down, she bent over and kissed their special flower girl, Farah on the cheek.

"Momma!" Farah exclaimed.

"My Baby Princess!" Sherry would never tire of hearing the endearment.

Frank choked back his own emotions. Today truly was a blessed day.

Reverend Law went through the simple, but sweet renewal ceremony. The congregation felt the sweet spirit in the sanctuary and witnessed the endearing love between Frank and Sherry.

"You may now kiss your bride," Reverend Law admonished.

"With all my heart, I love you, Sherry."

"With all my heart, I love you, Frank." Sherry looked up, their eyes magnetically fastened. Frank leaned in and covered her lips with his. The kiss intensified, almost electric. It mattered not that they were in church with a congregation of people staring at them. Sherry felt joyfully dizzy with a sensation that was indescribable. Frank felt a spark of fire, desiring more and more of his wife. He could never get enough of her. Their love had been restored, renewed and revived. The passion was more intense than ever before. They had found their rhythm of love again.

The family structure wasn't perfect, but at last, it was joyful and loving. Peter, now back in church, working in the youth ministry, alongside Elaine. The couple would be marrying in a few months. Timothy was seriously dating Anna. He had used his recent journey of overcoming immorality by starting a successful blog, an effort to help others who had walked in his shoes. Daniel was enjoying college, but home almost every other weekend to spend quality time with Molly and his family. Their love was solid. Miraculously, Molly was blessed with a huge donation from the church, friends, family and complete strangers, now making it possible to have the surgery that could possibly make her walk again, or at least have feelings in her lower part of the body. In addition, Farah, now two and all over the place, was a delight to the family. She brought such energy and excitement in the home, making Frank and Sherry both feel young again.

The oppression that hovered over their family like a permanent cloud had now been lifted. The dysfunctional family had been pieced back together by the hands of the True Potter. Though none of them were perfect, their Perfect Father loved them all, flaws and all. Jesus came to set those who were oppressed, free. The Reed Family was free indeed and **NO LONGER OPPRESSED!**

Dear Reader,

This has truly been a ride! This last book in the Freedom Series ministered to the depths of my soul. Jesus said I came to destroy the works of the devil. A major work of the devil is to oppress God's people. He oppresses us through sickness, poverty, emotional distress, addictions, sexual sins, jobs or lack of jobs, un-forgiveness, past hurts and trauma, church-hurts, and so many other things. However, the devil doesn't have the last word—God does! Greater is He that is in me than he that is in the world!

Frank and Sherry were their own worst enemies. Frank strayed while Sherry stayed in the past. She was bitter and couldn't forgive. She couldn't move on. So many of us are like that and we cannot move on. We have been hurt and mistreated, and instead of forgiving and allowing God to heal us, we stay stuck in that hurt. Stuck in that anger. That was Peter. He was mad at everything and everybody. He blamed God when he opened the door for the enemy to come in.

Timothy was a hard character for me to write about. It's hard dealing with an issue so accepted by so many people, including Christians. Yet, Timothy's issue is no greater or less than any other issue called sin. Whether it is lying, murdering, stealing, adultery... it's all sin and sin keeps us from God. It keeps us from entering into Heaven. We cannot look down on Timothy or anyone else living in sin. We should pray for them and love them through it. That was hard for Sherry. At the end of the day, we can only raise our children in the admonition and training of God. When they are older, we believe God's Word...they will not depart from it.

I pray that you were blessed by this book and encouraged. I admonish you to not be judgmental, but loving toward those who had fallen short of God's glory, lest forgetting that you too have fallen. But, thanks be to God, who picks us up, dust us off, cleans us up and send us right back out there to do His work.

God anointed Jesus Christ with the Holy Spirit and power, who went about doing good and healing all who were oppressed by the devil, for God was with Him. Acts 10:38. Thank You, God for *healing us, spiritually, mentally, physically and financially, all those who are oppressed by the devil. Free us so we are no longer captive, no longer brokenhearted, and no longer oppressed in Jesus' name, amen.*

*I would love to hear from you, please email me at: rlwbooks@ gmail.com or visit my website: RaiLindsayWallace. Also, please take the time to give me a 5-star rating on Amazon.com if my book was a blessing to you. I greatly appreciate it.*

God bless you richly,

*Rai*

PS: Coming soon....**Pastor Cannon Series (4 books)**. Find out about the Pastor Cannon's children: Leela, Cassi, Reese, and Jay. Each PK (Pastor's kid) travels different paths in discovering their individual callings, overcoming many obstacles and challenges along the way, and finding unexpected love.

*Finally Reader,*

*If you do not know Jesus as your personal, Lord and Savior, or if you have backslid, God is waiting on you with open arms to accept you into the family. He loves you and desires to take care of you, from now and into eternity. Accept His gift. Accept Jesus into your heart...today!*

**"If you confess with your mouth the Lord Jesus and believe in your heart that God has raised Him from the dead, you will be saved. For with the heart, one believes unto righteousness, and with the mouth, confession is made unto salvation. For whoever calls on the name of the Lord shall be saved."**
Romans: 10:9,10

*Prayer:*
*Father God, I am a sinner in need of a Savior. I confess with my mouth the Lord Jesus and believe in my heart that God raised Him from the dead. I accept your gift of salvation by accepting Jesus Christ as my Lord and Savior. Fill me with Your Spirit, so I may walk in the path You have for me to walk. I surrender my heart, my mind, my soul and my spirit to You. I am Yours, Lord. Thank You for making my heart Your home. In Jesus' name, Amen.*

# Discussion Questions:

1. Sometimes it takes something tragic to bring us to our knees, to bring us to back to God. For Peter, it was the belief of losing two unborn babies, and almost losing his brother. Did it take something tragic for you to give your life to Christ? If so, explain why or why not.

2. Sherry struggled with forgiving her husband Frank for his infidelity. She wanted to make him pay for his wrongs. Why is it so hard to forgive others, when Christ forgave us for our sins?

3. Homosexuality is a touchy subject. Especially since it is so accepted in the world. What are your views on homosexuality? Should the church make allowances for this lifestyle? Why or why not?

4. Peter walked away from God because he felt that God wasn't there for him. Have there ever been times in your life that God seemed so far away? Were there times when it seemed that He had turned a deaf ear to your prayers? If so, explain how did you get past it.

5. Daniel was a peacemaker. He wanted everybody around him to be happy. Thus, he often neglected to make himself happy. Do you know somebody like that? List a pro and con of being a people-pleaser.

6. Frank's mother, a lonely widow, found it hard in sharing her son. Therefore, she resented Sherry. It's hard for a mother to take a backseat to her child's spouse. What

are ways that could help mothers transitioned after a child marries?

7. Frank was left with the responsibility of caring for his child, from another mother. How would you handle it if you were put into that position? Explain.

8. Do you ever feel like your family is a fraud? Or do you know of a family that is a fraud? Why is it difficult to be our authentic selves? Especially, when God sees who we really are behind closed doors.

9. Family is very important. Can family members come together, in love, despite their spiritual differences and still be united as one? Explain.

10. Frank moved out. Both he and Sherry were unhappy. Do you think separation is good for couples going through trust issues? What are some ways Frank and Sherry could have worked things out without either of them leaving?

11. Daniel was willing to join the army and marry Molly, so that she could have the needed surgery. Do you think that under the circumstances that you would do the same to help a loved one out? Perhaps, not military, but sacrifice your career job or something very important, for the sake of the family.

# About The Author

Rai Lindsay-Wallace is from Columbia, South Carolina, where she lives with her devoted husband, Kent. Together, the Wallace's have three amazing children and five grandchildren. Rai is retired and spends much of her time ministering, writing inspiration fiction, singing, and writing music with her husband. She is also a graduate of The Ministerial Seminary of America, LLC, as a licensed Christian Minister. She is a pastor at God's House of Healing. Her mission is to spread the message of love, hope, and healing to the churched and un-churched through creative writings and ministering the Gospel of Jesus Christ. For more info, visit *RaiLindsayWallace.com or email her at rlwbooks@gmail.com.*

**Additional Books by Rai:**
*No Longer Captive*
*No Longer Brokenhearted*
*No Longer Oppressed*
*For Such a Time as This*

*Sunset/Sunrise (Will be republished)*
*Destiny*

*Coming soon...*
*Pastor's Daughter – Leela (January 2018)*
*Pastor's Daughter II– Cassi*
*Pastor's Son – Reese*
*Pastor's Son II – Jay*